Other Isak Dinesen titles available in Vintage:

Ehrengard

Last Tales

Out of Africa

Seven Gothic Tales

Shadows on the Grass

Winter's Tales

Anecdotes of Destiny

Anecdotes
of
Destiny

ISAK DINESEN

VINTAGE BOOKS
A DIVISION OF RANDOM HOUSE • NEW YORK

FIRST VINTAGE BOOKS EDITION,
December 1985

Anecdotes of Destiny *copyright © 1958 by*
Isak Dinesen. "The Immortal Story" copyright © 1953
by The Curtis Publishing Company.

Ehrengard *copyright © 1963 by Rungstedlundfonden.*
"The Secret of Rosenbad" copyright © 1962 by
The Curtis Publishing Company.

Library of Congress Cataloging-in-Publication Data
Dinesen, Isak, 1885–1962.
    Anecdotes of destiny; Ehrengard.
    I. Dinesen, Isak, 1885–1962. Ehrengard. 1985.
II. Title.   III. Title: Anecdotes of destiny.   IV. Title:
Ehrengard.
PR6003.L545A6   1985   839.8′ 1372   85-13591
ISBN 0-394-74215-X (pbk.)

Contents

The Diver — 3

Babette's Feast — 23

Tempests — 71

The Immortal Story — 155

The Ring — 235

The Diver

Mira Jama told this story:

In Shiraz lived a young student of theology by the name of Saufe who was highly gifted and pure of heart. As he read and re-read the Koran he became so absorbed in the thought of the angels that his soul dwelt with them more than with his mother or his brothers, his teachers or fellow-students or any other people of Shiraz.

He repeated to himself the words of the Holy Book: ". . . by the angels, who tear forth the souls of men with violence, and by those who draw forth the souls of others with gentleness, by those who glide swimmingly through the air with the commands of God, by those who precede and usher the righteous into Paradise, and by those who subordinately govern the affairs of this world . . ."

"The throne of God," he thought, "will needs be placed so sky-high that the eye of man cannot reach it, and the mind of man reels before it. But the radiant angels move between God's azure halls and our dark houses and schoolrooms. It should be possible to us to see them and communicate with them.

"Birds," he reflected, "must be, of all creatures, most like angels. Says not the Scripture: 'Whatever moveth both in heaven and on earth worshippeth God, and the angels also'—and surely the birds move both in heaven and on earth. Says it not further, of the angels: 'They are not elated with pride so as to disdain their service, they sing, and perform that which they are commanded'—and surely the birds do the same. If we endeavor to imitate the birds in all this, we shall become more like the angels than we are now.

"But in addition to these things, birds have wings, as have the angels. It would be good if men could make wings for themselves, to lift them into high regions, where dwells a clear and eternal light. A bird, if she strains the capacity of her wings to the utmost, may meet or pass an angel upon one of the wild paths of the ether. Perhaps the wing of the swallow has brushed an angel's foot, or the gaze of the eagle, at the moment when her strength was almost exhausted, has met the calm eyes of one of God's messengers.

"I shall," he decided, "employ my time and my learning in the task of constructing such wings for my fellow-men."

So he made up his mind that he would leave Shiraz to study the ways of the winged creatures.

Till now he had, by teaching rich men's sons and by copying out ancient manuscripts, supported his mother and his small brothers, and they complained that they would become poor without him. But he argued that, some time, his achievement would compensate them manifold for the privations of the present. His teachers, who had foreseen a fine career for him, came to see him and expostulated with him that, since the world had gone on for so long without men communicating with angels, it must be meant to do so, and might do so in the future as well.

The young Softa respectfully contradicted them.

"Until this day," he said, "nobody has seen the trekking-birds take their way toward such warmer spheres as do not exist, or the rivers break their course through rocks and plains to run into an ocean which is not to be found. For God does not create a longing or a hope without having a fulfilling reality ready for them. But our longing is our pledge, and blessed are the homesick, for they shall come home. Also," he cried out, carried away by his own course of thought, "how much better would not the world of man go, if he could consult with angels and from them learn to understand the pattern of the universe, which they read with ease because they see it from above!"

So strong was his faith in his undertaking that in the end his teachers gave up opposing him, and reflected that the fame of their pupil might, in time to come, make them themselves famous with him.

The young Softa now for a whole year stayed with the birds. He made his bed in the long grass of the plain, wherein the quail chirps; he climbed the old trees, in which the ring-dove and the thrush build; found for himself a seat in the foliage and sat so still there that he did not disturb them at all. He wandered in high mountains and, just below the snow-line, neighbored with a pair of eagles, watching them come and go.

He returned to Shiraz with much insight and knowledge gathered, and set himself to work upon his wings.

In the Koran he read: "Praise be unto God, who maketh the angels, furnished with two, or three, or four pairs of wings," and resolved to make for himself three pairs, one for his shoulders, one for his waist and one for his feet. During his wanderings he had collected many hundred flight-feathers of eagles, swans and buzzards; he shut himself up with these and worked with such zeal that for a long time he did not see or speak to anyone. But he sang as he worked, and the passers-by stopped and listened, and said: "This young Softa praises God and performs that which is commanded."

But when he had finished his first pair of wings, tried them on and felt their uplifting power, he could not keep his triumph to himself, but spoke of it to his friends.

At first the great people of Shiraz, the divines and high officials smiled at the rumor of his feat. But as the rumors spread, and were asserted by many young people, they grew alarmed.

"If indeed," they said to one another, "this flying boy meets and communicates with angels, the people of Shiraz, as is their wont when anything unusual happens, will go mad with wonder and joy. And who knows what new and revolutionary things the angels may not tell him? For after all," they remarked, "there may be angels in heaven."

They pondered the matter, and the oldest amongst them, a minister to the King whose name was Mirzah Aghai, said: "This young man is dangerous, in as much as he has great dreams. But he is harmless, and will be easy to handle, in as much as he has neglected the study of our real world, in which dreams are tested. We will, in one single lesson, both prove and disprove to him the existence of angels. Or are there no young women in Shiraz?"

The next day he sent for one of the King's dancers, whose name was Thusmu. He explained to her as much of the case as he thought it good for her to know and promised to reward her if she obeyed him. But if she failed, another young dancing-girl, her friend, would be promoted to her place within the royal dancing-troup, at the festival of gathering roses for making attar.

In this way it came to pass that one night, when the Softa had gone up on the roof of his house to look at the stars and calculate how fast he might travel from one of them to the other, he heard his name softly called behind him, and as he turned round caught sight of a slim radiant shape in a robe of gold and silver, who stood up erect, her feet close together, on the edge of the roof.

The young man had his mind filled with the idea of angels; he did not doubt the identity of his visitor, and was not even much surprised, but only over-whelmed with joy. He sent one glance to the sky, to see if the flight of the angel had not left a shining wake therein, and the while the people below pulled down the ladder by which the dancer had ascended his roof. Then he fell down on his knees before her.

She bent her head kindly to him, and looked at him with dark, thick-fringed eyes. "You have carried me in your heart a long time, my servant Saufe," she whispered. "I have come now to inspect that small lodging of mine. How long I shall stay with you in your house depends upon your humility and upon your readiness to carry out my will."

She then sat down cross-legged on the roof, while he still remained on his knees, and they talked together.

"We angels," she said, "do not really need wings to move between heaven and earth, but our own limbs suffice. If you and I become real friends it will be the same with you, and you may destroy the wings on which you are working."

All trembling with ecstasy he asked her how such flight could possibly be performed against all laws of science. She laughed at him, with a laughter like a little clear bell.

"You men," she said, "love laws and argument, and have great faith in the words that come out through your beards. But I am going to convince you that we have a mouth for sweeter debates, and a sweeter mouth for debates. I am going to teach you how angels and men arrive at perfect understanding without argument, in the heavenly manner." And this she did.

For a month the Softa's happiness was so great that his heart gave way beneath it. He forgot all about his work, as time after time he gave himself up to the celestial understanding. He said to Thusmu: "I see now how right was the angel Eblis, who said to God: 'I am more excellent than Adam. Thou hast created him of clay only, but thou hast created me of fire.'" And again he quoted the Scripture to her and sighed: "'Whoever is an ememy to the angels is an enemy to God.'"

He kept the angel in his house, for she had told him that the sight of her loveliness would blind the uninitiated people of Shiraz. Only in the night did she go with him to the house-top, and together they looked at the new moon.

Now it happened that the dancer became very fond of the theologian, for he had a lovely face, and his unexpended vigor made him a great lover. She began to believe him capable of anything. Also she had gathered from her talk with the old minister that he held the boy and his wings in fear, as perilous to himself, his colleagues and the state, and she reflected that she would like to see the old minister, his colleagues and the state perish. Her tenderness for her young friend made her heart almost as soft as his.

When the moon grew full and all the town lay bathed in her light, the two sat close together on the roof. He let his hands run over her and said: "Since I met you, my hands have acquired a life of their own. I realize that God, when He gave men hands, showed them as great a loving-kindness as if He had given them wings." And he lifted up his hands and looked at them.

"Blaspheme not," said she and sighed a little. "It is not I but you who are an angel, and indeed your hands have wonderful strength and life in them. Let me feel so once more, and then show me, tomorrow, the grand things which you have made with them."

To please her he brought her, the next day, all veiled, to his workshop. Then he saw that rats had eaten his eagles' flight-feathers and that the frame of his wings was broken and scattered about. He looked at them and remembered the time when he had worked upon them. But the dancer wept.

"I did not know that this was what he meant to

do," she cried, "and is not Mirzah Aghai a bad man!"

Astounded the Softa asked her what she meant, and in her sorrow and indignation she told him all.

"And oh, my love," she said, "I cannot fly, although they tell me that when I dance I am of an extraordinary lightness. Be not angry with me, but remember that Mirzah Aghai and his friends are great people, against whom a poor girl can do nothing. And they are rich, and own lovely things. And you cannot expect a dancing-girl to be an angel."

At that he fell upon his face and did not speak a word. Thusmu sat down beside him and her tears dropped in his hair as she wound it round her fingers.

"You are such a wonderful boy," she said. "With you everything is great and sweet and truly heavenly, and I love you. So do not worry, dear."

He lifted his head, looked at her and said: "God has appointed none but angels to preside over hell-fire."

"There is nobody," said she, "who recites from the Holy Book as beautifully as you."

Again he looked at her. "And if," he said, "thou didst behold when the angels cause the unbelievers to die. They strike their faces and say unto them: 'Taste ye pain of burning, this shall ye suffer for what your hands have done.'"

After a while she said: "Perhaps you can still repair the wings and they may be as good as new."

"I cannot repair them," he said, "and now that your work is done you must go, since it will be dangerous to you to stay with me. For Mirzah Aghai and his friends are great men. And you are to dance at the festival of gathering roses for making attar."

"Do you forget Thusmu?" said she.

"No," said he.

"Will you come and see me dance?" she asked.

"Yes, if I can," he answered.

"I shall always," she said gravely, as she got up, "hope that you will come. For without hope one cannot dance."

And with that she went away sadly.

Saufe now could not stay in his house; he left the door of his workshop open and wandered about in the town. But he could not stay in the town, so went away to the woods and the plains. But he could not bear the sight or song of the birds and soon returned to the streets. Here at times he stopped in his wanderings in front of a bird-seller's shop and for a long while watched the birds in their cages.

When his friends talked to him he did not recognize them. But when boys in the streets laughed at him and cried: "Behold the Softa who believed Thusmu to be an angel," he stood still, looked at them and said: "I believe so still. It is not my faith in the dancer that I have lost, but my faith in the angels. Today I cannot remember how, when I was young, I imagined the angels to look. I feel that they will be terrible to behold. Whoever is an enemy to the angels is an enemy to God, and whoever is an enemy to God has no hope left. I have no hope, and without hope you cannot fly. This is what makes me restless."

In this way the unfortunate Softa roamed about for

a year. I myself, when I was a small boy, have met him in the streets, wrapped in his shabby black cloak and in a darker cloak of everlasting loneliness.

At the end of the year he went away, and was no more seen in Shiraz.

"This," said Mira Jama, "is the first part of my story."

But it befell, many years later, when as a youth I first began to tell tales to delight the world and make it wiser, that I traveled to the sandy seashores, to the villages of the pearl-fishers, in order to hear the adventures of these men, and to make them mine.

For many things happen to those who dive to the bottom of the sea. Pearls in themselves are things of mystery and adventure; if you follow the career of a single pearl it will give you material for a hundred tales. And pearls are like poets' tales: disease turned into loveliness, at the same time transparent and opaque, secrets of the depths brought to light to please young women, who will recognize in them the deeper secrets of their own bosoms.

Later in life I have recounted to Kings, with much success, the stories which were first told me by these meek and simple fishermen.

Now within their narratives a name came back so often that I grew curious, and begged them to tell me more about the person who wore it. Then they informed me that the man had become famous amongst them because of his audacity and of his exceptional and inexplicable luck. In fact, the name, Elnazred, which they had given him, in their dialect meant "the successful" or "the happy and content" person. He would dive down into greater depths and stay down there longer than any other fisherman, and he never failed to bring up such oysters as contained the finest pearls. It was believed in the pearl-fishers' villages that he had got, in the deep water, a friend—maybe some fair young mermaid or maybe again some demon of the sea—to guide him. While the other fishermen were exploited by their trading companies and would remain poor all their time, the happy person had made a neat fortune for himself, had purchased a house and a garden inland, brought his mother to live there, and married off his brothers. But he still kept for his own use a small hut on the beach. In spite of his demoniacal reputation he was, it seemed, on dry land and in daily life, a peaceful man.

I am a poet, and something in these reports brought back to me tales of long ago. I resolved to look up this successful person and to make him tell me about himself. First, I sought him in vain in his pleasant house and garden; then one night I walked along the beach to his hut.

The moon was full in the sky, the long gray waves came in one by one, and everything around me seemed to agree to keep a secret. I looked at it all, and felt that I was going to hear, and to compose, a beautiful story.

The man I sought was not in his hut, but was sitting on the sand, gazing at the sea and from time to time throwing a pebble into it. The moon shone upon him, and I saw that he was a pretty, fat man, and that his tranquil countenance did indeed express harmony and happiness.

I saluted him with reverence, told him my name and explained that I was out for a walk in the clear, warm night. He returned my greeting courteously and benevolently and informed me that I was already known to him by repute as a youth keen to perfect himself in the art of story-telling. He then invited me to sit down on the sand beside him. He talked for a while of the moon and the sea. After a pause he remarked that it was a long time since he had heard a tale told. Would I, as we were sitting so pleasantly together in the clear, warm night, tell him a story?

I was eager to prove my skill, and also trusted that it might serve to forward my purpose with him. So I searched my memory for a good tale. Somehow, I do not know why, the story of the Softa Saufe had been running in my mind. Now in a low, sweet voice, concordant with the moon and the waves, I began:

"In Shiraz lived a young student of theology . . ."

The happy man listened quietly and attentively. But as I came to the passage of the lovers on the house-top and named the dancer Thusmu, he lifted up his hand and looked at it. I had taken much trouble in inventing this pretty moonlight scene, and it was dear to my poet's heart; I recognized the gesture and in great surprise and alarm cried out: "You are the Softa of Shiraz!"

"Yes," said the happy man.

It is to a poet a thing of awe to find that his story is true. I was only a boy and a novice at my art; the hair rose on my head and I nearly got up and ran away. But something in the happy man's voice held me to the spot.

"Once," he said, "I had the welfare of the Softa Saufe, of whom you have just told me, much at heart. By this time I had almost forgotten him. But I am pleased to know that he has got into a story, for that is probably what he was made for, and in future I shall leave him therein confidently. Go on with your tale, Mira Jama, story-teller, and let me hear the end of it."

I trembled at his demand, but again his manner fascinated me and enabled me to take up the thread of my story. At first I felt that he was bestowing an honor upon me and soon, as I went on, that I was bestowing an honor upon him as well. The triumph of the story-teller filled my heart. I told my story very movingly and when I had finished it, there upon that lean sea-sand, with only myself and him under the full moon, my face was bathed in tears.

The happy man comforted me and begged me not to take a story too much to heart. So when I had regained my voice I beseeched him to tell me all that had happened to him after he left Shiraz. For his experiences in the deep sea, and the luck which had brought him wealth and fame amongst men, would be sure to make as lovely a story as the one I had told him, and a more cheerful one. Princes, great ladies, dancers, I explained to him, love a sad tale, so do the beggars by the city walls. But I meant to be a story-teller to the whole world, and the men of business and their wives will demand a tale that ends well.

The happy man was silent for a while.

"What happened to me," he then answered me, "after I left Shiraz, makes no story at all.

"I am famous amongst men," he said, "because I am capable of staying at the bottom of the sea longer than they. This capacity, if you will, is a small heritage from the Softa of whom you have told me. But that makes no story. The fishes have been kind to me, and they betray nobody. So that makes no story.

"All the same," he went on after a longer silence, "in return for your tale, and so as not to discourage a young poet, although it makes no story, I shall tell you what happened to me after I left Shiraz." He then began his narration and I listened to him.

"I shall leave out the explanation of how I got away from Shiraz and came here, and take up the account of my experiences only where it will please the men of business and their wives.

"For when I first went down to the bottom of the sea, in search of a certain rare pearl of which at the time I thought much, an old cowfish with horn-rimmed spectacles took me in hand. As a very small fish she had been caught in the net of two old fishermen, and had spent a whole night there, in the bilge water of their boat, listening to the talk of these men, who must have been pious and profound people. But in the morning, when the net was lifted ashore, she slipped through the meshes and swam away. Since then she smiles at the other fishes' distrust of men. For really, she explains, if a fish knows how to behave herself, she can easily manage them. She has even come to take an interest in the nature and the customs of man, and often lectures upon these to an audience of fishes. She also likes to discuss them with me.

"I owe her much, for she holds a great position in the sea, and as her protégé I have been received everywhere; I owe to her also much of the wealth and fame which have made me, as you have been told, a happy man. I owe her more than that, for in our long talks together she has imparted to me the philosophy which has set me at rest.

"This is what she advocates:

"'The fish,' she proclaims, 'amongst all creatures is the one most carefully and accurately made in the image of the Lord. All things work together for the good of her, and from this we may conclude that she is called according to his purpose.

"'Man can move but in one plane, and is tied to the earth. Still the earth supports him only by the narrow space under the soles of his two feet; he must bear his own weight and sigh beneath it. He must, so I gathered from the talk of my old fishermen, climb the hills of the earth laboriously; it may happen to him to tumble down from them, and the earth then receives him with hardness. Even the birds, which have wings to them, if they do not strain their wings are betrayed by the air wherein they are set, and flung down.

"'We fish are upheld and supported on all sides.

We lean confidently and harmoniously upon our element. We move in all dimensions, and whatever course we take, the mighty waters out of reverence for our virtue change shape accordingly.

" 'We have no hands, so cannot construct anything at all, and are never tempted by vain ambition to alter anything whatever in the universe of the Lord. We sow not and toil not; therefore no estimates of ours will turn out wrong, and no expectations fail. The greatest amongst us in their spheres have reached perfect darkness. And the pattern of the universe we read with ease, because we see it from below.

" 'We carry with us, in these our floatings about, an account of events excellently suited to prove to us our privileged position and to maintain our fellow-feeling. It is known to man also and even takes up an important place in his history, but in accordance with his infantile conception of things in general, he has but a muddled understanding of it. I shall record it to you.

" 'When God had created heaven and earth, the earth caused him sore disappointment. Man, capable of falling, fell almost immediately, and with him all that was in the dry land. And it repented the Lord that he had made man, and the beasts of the earth, and the fowls of the air.

" 'But the fish did not fall, and never will fall, for how or whereto would we fall? So the Lord looked kindly at His fish and was comforted by the sight of them, since amongst all creation they alone had not disappointed him.

" 'He resolved to reward the fish according to their merit. So all the fountains of the great deep were broken up, and the windows of heaven were opened, and the waters of the flood came upon the earth. And the waters prevailed and were increased, and all the high hills that were under the whole heaven were covered. And the waters prevailed exceedingly, and all flesh died that moved upon the earth, both of fowl and of cattle, and of beast and of every man. All that was on dry land died.

" 'I shall not, in giving you this report, dwell long upon the pleasantness of that age and state. For I have got compassion with man, and besides tact. You yourself, before you found your way to us, may have set your heart upon cattle, camels and horses, or you may have kept pigeons and pea-fowl. You are young, and may recently have been attached to some such creature, of your own species and yet somehow like a bird, as you name a young woman. (Although, by the way, it would be better for you if it were not so, for I remember the words of my fishermen: that a young woman will make her lover taste the pain of burning, and you might otherwise come to take an interest in one of my own nieces, quite unusually salty young creatures, who will never make a lover taste any pain of burning.) I shall but briefly mention that we did have a hundred and fifty days of abundance, and that blessed plenty appeared with full horn.

" 'I shall further—this time for my own sake—in the wise and proven manner of the fish, pass lightly over the fact that man, although fallen and corrupted, once more succeeded, by craft, in coming out on top.

" 'It does, however, remain open to doubt whether,

through this apparent triumph, man obtained true welfare. How will real security be obtained by a creature ever anxious about the direction in which he moves, and attaching vital importance to his rising or falling? How can equilibrium be obtained by a creature which refuses to give up the idea of hope and risk?

" 'We fish rest quietly, on all sides supported, within an element which all the time accurately and unfailingly evens itself out. An element which may be said to have taken over our personal existence, in as much as, regardless of individual shape and whether we be flat fish or round fish, our weight and body are calculated according to the quantity of our surroundings which we displace.

" 'Our experience has proved to us, as your own will some time do it to you, that one may quite well float without hope, ay, that one will even float better without it. Therefore, also, our creed states that with us all hope is left out.

" 'We run no risks. For our changing of place in existence never creates, or leaves after it, what man calls a way, upon which phenomenon—in reality no phenomenon but an illusion—he will waste inexplicable passionate deliberation.

" 'Man, in the end, is alarmed by the idea of time, and unbalanced by incessant wanderings between past and future. The inhabitants of a liquid world have brought past and future together in the maxim: *Après nous le déluge.*' "

Babette's Feast

1. *Two Ladies of Berlevaag*

In Norway there is a fjord—a long narrow arm of the sea between tall mountains—named Berlevaag Fjord. At the foot of the mountains the small town of Berlevaag looks like a child's toy-town of little wooden pieces painted gray, yellow, pink and many other colors.

Sixty-five years ago two elderly ladies lived in one of the yellow houses. Other ladies at that time wore a bustle, and the two sisters might have worn it as gracefully as any of them, for they were tall and willowy. But they had never possessed any article of fashion; they had dressed demurely in gray or black all their lives. They were christened Martine and Philippa, after Martin Luther and his friend Philip Melanchton. Their father had been a Dean and a prophet, the founder of a pious ecclesiastic party or sect, which was known and looked up to in all the country of Norway. Its members renounced the pleasures of this world, for the earth and all that it held to them was but a kind of illusion, and the true reality was the New Jerusalem toward which they were longing. They swore not at all, but their communication was yea yea and nay nay, and they called one another Brother and Sister.

The Dean had married late in life and by now had long been dead. His disciples were becoming fewer in number every year, whiter or balder and harder of hearing; they were even becoming somewhat querulous and quarrelsome, so that sad little schisms would arise in the congregation. But they still gathered together to read and interpret the Word. They had all known the Dean's daughters as little girls; to them they were even now very small sisters, precious for their dear father's sake. In the yellow house they felt that their Master's spirit was with them; here they were at home and at peace.

These two ladies had a French maid-of-all-work, Babette.

It was a strange thing for a couple of Puritan women in a small Norwegian town; it might even seem to call for an explanation. The people of Berlevaag found the explanation in the sisters' piety and kindness of heart. For the old Dean's daughters spent their time and their small income in works of charity; no sorrowful or distressed creature knocked on their door in vain. And Babette had come to that door twelve years ago as a friendless fugitive, almost mad with grief and fear.

But the true reason for Babette's presence in the two sisters' house was to be found further back in time and deeper down in the domain of human hearts.

II. *Martine's Lover*

As young girls, Martine and Philippa had been extraordinarily pretty, with the almost supernatural fairness of flowering fruit trees or perpetual snow. They were never to be seen at balls or parties, but people turned when they passed in the streets, and the young men of Berlevaag went to church to watch them walk up the aisle. The younger sister also had a lovely voice, which on Sundays filled the church with sweetness. To the Dean's congregation earthly love, and marriage with it, were trivial matters, in themselves nothing but illusions; still it is possible that more than one of the elderly Brothers had been prizing the maidens far above rubies and had suggested as much to their father. But the Dean had declared that to him in his calling his daughters were his right and left hand. Who could want to bereave him of them? And the fair girls had been brought up to an ideal of heavenly love; they were all filled with it and did not let themselves be touched by the flames of this world.

All the same they had upset the peace of heart of two gentlemen from the great world outside Berlevaag.

There was a young officer named Lorens Loewenhielm, who had led a gay life in his garrison town and had run into debt. In the year of 1854, when Martine was eighteen and Philippa seventeen, his angry father sent him on a month's visit to his aunt in her old country house of Fossum near Berlevaag, where he would have time to meditate and to better his ways. One day he rode into town and met Martine in the marketplace. He looked down at the pretty girl, and she looked up at the fine horseman. When she had passed him and disappeared he was not certain whether he was to believe his own eyes.

In the Loewenhielm family there existed a legend to the effect that long ago a gentleman of the name had married a Huldre, a female mountain spirit of Norway, who is so fair that the air round her shines and quivers. Since then, from time to time, members of the family had been second-sighted. Young Lorens till now had not been aware of any particular spiritual gift in his own nature. But at this one moment there rose before his eyes a sudden, mighty vision of a higher and purer life, with no creditors, dunning letters or parental lectures, with no secret, unpleasant pangs of conscience and with a gentle, golden-haired angel to guide and reward him.

Through his pious aunt he got admission to the Dean's house, and saw that Martine was even lovelier without a bonnet. He followed her slim figure with adoring eyes, but he loathed and despised the figure which he himself cut in her nearness. He was amazed and shocked by the fact that he could find nothing at all to say, and no inspiration in the glass of water before him. "Mercy and Truth, dear brethren, have met together," said the Dean. "Righteousness and Bliss have kissed one another." And the young man's thoughts were with the moment when Lorens and Martine should be kissing each other. He repeated his visit time after time, and each time seemed to himself to grow smaller and more insignificant and contemptible.

When in the evening he came back to his aunt's house he kicked his shining riding-boots to the corners of his room; he even laid his head on the table and wept.

On the last day of his stay he made a last attempt to communicate his feelings to Martine. Till now it had been easy for him to tell a pretty girl that he loved her, but the tender words stuck in his throat as he looked into this maiden's face. When he had said good-bye to the party, Martine saw him to the door with a candlestick in her hand. The light shone on her mouth and threw upwards the shadows of her long eyelashes. He was about to leave in dumb despair when on the threshold he suddenly seized her hand and pressed it to his lips.

"I am going away forever!" he cried. "I shall never, never see you again! For I have learned here that Fate is hard, and that in this world there are things which are impossible!"

When he was once more back in his garrison town he thought his adventure over, and found that he did not like to think of it at all. While the other young officers talked of their love affairs, he was silent on his. For seen from the officers' mess, and so to say with its eyes, it was a pitiful business. How had it come to pass that a lieutenant of the hussars had let himself be defeated and frustrated by a set of long-faced sectarians, in the bare-floored rooms of an old Dean's house?

Then he became afraid; panic fell upon him. Was it the family madness which made him still carry with him the dream-like picture of a maiden so fair that she made the air round her shine with purity and holiness? He did not want to be a dreamer; he wanted to be like his brother-officers.

So he pulled himself together, and in the greatest effort of his young life made up his mind to forget what had happened to him in Berlevaag. From now on, he resolved, he would look forward, not back. He would concentrate on his career, and the day was to come when he would cut a brilliant figure in a brilliant world.

His mother was pleased with the result of his visit to Fossum, and in her letters expressed her gratitude to his aunt. She did not know by what queer, winding roads her son had reached his happy moral standpoint.

The ambitious young officer soon caught the attention of his superiors and made unusually quick advancement. He was sent to France and to Russia, and on his return he married a lady-in-waiting to Queen Sophia. In these high circles he moved with grace and ease, pleased with his surroundings and with himself. He even in the course of time benefited from words and turns which had stuck in his mind from the Dean's house, for piety was now in fashion at Court.

In the yellow house of Berlevaag, Philippa sometimes turned the talk to the handsome, silent young man who had so suddenly made his appearance, and so suddenly disappeared again. Her elder sister would then answer her gently, with a still, clear face, and find other things to discuss.

III. *Philippa's Lover*

A year later a more distinguished person even than Lieutenant Loewenhielm came to Berlevaag.

The great singer Achille Papin of Paris had sung for a week at the Royal Opera of Stockholm, and had carried away his audience there as everywhere. One evening a lady of the Court, who had been dreaming of a romance with the artist, had described to him the wild, grandiose scenery of Norway. His own romantic nature was stirred by the narration, and he had laid his way back to France round the Norwegian coast. But he felt small in the sublime surroundings; with nobody to talk to he fell into that melancholy in which he saw himself as an old man, at the end of his career, till on a Sunday, when he could think of nothing else to do, he went to church and heard Philippa sing.

Then in one single moment he knew and understood all. For here were the snowy summits, the wild flowers and the white Nordic nights, translated into his own language of music, and brought him in a young woman's voice. Like Lorens Loewenhielm he had a vision.

"Almighty God," he thought, "Thy power is without end, and Thy mercy reacheth unto the clouds! And here is a prima donna of the opera who will lay Paris at her feet."

Achille Papin at this time was a handsome man of forty, with curly black hair and a red mouth. The idolization of nations had not spoilt him; he was a kind-hearted person and honest toward himself.

He went straight to the yellow house, gave his name—which told the Dean nothing—and explained that he was staying in Berlevaag for his health, and the while would be happy to take on the young lady as a pupil.

He did not mention the Opera of Paris, but described at length how beautifully Miss Philippa would come to sing in church, to the glory of God.

For a moment he forgot himself, for when the Dean asked whether he was a Roman Catholic he answered according to truth, and the old clergyman, who had never seen a live Roman Catholic, grew a little pale. All the same the Dean was pleased to speak French, which reminded him of his young days when he had studied the works of the great French Lutheran writer, Lefèvre d'Etaples. And as nobody could long withstand Achille Papin when he had really set his heart on a matter, in the end the father gave his consent, and remarked to his daughter: "God's paths run across the sea and the snowy mountains, where man's eye sees no track."

So the great French singer and the young Norwegian novice set to work together. Achille's expectation grew into certainty and his certainty into ecstasy. He thought: "I have been wrong in believing that I was growing old. My greatest triumphs are before me! The world will once more believe in miracles when she and I sing together!"

After a while he could not keep his dreams to himself, but told Philippa about them.

She would, he said, rise like a star above any diva of the past or present. The Emperor and Empress, the Princes, great ladies and *bels esprits* of Paris would listen to her, and shed tears. The common people too would worship her, and she would bring consolation and strength to the wronged and oppressed. When she left the Grand Opera upon her master's arm, the crowd would unharness her horses, and themselves draw her to the Café Anglais, where a magnificent supper awaited her.

Philippa did not repeat these prospects to her father or her sister, and this was the first time in her life that she had had a secret from them.

The teacher now gave his pupil the part of Zerlina in Mozart's opera *Don Giovanni* to study. He himself, as often before, sang Don Giovanni's part.

He had never in his life sung as now. In the duet of the second act—which is called the seduction duet —he was swept off his feet by the heavenly music and the heavenly voices. As the last melting note died away he seized Philippa's hands, drew her toward him and kissed her solemnly, as a bridegroom might kiss his bride before the altar. Then he let her go. For the moment was too sublime for any further word or movement; Mozart himself was looking down on the two.

Philippa went home, told her father that she did not want any more singing lessons and asked him to write and tell Monsieur Papin so.

The Dean said: "And God's paths run across the rivers, my child."

When Achille got the Dean's letter he sat immovable for an hour. He thought: "I have been wrong. My day is over. Never again shall I be the divine Papin. And this poor weedy garden of the world has lost its nightingale!"

A little later he thought: "I wonder what is the

matter with that hussy? Did I kiss her, by any chance?"

In the end he thought: "I have lost my life for a kiss, and I have no remembrance at all of the kiss! Don Giovanni kissed Zerlina, and Achille Papin pays for it! Such is the fate of the artist!"

In the Dean's house Martine felt that the matter was deeper than it looked, and searched her sister's face. For a moment, slightly trembling, she too imagined that the Roman Catholic gentleman might have tried to kiss Philippa. She did not imagine that her sister might have been surprised and frightened by something in her own nature.

Achille Papin took the first boat from Berlevaag.

Of this visitor from the great world the sisters spoke but little; they lacked the words with which to discuss him.

IV. *A Letter from Paris*

Fifteen years later, on a rainy June night of 1871, the bell-rope of the yellow house was pulled violently three times. The mistresses of the house opened the door to a massive, dark, deadly pale woman with a bundle on her arm, who stared at them, took a step forward and fell down on the doorstep in a dead swoon. When the frightened ladies had restored her to life she sat up, gave them one more glance from her sunken eyes and, all the time without a word, fumbled in her wet clothes and brought out a letter which she handed to them.

The letter was addressed to them all right, but it was written in French. The sisters put their heads together and read it. It ran as follows:

Ladies!

Do you remember me? Ah, when I think of you I have the heart filled with wild lilies-of-the-valley! Will the memory of a Frenchman's devotion bend your hearts to save the life of a Frenchwoman?

The bearer of this letter, Madame Babette Hersant, like my beautiful Empress herself, has had to flee from Paris. Civil war has raged in our streets. French hands have shed French blood. The noble Communards, standing up for the Rights of Man, have been crushed and annihilated. Madame Hersant's husband and son, both eminent ladies' hairdressers, have been shot. She herself was arrested as a Pétroleuse—(which word is used here for women who set fire to houses with petroleum)—and has narrowly escaped the blood-stained hands of General Galliffet. She has lost all she possessed and dares not remain in France.

A nephew of hers is cook to the boat *Anna Colbioernsson*, bound for Christiania—(as I believe, the capital of Norway)—and he has obtained shipping opportunity for his aunt. This is now her last sad resort!

Knowing that I was once a visitor to your magnificent country she comes to me, asks me if there be any good people in Norway and begs me, if it be so, to supply her with a letter to them. The two words of 'good people' immediately bring before my eyes your picture, sacred to my heart. I send her to you. How she is to get from Christiania to Berlevaag I know not, having forgotten the map of Norway. But she is a Frenchwoman, and you will find that in her misery she has still got resourcefulness, majesty and true stoicism.

I envy her in her despair: she is to see your faces.

As you receive her mercifully, send a merciful thought back to France.

For fifteen years, Miss Philippa, I have grieved that your voice should never fill the Grand Opera of Paris. When tonight I think of you, no doubt surrounded by a gay and loving family, and of myself: gray, lonely, forgotten by those who once applauded and adored me, I feel that you may have chosen the better part in life. What is fame? What is glory? The grave awaits us all!

And yet, my lost Zerlina, and yet, soprano of the snow! As I write this I feel that the grave is not the end. In Paradise I shall hear your voice again. There you will sing, without fears or scruples, as God meant you to sing. There you will be the great artist that God meant you to be. Ah! how you will enchant the angels.

Babette can cook.

Deign to receive, my ladies, the humble homage of the friend who was once

Achille Papin

At the bottom of the page, as a P.S. were neatly

printed the first two bars of the duet between Don Giovanni and Zerlina, like this:

The two sisters till now had kept only a small servant of fifteen to help them in the house and they felt that they could not possibly afford to take on an elderly, experienced housekeeper. But Babette told them that she would serve Monsieur Papin's good people for nothing, and that she would take service with nobody else. If they sent her away she must die. Babette remained in the house of the Dean's daughters for twelve years, until the time of this tale.

v. *Still Life*

Babette had arrived haggard and wild-eyed like a hunted animal, but in her new, friendly surroundings she soon acquired all the appearance of a respectable and trusted servant. She had appeared to be a beggar; she turned out to be a conqueror. Her quiet countenance and her steady, deep glance had magnetic qualities; under her eyes things moved, noiselessly, into their proper places.

Her mistresses at first had trembled a little, just as the Dean had once done, at the idea of receiving a Papist under their roof. But they did not like to worry a hard-tried fellow-creature with catechization;

neither were they quite sure of their French. They silently agreed that the example of a good Lutheran life would be the best means of converting their servant. In this way Babette's presence in the house became, so to say, a moral spur to its inhabitants.

They had distrusted Monsieur Papin's assertion that Babette could cook. In France, they knew, people ate frogs. They showed Babette how to prepare a split cod and an ale-and-bread-soup; during the demonstration the Frenchwoman's face became absolutely expressionless. But within a week Babette cooked a split cod and an ale-and-bread-soup as well as anybody born and bred in Berlevaag.

The idea of French luxury and extravagance next had alarmed and dismayed the Dean's daughters. The first day after Babette had entered their service they took her before them and explained to her that they were poor and that to them luxurious fare was sinful. Their own food must be as plain as possible; it was the soup-pails and baskets for their poor that signified. Babette nodded her head; as a girl, she informed her ladies, she had been cook to an old priest who was a saint. Upon this the sisters resolved to surpass the French priest in asceticism. And they soon found that from the day when Babette took over the housekeeping its cost was miraculously reduced, and the soup-pails and baskets acquired a new, mysterious power to stimulate and strengthen their poor and sick.

The world outside the yellow house also came to acknowledge Babette's excellence. The refugee never learned to speak the language of her new country, but in her broken Norwegian she beat down the prices of Berlevaag's flintiest tradesmen. She was held in awe on the quay and in the marketplace.

The old Brothers and Sisters, who had first looked askance at the foreign woman in their midst, felt a happy change in their little sisters' life, rejoiced at it and benefited by it. They found that troubles and cares had been conjured away from their existence, and that now they had money to give away, time for the confidences and complaints of their old friends and peace for meditating on heavenly matters. In the course of time not a few of the brotherhood included Babette's name in their prayers, and thanked God for the speechless stranger, the dark Martha in the house of their two fair Marys. The stone which the builders had almost refused had become the headstone of the corner.

The ladies of the yellow house were the only ones to know that their cornerstone had a mysterious and alarming feature to it, as if it was somehow related to the Black Stone of Mecca, the Kaaba itself.

Hardly ever did Babette refer to her past life. When in early days the sisters had gently condoled her upon her losses, they had been met with that majesty and stoicism of which Monsieur Papin had written. "What will you ladies?" she had answered, shrugging her shoulders. "It is Fate."

But one day she suddenly informed them that she had for many years held a ticket in a French lottery, and that a faithful friend in Paris was still renewing it for her every year. Some time she might win the *grand prix* of ten thousand francs. At that they felt that their cook's old carpetbag was made from a magic carpet; at a given moment she might mount it and be carried off, back to Paris.

And it happened when Martine or Philippa spoke to Babette that they would get no answer, and would wonder if she had even heard what they said. They would find her in the kitchen, her elbows on the table and her temples on her hands, lost in the study of a heavy black book which they secretly suspected to be a popish prayer-book. Or she would sit immovable on the three-legged kitchen chair, her strong hands in her lap and her dark eyes wide open, as enigmatical and fatal as a Pythia upon her tripod. At such moments they realized that Babette was deep, and that in the soundings of her being there were passions, there were memories and longings of which they knew nothing at all.

A little cold shiver ran through them, and in their hearts they thought: "Perhaps after all she had indeed been a Pétroleuse."

vi. *Babette's Good Luck*

The fifteenth of December was the Dean's hundredth anniversary.

His daughters had long been looking forward to this day and had wished to celebrate it, as if their dear father were still among his disciples. Therefore it had been to them a sad and incomprehensible thing that in this last year discord and dissension had been raising their heads in his flock. They had endeavored to make peace, but they were aware that they had failed. It was as if the fine and lovable vigor of their father's personality had been evaporating, the way Hoffmann's anodyne will evaporate when left on the shelf in a bottle without a cork. And his departure had left the door ajar to things hitherto unknown to the two sisters, much younger than his spiritual children. From a past half a century back, when the unshepherded sheep had been running astray in the mountains, uninvited dismal guests pressed through the opening on the heels of the worshippers and seemed to darken the little rooms and to let in the cold. The sins of old Brothers and Sisters came, with late piercing repentance like a toothache, and the sins of others against them came back with bitter resentment, like a poisoning of the blood.

There were in the congregation two old women who before their conversion had spread slander upon each other, and thereby to each other ruined a marriage and an inheritance. Today they could not remember happenings of yesterday or a week ago, but they remembered this forty-year-old wrong and kept going through the ancient accounts; they scowled at each other. There was an old Brother who suddenly called to mind how another Brother, forty-five years ago, had cheated him in a deal; he could have wished to dismiss the matter from his mind, but it stuck there like a deep-seated, festering splinter. There was a gray, honest skipper and a furrowed, pious widow, who in their young days, while she was the wife of another man, had been sweethearts. Of late each had begun to grieve, while shifting the burden of guilt from his own shoulders to those of the other and back again, and to worry about the possible terrible consequences, through all eternity, to himself, brought upon him by one who had pretended to hold him dear. They grew pale at the meetings in the yellow house and avoided each other's eyes.

As the birthday drew nearer, Martine and Philippa felt the responsibility growing heavier. Would their ever-faithful father look down to his daughters and call them by name as unjust stewards? Between them they talked matters over and repeated their father's saying: that God's paths were running even across the salt sea, and the snow-clad mountains, where man's eye sees no track.

One day of this summer the post brought a letter from France to Madame Babette Hersant. This in itself was a surprising thing, for during these twelve years Babette had received no letter. What, her mistresses wondered, could it contain? They took it into the kitchen to watch her open and read it. Babette opened it, read it, lifted her eyes from it to her ladies' faces and told them that her number in the French lottery had come out. She had won ten thousand francs.

The news made such an impression on the two sisters that for a full minute they could not speak a word. They themselves were used to receiving their modest pension in small instalments; it was difficult to them even to imagine the sum of ten thousand francs in a pile. Then they pressed Babette's hand, their own hands trembling a little. They had never before pressed the hand of a person who the moment before had come into possession of ten thousand francs.

After a while they realized that the happenings concerned themselves as well as Babette. The country of France, they felt, was slowly rising before their servant's horizon, and correspondingly their own existence was sinking beneath their feet. The ten thousand francs which made her rich—how poor did they not make the house she had served! One by one old forgotten cares and worries began to peep out at them from the four corners of the kitchen. The congratulations died on their lips, and the two pious women were ashamed of their own silence.

During the following days they announced the news to their friends with joyous faces, but it did them good to see these friends' faces grow sad as they listened to them. Nobody, it was felt in the Brotherhood, could really blame Babette: birds will return to their nests and human beings to the country of their birth. But did that good and faithful servant realize that in going away from Berlevaag she would be leaving many old and poor people in distress? Their little sisters would have no more time for the sick and sorrowful. Indeed, indeed, lotteries were ungodly affairs.

In due time the money arrived through offices in Christiania and Berlevaag. The two ladies helped

Babette to count it, and gave her a box to keep it in. They handled, and became familiar with, the ominous bits of paper.

They dared not question Babette upon the date of her departure. Dared they hope that she would remain with them over the fifteenth of December?

The mistresses had never been quite certain how much of their private conversation the cook followed or understood. So they were surprised when on a September evening Babette came into the drawing room, more humble or subdued than they had ever seen her, to ask a favor. She begged them, she said, to let her cook a celebration dinner on the Dean's birthday.

The ladies had not intended to have any dinner at all. A very plain supper with a cup of coffee was the most sumptuous meal to which they had ever asked any guest to sit down. But Babette's dark eyes were as eager and pleading as a dog's; they agreed to let her have her way. At this the cook's face lighted up.

But she had more to say. She wanted, she said, to cook a French dinner, a real French dinner, for this one time. Martine and Philippa looked at each other. They did not like the idea; they felt that they did not know what it might imply. But the very strangeness of the request disarmed them. They had no arguments wherewith to meet the proposition of cooking a real French dinner.

Babette drew a long sigh of happiness, but still she did not move. She had one more prayer to make.

She begged that her mistresses would allow her to pay for the French dinner with her own money.

"No, Babette!" the ladies exclaimed. How could she imagine such a thing? Did she believe that they would allow her to spend her precious money on food and drink—or on them? No, Babette, indeed.

Babette took a step forward. There was something formidable in the move, like a wave rising. Had she stepped forth like this, in 1871, to plant a red flag on a barricade? She spoke, in her queer Norwegian, with classical French eloquence. Her voice was like a song.

Ladies! Had she ever, during twelve years, asked you a favor? No! And why not? Ladies, you who say your prayers every day, can you imagine what it means to a human heart to have no prayer to make? What would Babette have had to pray for? Nothing! Tonight she had a prayer to make, from the bottom of her heart. Do you not then feel tonight, my ladies, that it becomes you to grant it her, with such joy as that with which the good God has granted you your own?

The ladies for a while said nothing. Babette was right; it was her first request these twelve years; very likely it would be her last. They thought the matter over. After all, they told themselves, their cook was now better off than they, and a dinner could make no difference to a person who owned ten thousand francs.

Their consent in the end completely changed Babette. They saw that as a young woman she had been beautiful. And they wondered whether in this hour they themselves had not, for the very first time, become to her the "good people" of Achille Papin's letter.

VII. *The Turtle*

In November Babette went for a journey.

She had preparations to make, she told her mistresses, and would need a leave of a week or ten days. Her nephew, who had once got her to Christiania, was still sailing to that town; she must see him and talk things over with him. Babette was a bad sailor; she had spoken of her one sea-voyage, from France to Norway, as of the most horrible experience of her life. Now she was strangely collected; the ladies felt that her heart was already in France.

After ten days she came back to Berlevaag.

Had she got things arranged as she wished? the ladies asked. Yes, she answered, she had seen her nephew and given him a list of the goods which he was to bring her from France. To Martine and Philippa this was a dark saying, but they did not care to talk of her departure, so they asked her no more questions.

Babette was somewhat nervous during the next weeks. But one December day she triumphantly announced to her mistresses that the goods had come to Christiania, had been transshipped there, and on this very day had arrived at Berlevaag. She had, she added, engaged an old man with a wheelbarrow to have them conveyed from the harbor to the house.

But what goods, Babette? the ladies asked. Why, Mesdames, Babette replied, the ingredients for the birthday dinner. Praise be to God, they had all arrived in good condition from Paris.

By this time Babette, like the bottled demon of the fairy tale, had swelled and grown to such dimensions that her mistresses felt small before her. They now saw the French dinner coming upon them, a thing of incalculable nature and range. But they had never in their life broken a promise; they gave themselves into their cook's hands.

All the same when Martine saw a barrow load of bottles wheeled into the kitchen, she stood still. She touched the bottles and lifted up one. "What is there in this bottle, Babette?" she asked in a low voice. "Not wine?" "Wine, Madame!" Babette answered. "No, Madame. It is a Clos Vougeot 1846!" After a moment she added: "From Philippe, in Rue Montorgueil!" Martine had never suspected that wines could have names to them, and was put to silence.

Late in the evening she opened the door to a ring, and was once more faced with the wheelbarrow, this time with a red-haired sailor-boy behind it, as if the old man had by this time been worn out. The youth grinned at her as he lifted a big, undefinable object from the barrow. In the light of the lamp it looked like some greenish-black stone, but when set down on the kitchen floor it suddenly shot out a snake-like head and moved it slightly from side to side. Martine had seen pictures of tortoises, and had even as a child owned a pet tortoise, but this thing was monstrous in size and terrible to behold. She backed out of the kitchen without a word.

She dared not tell her sister what she had seen. She passed an almost sleepless night; she thought of her father and felt that on his very birthday she and her sister were lending his house to a witches' sabbath. When at last she fell asleep she had a terrible dream, in which she saw Babette poisoning the old Brothers and Sisters, Philippa and herself.

Early in the morning she got up, put on her gray cloak and went out in the dark street. She walked from house to house, opened her heart to her Brothers and Sisters, and confessed her guilt. She and Philippa, she said, had meant no harm; they had granted their servant a prayer and had not foreseen what might come of it. Now she could not tell what, on her father's birthday, her guests would be given to eat or drink. She did not actually mention the turtle, but it was present in her face and voice.

The old people, as has already been told, had all known Martine and Philippa as little girls; they had seen them cry bitterly over a broken doll. Martine's tears brought tears into their own eyes. They gathered in the afternoon and talked the problem over.

Before they again parted they promised one another that for their little sisters' sake they would, on the great day, be silent upon all matters of food and drink. Nothing that might be set before them, be it even frogs or snails, should wring a word from their lips.

"Even so," said a white-bearded Brother, "the tongue is a little member and boasteth great things. The tongue can no man tame; it is an unruly evil, full of deadly poison. On the day of our master we will cleanse our tongues of all taste and purify them of all delight or disgust of the senses, keeping and preserving them for the higher things of praise and thanksgiving."

So few things ever happened in the quiet existence of the Berlevaag brotherhood that they were at this moment deeply moved and elevated. They shook hands on their vow, and it was to them as if they were doing so before the face of their Master.

VIII. *The Hymn*

On Sunday morning it began to snow. The white flakes fell fast and thick; the small windowpanes of the yellow house became pasted with snow.

Early in the day a groom from Fossum brought the two sisters a note. Old Mrs. Loewenhielm still resided in her country house. She was now ninety years old and stone-deaf, and she had lost all sense of smell or taste. But she had been one of the Dean's first supporters, and neither her infirmity nor the sledge journey would keep her from doing honor to his memory. Now, she wrote, her nephew, General Lorens Loewenhielm, had unexpectedly come on a visit; he had spoken with deep veneration of the Dean, and she begged permission to bring him with her. It would do him good, for the dear boy seemed to be in somewhat low spirits.

Martine and Philippa at this remembered the young officer and his visits; it relieved their present anxiety to talk of old happy days. They wrote back that General Loewenhielm would be welcome. They also called in Babette to inform her that they would now be twelve for dinner; they added that their latest guest had lived in Paris for several years. Babette seemed pleased with the news, and assured them that there would be food enough.

The hostesses made their little preparations in the sitting room. They dared not set foot in the kitchen, for Babette had mysteriously nosed out a cook's mate from a ship in the harbor—the same boy, Martine realized, who had brought in the turtle—to assist her in the kitchen and to wait at table, and now the dark woman and the red-haired boy, like some witch with her familiar spirit, had taken possession of these regions. The ladies could not tell what fires had been burning or what cauldrons bubbling there from before daybreak.

Table linen and plate had been magically mangled and polished, glasses and decanters brought, Babette only knew from where. The Dean's house did not possess twelve dining-room chairs, the long horse-hair-covered sofa had been moved from the parlor to the dining room, and the parlor, ever sparsely furnished, now looked strangely bare and big without it.

Martine and Philippa did their best to embellish the domain left to them. Whatever troubles might be in wait for their guests, in any case they should not be cold; all day the sisters fed the towering old stove with birch-knots. They hung a garland of juniper round their father's portrait on the wall, and placed candlesticks on their mother's small working table beneath it; they burned juniper-twigs to make the room smell nice. The while they wondered if in this weather the sledge from Fossum would get through. In the end they put on their old black best frocks and their confirmation gold crosses. They sat down, folded their hands in their laps and committed themselves unto God.

The old Brothers and Sisters arrived in small groups and entered the room slowly and solemnly.

This low room with its bare floor and scanty furniture was dear to the Dean's disciples. Outside its windows lay the great world. Seen from in here the great world in its winter-whiteness was ever prettily bordered in pink, blue and red by the row of hyacinths on the window-sills. And in summer, when the windows were open, the great world had a softly moving frame of white muslin curtains to it.

Tonight the guests were met on the doorstep with warmth and sweet smell, and they were looking into the face of their beloved Master, wreathed with evergreen. Their hearts like their numb fingers thawed.

One very old Brother, after a few moments' silence, in his trembling voice struck up one of the Master's own hymns:

> *"Jerusalem, my happy home*
> *name ever dear to me . . ."*

One by one the other voices fell in, thin quivering women's voices, ancient seafaring Brothers' deep growls, and above them all Philippa's clear soprano, a little worn with age but still angelic. Unwittingly the choir had seized one another's hands. They sang the hymn to the end, but could not bear to cease and joined in another:

> *"Take not thought for food or raiment*
> *careful one, so anxiously . . ."*

The mistresses of the house somewhat reassured by it, the words of the third verse:

> *"Wouldst thou give a stone, a reptile*
> *to thy pleading child for food? . . ."*

went straight to Martine's heart and inspired her with hope.

In the middle of this hymn sledge bells were heard outside; the guests from Fossum had arrived.

Martine and Philippa went to receive them and saw them into the parlor. Mrs. Loewenhielm with age had become quite small, her face colorless like parchment, and very still. By her side General Loewenhielm, tall, broad and ruddy, in his bright uniform, his breast covered with decorations, strutted and shone like an ornamental bird, a golden pheasant or a peacock, in this sedate party of black crows and jackdaws.

ix. *General Loewenhielm*

General Loewenhielm had been driving from Fossum to Berlevaag in a strange mood. He had not visited this part of the country for thirty years. He had come now to get a rest from his busy life at Court, and he had found no rest. The old house of Fossum was peaceful enough and seemed somehow pathetically small after the Tuileries and the Winter Palace. But it held one disquieting figure: young Lieutenant Loewenhielm walked in its rooms.

General Loewenhielm saw the handsome, slim figure pass close by him. And as he passed, the boy gave the elder man a short glance and a smile, the haughty, arrogant smile which youth gives to age. The General might have smiled back, kindly and a little sadly, as age smiles at youth, if it had not been that he was really in no mood to smile; he was, as his aunt had written, in low spirits.

General Loewenhielm had obtained everything that he had striven for in life and was admired and envied by everyone. Only he himself knew of a queer fact, which jarred with his prosperous existence: that he was not perfectly happy. Something was wrong somewhere, and he carefully felt his mental self all over, as one feels a finger over to determine the place of a deep-seated, invisible thorn.

He was in high favor with royalty, he had done

well in his calling, he had friends everywhere. The thorn sat in none of these places.

His wife was a brilliant woman and still good-looking. Perhaps she neglected her own house a little for her visits and parties; she changed her servants every three months and the General's meals at home were served unpunctually. The General, who valued good food highly in life, here felt a slight bitterness against the lady, and secretly blamed her for the indigestion from which he sometimes suffered. Still the thorn was not here either.

Nay, but an absurd thing had lately been happening to General Loewenhielm: he would find himself worrying about his immortal soul. Did he have any reason for doing so? He was a moral person, loyal to his king, his wife and his friends, an example to everybody. But there were moments when it seemed to him that the world was not a moral, but a mystic, concern. He looked into the mirror, examined the row of decorations on his breast and sighed to himself: "Vanity, vanity, all is vanity!"

The strange meeting at Fossum had compelled him to make out the balance-sheet of his life.

Young Lorens Loewenhielm had attracted dreams and fancies as a flower attracts bees and butterflies. He had fought to free himself of them; he had fled and they had followed. He had been scared of the Huldre of the family legend and had declined her invitation to come into the mountain; he had firmly refused the gift of second sight.

The elderly Lorens Loewenhielm found himself

wishing that one little dream would come his way, and a gray moth of dusk look him up before night-fall. He found himself longing for the faculty of second sight, as a blind man will long for the normal faculty of vision.

Can the sum of a row of victories in many years and in many countries be a defeat? General Loewenhielm had fulfilled Lieutenant Loewenhielm's wishes and had more than satisfied his ambitions. It might be held that he had gained the whole world. And it had come to this, that the stately, worldly-wise older man now turned toward the naïve young figure to ask him, gravely, even bitterly, in what he had profited? Some-where something had been lost.

When Mrs. Loewenhielm had told her nephew of the Dean's anniversary and he had made up his mind to go with her to Berlevaag, his decision had not been an ordinary acceptance of a dinner invitation.

He would, he resolved, tonight make up his ac-count with young Lorens Loewenhielm, who had felt himself to be a shy and sorry figure in the house of the Dean, and who in the end had shaken its dust off his riding boots. He would let the youth prove to him, once and for all, that thirty-one years ago he had made the right choice. The low rooms, the haddock and the glass of water on the table before him should all be called in to bear evidence that in their milieu the existence of Lorens Loewenhielm would very soon have become sheer misery.

He let his mind stray far away. In Paris he had once won a *concours hippique* and had been feted by high French cavalry officers, princes and dukes among them. A dinner had been given in his honor at the finest restaurant of the city. Opposite him at table was a noble lady, a famous beauty whom he had long been courting. In the midst of dinner she had lifted her dark velvet eyes above the rim of her champagne glass and without words had promised to make him happy. In the sledge he now all of a sudden remembered that he had then, for a second, seen Martine's face before him and had rejected it. For a while he listened to the tinkling of the sledge bells, then he smiled a little as he reflected how he would tonight come to dominate the conversation round that same table by which young Lorens Loewenhielm had sat mute.

Large snowflakes fell densely; behind the sledge the tracks were wiped out quickly. General Loewenhielm sat immovable by the side of his aunt, his chin sunk in the high fur collar of his coat.

x. *Babette's Dinner*

As Babette's red-haired familiar opened the door to the dining room, and the guests slowly crossed the threshold, they let go one another's hands and became silent. But the silence was sweet, for in spirit they still held hands and were still singing.

Babette had set a row of candles down the middle of the table; the small flames shone on the black coats and frocks and on the one scarlet uniform, and were reflected in clear, moist eyes.

General Loewenhielm saw Martine's face in the candlelight as he had seen it when the two parted, thirty years ago. What traces would thirty years of Berlevaag life have left on it? The golden hair was now streaked with silver; the flower-like face had slowly been turned into alabaster. But how serene was the forehead, how quietly trustful the eyes, how pure and sweet the mouth, as if no hasty word had ever passed its lips.

When all were seated, the eldest member of the congregation said grace in the Dean's own words:

> *"May my food my body maintain,*
> *may my body my soul sustain,*
> *may my soul in deed and word*
> *give thanks for all things to the Lord."*

At the word of "food" the guests, with their old heads bent over their folded hands, remembered how they had vowed not to utter a word about the subject, and in their hearts they reinforced the vow: they would not even give it a thought! They were sitting down to a meal, well, so had people done at the wedding of Cana. And grace has chosen to manifest itself there, in the very wine, as fully as anywhere.

Babette's boy filled a small glass before each of the party. They lifted it to their lips gravely, in confirmation of their resolution.

General Loewenhielm, somewhat suspicious of his wine, took a sip of it, startled, raised the glass first to his nose and then to his eyes, and sat it down bewildered. "This is very strange!" he thought. "Amontillado! And the finest Amontillado that I have ever tasted." After a moment, in order to test his senses, he took a small spoonful of his soup, took a second spoonful and laid down his spoon. "This is exceedingly strange!" he said to himself. "For surely I am eating turtle-soup—and what turtle-soup!" He was seized by a queer kind of panic and emptied his glass.

Usually in Berlevaag people did not speak much while they were eating. But somehow this evening tongues had been loosened. An old Brother told the story of his first meeting with the Dean. Another went through that sermon which sixty years ago had brought about his conversion. An aged woman, the one to whom Martine had first confided her distress, reminded her friends how in all afflictions any Brother or Sister was ready to share the burden of any other.

General Loewenhielm, who was to dominate the conversation of the dinner table, related how the Dean's collection of sermons was a favorite book of the Queen's. But as a new dish was served he was silenced. "Incredible!" he told himself. "It is Blinis Demidoff!" He looked round at his fellow-diners. They were all quietly eating their Blinis Demidoff, without any sign of either surprise or approval, as if they had been doing so every day for thirty years.

A Sister on the other side of the table opened on the subject of strange happenings which had taken place while the Dean was still amongst his children, and which one might venture to call miracles. Did they remember, she asked, the time when he had promised a Christmas sermon in the village the other side of the fjord? For a fortnight the weather had been so bad that no skipper or fisherman would risk the crossing. The villagers were giving up hope, but the Dean told them that if no boat would take him, he would come to them walking upon the waves. And behold! Three days before Christmas the storm stopped, hard frost set in, and the fjord froze from shore to shore—and this was a thing which had not happened within the memory of man!

The boy once more filled the glasses. This time the Brothers and Sisters knew that what they were given to drink was not wine, for it sparkled. It must be some kind of lemonade. The lemonade agreed with their exalted state of mind and seemed to lift them off the ground, into a higher and purer sphere.

General Loewenhielm again set down his glass, turned to his neighbor on the right and said to him: "But surely this is a Veuve Cliquot 1860?" His neighbor looked at him kindly, smiled at him and made a remark about the weather.

Babette's boy had his instructions; he filled the glasses of the Brotherhood only once, but he refilled the General's glass as soon as it was emptied. The General emptied it quickly time after time. For how is a man of sense to behave when he cannot trust his senses? It is better to be drunk than mad.

Most often the people in Berlevaag during the course of a good meal would come to feel a little heavy. Tonight it was not so. The *convives* grew lighter in weight and lighter of heart the more they ate and drank. They no longer needed to remind themselves of their vow. It was, they realized, when man has not only altogether forgotten but has firmly renounced all ideas of food and drink that he eats and drinks in the right spirit.

General Loewenhielm stopped eating and sat immovable. Once more he was carried back to that dinner in Paris of which he had thought in the sledge. An incredibly recherché and palatable dish had been served there; he had asked its name from his fellow diner, Colonel Galliffet, and the Colonel had smilingly told him that it was named "Cailles en Sarcophage." He had further told him that the dish had been invented by the chef of the very café in which they were dining, a person known all over Paris as the greatest culinary genius of the age, and—most surprisingly—a woman! "And indeed," said Colonel Galliffet, "this woman is now turning a dinner at the Café Anglais into a kind of love affair—into a love affair of the noble and romantic category in which one no longer distinguishes between bodily and spiritual appetite or satiety! I have, before now, fought a duel for the sake of a fair lady. For no woman in all Paris, my young friend, would I more willingly shed my blood!" General Loewenhielm turned to his neighbor on the left and said to him: "But this is Cailles en Sarcophage!" The neighbor, who had been listening to the description of a miracle, looked at him absent-mindedly, then nodded his head and answered: "Yes, Yes, certainly. What else would it be?"

From the Master's miracles the talk round the table

had turned to the smaller miracles of kindliness and helpfulness daily performed by his daughters. The old Brother who had first struck up the hymn quoted the Dean's saying: "The only things which we may take with us from our life on earth are those which we have given away!" The guests smiled—what nabobs would not the poor, simple maidens become in the next world!

General Loewenhielm no longer wondered at anything. When a few minutes later he saw grapes, peaches and fresh figs before him, he laughed to his neighbor across the table and remarked: "Beautiful grapes!" His neighbor replied: " 'And they came onto the brook of Eshcol, and cut down a branch with one cluster of grapes. And they bare it two upon a staff.' "

Then the General felt that the time had come to make a speech. He rose and stood up very straight.

Nobody else at the dinner table had stood up to speak. The old people lifted their eyes to the face above them in high, happy expectation. They were used to seeing sailors and vagabonds dead drunk with the crass gin of the country, but they did not recognize in a warrior and courtier the intoxication brought about by the noblest wine of the world.

XI. *General Loewenhielm's Speech*

"Mercy and truth, my friends, have met together," said the General. "Righteousness and bliss shall kiss one another."

He spoke in a clear voice which had been trained in drill grounds and had echoed sweetly in royal halls, and yet he was speaking in a manner so new to himself and so strangely moving that after his first sentence he had to make a pause. For he was in the habit of forming his speeches with care, conscious of his purpose, but here, in the midst of the Dean's simple congregation, it was as if the whole figure of General Loewenhielm, his breast covered with decorations, were but a mouthpiece for a message which meant to be brought forth.

"Man, my friends," said General Loewenhielm, "is frail and foolish. We have all of us been told that grace is to be found in the universe. But in our human foolishness and short-sightedness we imagine divine grace to be finite. For this reason we tremble . . . " Never till now had the General stated that he trembled; he was genuinely surprised and even shocked at hearing his own voice proclaim the fact. "We tremble before making our choice in life, and after having made it again tremble in fear of having chosen wrong. But the moment comes when our eyes are opened, and we see and realize that grace is infinite. Grace, my friends, demands nothing from us but that we shall await it with confidence and acknowledge it in gratitude. Grace, brothers, makes no conditions and singles out none of us in particular; grace takes us all to its bosom and proclaims general amnesty. See! that which we have chosen is given us, and that which we have refused is, also and at the same time, granted us. Ay, that which we have rejected is poured upon us abundantly. For mercy and truth have met together, and righteousness and bliss have kissed one another!"

The Brothers and Sisters had not altogether understood the General's speech, but his collected and inspired face and the sound of well-known and cherished words had seized and moved all hearts. In this way, after thirty-one years, General Loewenhielm succeeded in dominating the conversation at the Dean's dinner table.

Of what happened later in the evening nothing definite can here be stated. None of the guests later on had any clear remembrance of it. They only knew that the rooms had been filled with a heavenly light, as if a number of small halos had blended into one glorious radiance. Taciturn old people received the gift of tongues; ears that for years had been almost deaf were opened to it. Time itself had merged into eternity. Long after midnight the windows of the house shone like gold, and golden song flowed out into the winter air.

The two old women who had once slandered each other now in their hearts went back a long way, past the evil period in which they had been stuck, to those days of their early girlhood when together they had been preparing for confirmation and hand in hand had filled the roads round Berlevaag with singing. A Brother in the congregation gave another a knock in the ribs, like a rough caress between boys, and cried out: "You cheated me on that timber, you old scoundrel!" The Brother thus addressed almost collapsed in a heavenly burst of laughter, but tears ran from his eyes. "Yes, I did so, beloved Brother," he answered. "I did so." Skipper Halvorsen and Madam

Oppegaarden suddenly found themselves close together in a corner and gave one another that long, long kiss, for which the secret uncertain love affair of their youth had never left them time.

The old Dean's flock were humble people. When later in life they thought of this evening it never occurred to any of them that they might have been exalted by their own merit. They realized that the infinite grace of which General Loewenhielm had spoken had been allotted to them, and they did not even wonder at the fact, for it had been but the fulfillment of an ever-present hope. The vain illusions of this earth had dissolved before their eyes like smoke, and they had seen the universe as it really is. They had been given one hour of the millennium.

Old Mrs. Loewenhielm was the first to leave. Her nephew accompanied her, and their hostesses lighted them out. While Philippa was helping the old lady into her many wraps, the General seized Martine's hand and held it for a long time without a word. At last he said:

"I have been with you every day of my life. You know, do you not, that it has been so?"

"Yes," said Martine, "I know that it has been so."

"And," he continued, "I shall be with you every day that is left to me. Every evening I shall sit down, if not in the flesh, which means nothing, in spirit, which is all, to dine with you, just like tonight. For tonight I have learned, dear sister, that in this world anything is possible."

"Yes, it is so, dear brother," said Martine. "In this world anything is possible."

Upon this they parted.

When at last the company broke up it had ceased to snow. The town and the mountains lay in white, unearthly splendor and the sky was bright with thousands of stars. In the street the snow was lying so deep that it had become difficult to walk. The guests from the yellow house wavered on their feet, staggered, sat down abruptly or fell forward on their knees and hands and were covered with snow, as if they had indeed had their sins washed white as wool, and in this regained innocent attire were gamboling like little lambs. It was, to each of them, blissful to have become as a small child; it was also a blessed joke to watch old Brothers and Sisters, who had been taking themselves so seriously, in this kind of celestial second childhood. They stumbled and got up, walked on or stood still, bodily as well as spiritually hand in hand, at moments performing the great chain of a beatified *lanciers*.

"Bless you, bless you, bless you," like an echo of the harmony of the spheres rang on all sides.

Martine and Philippa stood for a long time on the stone steps outside the house. They did not feel the cold. "The stars have come nearer," said Philippa.

"They will come every night," said Martine quietly. "Quite possibly it will never snow again."

In this, however, she was mistaken. An hour later it again began to snow, and such a heavy snowfall had never been known in Berlevaag. The next morn-

ing people could hardly push open their doors against
the tall snowdrifts. The windows of the houses were
so thickly covered with snow, it was told for years
afterwards, that many good citizens of the town did
not realize that daybreak had come, but slept on till
late in the afternoon.

XII. *The Great Artist*

When Martine and Philippa locked the door they remembered Babette. A little wave of tenderness and
pity swept through them: Babette alone had had no
share in the bliss of the evening.

So they went out into the kitchen, and Martine
said to Babette: "It was quite a nice dinner, Babette."

Their hearts suddenly filled with gratitude. They
realized that none of their guests had said a single
word about the food. Indeed, try as they might, they
could not themselves remember any of the dishes
which had been served. Martine bethought herself of
the turtle. It had not appeared at all, and now seemed
very vague and far away; it was quite possible that it
had been nothing but a nightmare.

Babette sat on the chopping block, surrounded by
more black and greasy pots and pans than her mistresses had ever seen in their life. She was as white and
as deadly exhausted as on the night when she first
appeared and had fainted on their doorstep.

After a long time she looked straight at them and
said: "I was once cook at the Café Anglais."

Martine said again: "They all thought that it was a

nice dinner." And when Babette did not answer a word she added: "We will all remember this evening when you have gone back to Paris, Babette."

Babette said: "I am not going back to Paris."

"You are not going back to Paris?" Martine exclaimed.

"No," said Babette. "What will I do in Paris? They have all gone. I have lost them all, Mesdames."

The sisters' thoughts went to Monsieur Hersant and his son, and they said: "Oh, my poor Babette."

"Yes, they have all gone," said Babette. "The Duke of Morny, the Duke of Decazes, Prince Narishkine, General Galliffet, Aurélian Scholl, Paul Daru, the Princesse Pauline! All!"

The strange names and titles of people lost to Babette faintly confused the two ladies, but there was such an infinite perspective of tragedy in her announcement that in their responsive state of mind they felt her losses as their own, and their eyes filled with tears.

At the end of another long silence Babette suddenly smiled slightly at them and said: "And how would I go back to Paris, Mesdames? I have no money."

"No money?" the sisters cried as with one mouth.

"No," said Babette.

"But the ten thousand francs?" the sisters asked in a horrified gasp.

"The ten thousand francs have been spent, Mesdames," said Babette.

The sisters sat down. For a full minute they could not speak.

"But ten thousand francs?" Martine slowly whispered.

"What will you, Mesdames," said Babette with great dignity. "A dinner for twelve at the Café Anglais would cost ten thousand francs."

The ladies still did not find a word to say. The piece of news was incomprehensible to them, but then many things tonight in one way or another had been beyond comprehension.

Martine remembered a tale told by a friend of her father's who had been a missionary in Africa. He had saved the life of an old chief's favorite wife, and to show his gratitude the chief had treated him to a rich meal. Only long afterwards the missionary learned from his own black servant that what he had partaken of was a small fat grandchild of the chief's, cooked in honor of the great Christian medicine man. She shuddered.

But Philippa's heart was melting in her bosom. It seemed that an unforgettable evening was to be finished off with an unforgettable proof of human loyalty and self-sacrifice.

"Dear Babette," she said softly, "you ought not to have given away all you had for our sake."

Babette gave her mistress a deep glance, a strange glance. Was there not pity, even scorn, at the bottom of it?

"For your sake?" she replied. "No. For my own."

She rose from the chopping block and stood up before the two sisters.

"I am a great artist!" she said.

She waited a moment and then repeated: "I am a great artist, Mesdames."

Again for a long time there was deep silence in the kitchen.

Then Martine said: "So you will be poor now all your life, Babette?"

"Poor?" said Babette. She smiled as if to herself. "No, I shall never be poor. I told you that I am a great artist. A great artist, Mesdames, is never poor. We have something, Mesdames, of which other people know nothing."

While the elder sister found nothing more to say, in Philippa's heart deep, forgotten chords vibrated. For she had heard, before now, long ago, of the Café Anglais. She had heard, before now, long ago, the names on Babette's tragic list. She rose and took a step toward her servant.

"But all those people whom you have mentioned," she said, "those princes and great people of Paris whom you named, Babette? You yourself fought against them. You were a Communard! The General you named had your husband and son shot! How can you grieve over them?"

Babette's dark eyes met Philippa's.

"Yes," she said, "I was a Communard. Thanks be to God, I was a Communard! And those people whom I named, Mesdames, were evil and cruel. They let the people of Paris starve; they oppressed and wronged the poor. Thanks be to God, I stood upon a barricade; I loaded the gun for my menfolk! But all the same, Mesdames, I shall not go back to Paris, now that those people of whom I have spoken are no longer there."

She stood immovable, lost in thought.

"You see, Mesdames," she said, at last, "those people belonged to me, they were mine. They had been brought up and trained, with greater expense than you, my little ladies, could ever imagine or believe, to understand what a great artist I am. I could make them happy. When I did my very best I could make them perfectly happy."

She paused for a moment.

"It was like that with Monsieur Papin too," she said.

"With Monsieur Papin?" Philippa asked.

"Yes, with your Monsieur Papin, my poor lady," said Babette. "He told me so himself: 'It is terrible and unbearable to an artist,' he said, 'to be encouraged to do, to be applauded for doing, his second best.' He said: 'Through all the world there goes one long cry from the heart of the artist: Give me leave to do my utmost!' "

Philippa went up to Babette and put her arms round her. She felt the cook's body like a marble monument against her own, but she herself shook and trembled from head to foot.

For a while she could not speak. Then she whispered:

"Yet this is not the end! I feel, Babette, that this is not the end. In Paradise you will be the great artist that God meant you to be! Ah!" she added, the tears streaming down her cheeks. "Ah, how you will enchant the angels!"

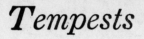

Tempests

1. *The Vision of the Tempest*

There was an old actor and theatre director whose name was Herr Soerensen. In his young days he had played in Copenhagen theatres; he had even got so far as to appear as Aristophanes in Adam Oehlenschlaeger's tragedy *Socrates* at the very Royal Theatre. But he was a man of a mighty, independent character, which demanded the creation and control of his own world around him. As a child he had been taken to stay with his mother's relations in Norway, and he had kept a deep, undying passion for the land of fells, which in his mind loomed heaven-aspiring and windswept, as back-drop and wings for *Hakon Jarl* and for Macbeth's and Ossian's Scotland. He read the Norwegian poet Wergeland and heard tell of the Norwegian folk's longing for great art, and his soul grew restless within him. Visions and voices filled him, a crown was indicated for him, and he received his orders to sally forth for the North. Late in life he abruptly pulled up his roots from the soft mould of Copenhagen to plant them afresh in stony ground, and at the time—about a hundred years ago—when steamers first began to ply regularly along the Norwegian coast he traveled with his own small company from town to town up and down the fjords.

His old Copenhagen friends discussed among themselves the sad come-down it must be for a Royal Copenhagen actor to appear on provincial stages with a half-trained cast and before a half-barbarous public. But Herr Soerensen himself delighted in his freedom;

his being blossomed in the swell of wind and wave, in dressing-rooms made from rough boards, in draughts and among tallow-dips. On gala nights he was the highly appreciated ambassador to the great powers, glittering with stars and royal favor, at other times, groaning away in his narrow berth and in the merciless hand of seasickness, he was their hard-tried prophet, Jonah in the belly of the whale. But always and everywhere he was the chosen one, the wanderer in his vocation.

Herr Soerensen in his nature had a kind of duplicity which might well confuse and disturb his surroundings and might even be called demoniacal, but with which he himself managed to exist on harmonious terms. He was on the one hand a wide-awake, shrewd and untiring businessman, with eyes at the back of his head, a fine nose for profit, and a completely matter-of-fact and detached outlook on his public and humanity in general. And he was at one and the same time his art's obedient servant, a humble old priest in the temple, with the words "*Domine, non sum dignus*" graven in his heart.

He did not, in his contracts, let himself be done for as much as a farthing. While laying on his mask in front of a dim, chipped mirror he might suddenly get a bright idea which put him in a position to steal a march on other folk. He played in many coarse farces (which in his time were called *Possen*), giving his audience their hearts' desire of capering, roaring and fantastic grimacing, and thanking them for their deafening applause with his hand on his heart and the sweetest of smiles on his lips—and all the time he had the evening's accounts, down to the smallest item, in his head.

But when, later at night, after having enjoyed his modest supper, with a little glass of schnapps thrown in, he ascended to his bedroom, candle in hand, up a staircase as steep and narrow as a hen-coop ladder, in spirit he moved as high as an old angel on Jacob's ladder. Up there he sat down again to table with Euripides, Lopez de Vega and Molière, with the poets of his own country's golden age, and with the one who most of all looked like a human being, with William Shakespeare himself. The immortal minds were his brethren and understood him as he them. In their circle he could let himself go, free and jubilant, or he could shed tears of deepest *weltschmerz*.

Herr Soerensen at times had been characterized by business connections as a shameless speculator. But in his relations to the immortals he was as chaste as a virgin.

Only a few close friends knew of his theory: that much which is unworthy in human life might be avoided if people would only accustom themselves to talking in verse. "It need not exactly rhyme," he said. "Nay, it really ought not to rhyme. Rhyming verse in the long run is an underhand attack on the true being of poetry. But we should express our feelings, and communicate with one another, in blank verse. For iambics gently sway our nature's rawness—to noble worth, and zealously divide—chatter and tripe and scandal's overspill—from gold and silver in the human speech." In the great moments of his existence Herr Soerensen himself thought in iambics.

Only the Registrar-General of Births and Deaths in Copenhagen—who had shown himself highly reluctant to the idea—knew of a codicil to his will, in accordance with which his old cranium would one day be polished and through the ages to come would figure on the stage as Yorick's skull.

Now one year it happened that Herr Soerensen in doing his accounts found his last season to have been more profitable than any previous one. The old manager felt that the great powers above had looked to him kindly and that in return he ought to do something for them. He determined to put into operation a life-old dream. He would produce *The Tempest* and himself play the part of Prospero.

No sooner had he taken this decision than he got up from his bed, dressed and went for a long walk in the night. He gazed at the stars above him and reflected that he had been led along strange ways. "Those wings for which all my life I have been longing and looking," he said to himself, "have now been granted me—in order that I may fold them together! My thanks to those in whose hands I have been, and am."

II. *A Part Assigned*

He lay wakeful through many a night, shifting his males and females here and there in the play's cast, as if they had been pieces in a choice game of chess.

At length, except for one single figure, he had the whole distribution of parts on his fingers and was pleased with it. But an Ariel he had not yet found, and he tore his hair in despair over his inability. Already in his mind he had tried his best artists in the part and in exasperation had flung them out of it again, when one day his eye fell on a young girl who had recently become a member of the troupe, and in a couple of small parts had won modest applause.

"My Lord and Judge," Herr Soerensen at the same instant cried out in his heart, "where have I had my eyes? Here have I been on my knees, imploring heaven to send me a serviceable air-spirit! I have been on the point of losing all hope and giving up! And all the time the most exquisite Ariel the world has ever known has been walking up and down under my nose without my recognizing him!" So moved was he that he overlooked his pupil's sex.

"My girl," he said to the young actress. "You are to play Ariel in *The Tempest*."

"Am I!" she cried.

"Yes," said Herr Soerensen.

The girl to whom he was talking was big, with a pair of clear, undaunted eyes, but with a peculiar reserved dignity in her manner. Herr Soerensen who, so far as the morals of his young actresses went, had preserved the high traditions of the Royal Copenhagen theatre, occasionally had noticed her just because she seemed difficult to approach. She was a pretty girl and to a chivalrous nature like that of Herr Soerensen there was something moving or pathetic in her face. Still no theatre man but one with the eyes of genius would ever have imagined her in the part of Ariel.

"She is somewhat skinny," Herr Soerensen thought, "because she has had to live on short commons, poor child. But it becomes her because the structure of her skeleton is exceptionally noble. If it be correct—as my Copenhagen director, of blessed memory, did hold forth to me—that woman is to man what poetry is to prose, then are the womenfolk we come across from day to day poems read aloud.—They're read aloud with taste, and please the ear—or else they're badly read, and grate and jar.—But this my gray-eyed lassie is a song."

"Now then, little one," he said, as he lit one of the fat cigars which were the only luxury he allowed himself. "Now we two will set to work, and set to work in earnest. We are here to serve Will Shakespeare, the Swan of Avon. And we are not going to think of ourselves at all, for we are nothing at all in ourselves. You are prepared to forget everything for his sake?"

The girl thought the matter over, blushed and said: "If only I am not too big."

Herr Soerensen looked her over observantly from head to foot and even walked round her once in order to become certain.

"To hell with stones and pounds," he burst out. "I could, *au contraire*, wish that there was more of you. For you are light in yourself, in the way of a gas balloon: the more one fills into it the higher it will go. Besides, surely our William is man enough to do away with such a hackneyed regulation as the law of gravity.

"And look at me now. I am a little man as I walk about on my dreary daily round. But do you think that once in the cloak of Prospero I shall look the same? Nay, the danger will then be that the stage will become too cramped for my stature; the rest of my cast will find it a bit of a tight fit. And when I order myself a new suit of clothes—which the Lord knows I need—the tailor who has had a seat in the pit will put up his price because he realizes that he will need to use extra material for my volume!

"I am aware," he continued after a long pause and in deep earnest, "that even among theatre managers there may be found those who have the heart—and the means—to let Ariel come swooping onto the stage on a wire from the wings. To hell with it! Such things to me are an abomination. It is the words of the poet which are to make Ariel fly. Ought we, who are our William's servants, to rely more on a bit of steel than on his heavenly stanzas! That, on this stage, shall come to happen only over Valdemar Soerensen's dead body!

"You are a bit slow in your movements," he went on. "That is as it should be. Rapid Ariel must not be, nor bustling. And when he answers Prospero:

> *I drink the air before me and return
> or e'er your pulse twice beat,*

the public will believe him. Certainly they will believe him. But, it shall not be because they think: 'Ay, maybe he can do it, the way he can hustle.' No, they must not be in doubt even for a fraction of a second, for they must at the very moment be blissfully a-tremble in their hearts and there cry out: 'Oh, what witchcraft!'

"Nay, I will tell you something, wench," Herr Soerensen took up the tale a moment after, mightily carried away by his own fantasy. "If one imagines— for one may imagine anything—that it happened that a girl had come into the world with a pair of wings to her back, and she came to me and begged for a part in a play, I should answer her: 'In the works of the poets there is a part for every single child of man, ergo, one for you too. Indeed, one will find more than one heroine in the kind of comedies we have to put up nowadays who might profit by losing a bit of her *avoir du pois!* The Lord be with you, you may play one of those. But Ariel, you cannot play be- cause already you have got wings to your back, and because, in stark reality and without any poetry at all, you are capable of flying!' "

III. *The Child of Love*

The girl who was to play Ariel had for some time known in her heart that she would be an actress.

Her mother sewed hats for ladies in a small fjord town, and the daughter sat beside her and dizzily felt that the swell in her own heart was like that in the water. Sometimes she thought that she would die from it. But she knew no more about the soundings of the heart than about those of the sea. She picked up her thimble and scissors with a pale face.

Her father had been a Scotch ship's captain, by name Alexander Ross, whose ship twenty years ago had suffered damage on her way to Riga and had had to lie up through the summer in the town harbor. During these summer months the big handsome man, who had sailed round the world and taken part in an Antarctic expedition, had created much stir and unrest among the townsfolk. And he had, in haste and with a will, such as he did everything, fallen in love with and married one of their loveliest girls, the seventeen-year-old daughter of a customs officer. The young maiden had defended herself in sweet emotion and confusion, but had still become Madam Ross before she knew where she was. "It's the sea that brought me, little heart of mine," he had whispered to her, in his queer, broken, adorable Norwegian. "Stop wave-beat, stop heart-beat."

Toward the end of the summer the captain's ship was cleared, he embraced and kissed his young bride, laid a pile of gold coins on her work table and promised her to come again before Christmas to take her with him to Scotland. She stood on the quay in the fine East Indian shawl he had given her, and saw him sail away. He had been one with her: now he became one with his ship. Since that day no one had seen or heard anything of him.

The young wife next spring, after the long terrible waiting of the winter months, realized that his ship had gone down, and that she was a widow. But the townsfolk began to talk: never had Captain Ross intended to come back. A little later it was said that he already had a wife at home in Scotland; his own crew had hinted at it.

There were those in the town who blamed a maiden who had been in such a hurry to throw herself into the arms of a foreign sea captain. Others felt sympathy for the forlorn Norwegian girl and would have liked to help and comfort her. But she was sensitive to something in their help and comfort that she did not want or could not bear. Even before her child was born, with the money her lover had given her when he left she established her little milliner's shop. She just put one single sovereign aside, for her child was to have an heirloom of pure gold from its father. From now on she kept back from her own family and her old acquaintances in town. She had nothing against them, but they would not leave her time to think of Alexander Ross. When once more it began to show green round the fjord she gave birth to a daughter who would, she thought, in years to come, help her in the task.

Madam Ross had had her daughter christened Malli because her husband had sung a song about a Scotch girl called Malli, who was all in all complete. But she told the customers who peered at the child lying within its cradle in the shop that this was a family name among her husband's kin; his mother had been called Malli. She ended up by believing it herself.

During the months in which she had been waiting in rising anxiety and finally, as it were, in deep darkness, the unborn child to her had been a sure proof that her husband was alive. It grew and kicked in her womb; it could not be a dead man's child. Now, after the rumors about her husband had reached her, to her the child slowly became a just as certain proof that he was dead. For a child so healthy, beautiful and gentle could not be a deceiver's gift to her. As Malli grew up she realized, without her mother having ever expressed it in words, nor having ever been able to express it, what a powerful, mystic, at the same time tragic and blissful importance her very existence had to that gentle, lonesome mother. So the two lived wonderfully quiet and secluded, and very happily, together.

When the girl grew older and now and then came out among people, she heard her father spoken of. She was quick-witted and had an ear for intonation and silence; she soon got wind of the sort of name Captain Ross had in the town. No one got to know what she felt about it. But she took her mother's side against the whole world with growing vigor. She stood guard over Madam Ross like an armed sentry, and she became exaggeratedly wise and demure in all she did. Without making it really clear even to herself, in her young heart she decided that never in the conduct of the daughter should people find any confirmation that the mother had let herself be seduced by a bad man.

But when Malli was alone she happily gave herself up to thoughts of her big, handsome father. For her he might well have been an adventurer, a privateer captain, like those one heard of in time of war—indeed even a corsair or a pirate! Below her quiet manner there lay a vital, concealed gaiety and arrogance; in her contempt for the townspeople was mingled forbearance for her own mother. She herself, and Alexander Ross, knew better than they.

Madam Ross was proud of her obedient, thoughtful child, and in the eyes of the town became somewhat ludicrous in her maternal vanity. She had Malli taught English by an old spinster who was still sitting about in the fjord town after coming there a generation ago as governess to Baron Loewenskiold's daughters. In the dried-up, beaky-nosed Englishwoman's small room above a grocer's shop Malli learned her father's tongue. And up here a meeting took place, fateful for the girl: one day she also read Shakespeare. With trembling voice and with tears in her eyes the old maid read out her bard to the young one, the exiled woman asserted her lineage and her wealth, and with majestic dignity introduced the milliner's daughter to a circle of noble and brilliant compatriots. From then on Malli saw her hero Alexander Ross as a Shakespearean hero. In her heart she cried out with Philip Faulconbridge:

> "*Madam, I would not wish a better father.*
> *Some sins do bear their privilege on earth,*
> *And so doth yours . . .*"

Malli as a child had been tall for her age, but she was late in developing into womanhood. Even when at the age of sixteen she was confirmed she looked like a lanky boy. When she grew up she grew beautiful. No human being has a richer experience than

the unlovely, awkward girl who in the course of a
few months turns into a beautiful young maiden. It
is both a glorious surprise and a fulfilled expectation,
both a favor and a well-deserved promotion. The
ship has been becalmed, or has tossed in stormy cur-
rents; now the white sails fill and she stands out for
open sea. The speed itself gives an even keel.

Malli sailed her high and mighty course, as daringly
and surely as if Captain Ross in person had stood at
the helm. The young men turned round to look at her
in the street, and there were those who imagined
that her exceptional position would make her an easy
prey. But in this they were mistaken. The maiden
might well consent to be a corsair's daughter, but by
no means would she consent to be a corsair's prize.
As a child she had been soft-hearted; as a young girl
she was without mercy. "No," she told herself. "It is
they that shall be my victims." All the same the unaccustomed admiration, the new defensive and offensive brought unrest to the first years of her youth.
And as now here Malli's story is being written and
read, one is free to imagine that had it drawn out
longer she would have become what the French call
une lionne, a lioness. In the story itself she is but a
lion cub, somewhat whelp-like in movement and, up
to the last chapter, uncertain in her estimation of her
own strength.

iv. *Madam Ross*

It so happened that one evening in the town's small
theatre. Malli saw Herr Soerensen's company give a

performance. All the vigor and longing in her, which for years had been forcibly mastered, were released into perfect clarity and bliss, just as if she had been struck right in the heart by a divine arrow. Before the performance came to an end she had reached her irrevocable decision: she would become an actress.

As she was walking home from the theatre the street heaved and swung beneath her and round her. In her little room she took down her books, and the room became a starry night above Verona and a crypt there. It grew verdant and filled with the sweet song and music of the forest of Arden, and deep Mediterranean waves here rolled blue round Cyprus. Secretly, with trembling heart as if she were facing doomsday, she shortly afterwards made her way to the little hotel where Herr Soerensen had settled in, was admitted into his presence and recited to him some of the parts she had taught herself.

Herr Soerensen listened to her, looked at her, looked again and said to himself: "There is something there!" So much was there that he would not let the girl go away, but took her on at a small consideration for three months. "Let her," he thought, "ripen awhile unnoticed in the atmosphere of the stage. And then let's see." Malli could now reveal her decision to her mother, and the neighbors too soon got news of it.

To the townsfolk the life and calling of an actress was something utterly foreign and in itself dubious. Also Malli's special position caused her to be harshly judged or ridiculed. But so sure of herself was the girl that while till now she had at all times been accurately aware of what the town was thinking and opining, and had kept her account of it, she now completely overlooked it or bothered about it not at all. She was genuinely surprised at her own mother's dismay the day she laid her plan before her.

Madam Ross had never needed to constrain her daughter's nature and had none of an ordinary mother's authority. In her present conflict with her daughter she became as if deranged with horror and grief, while on her side Malli was completely unbending. It came to a couple of great wild scenes between the two, and it might have ended with one or the other of them walking into the fjord.

In this hour Malli received support where she could least have expected it. Her dead or disappeared father himself became her ally.

Madam Ross had loved her man and had believed in him without ever having understood him. Now, whether in punishment or reward, through all eternity she must love and believe in what she did not understand. Had Malli's purpose lain within the scope of her own conceptions, she might have found a means to combat it. But confronted with this wild, carefree madness she was carried off her feet, dizzy with sweet and strange memories and associations. During the time in which she strove against her daughter's obsession she inexplicably lived her short marriage over again. It was from day to day the same surprises and emotions: a foreign, rich and enrapturing power, that had once taken her by storm, again surrounded her on all sides. Malli's manner grew as insinuating and enticing as that of her lover of twenty years ago. Madam Ross remembered that Alexander, the strong, handsome seafarer, had knelt down before her and had whispered up to her: "Nay, let me lie here. This is the most fitting place of all." She fell in love with her daughter as she had once fallen in love with the father, so that she forgot that years had passed and that her own hair had grown gray in their passing. She blushed and blanched in Malli's presence and trembled when the girl left her; she felt her own will impotent before her child's gaze and voice, and there was in this impotence a dreamlike, resurrected bliss.

When finally in a stormy and tearful interview she gave the girl her blessing, it was to her as if she were being wed again. From now on she was incapable of grieving or fearing as the town expected her to do. The day Malli went away with Herr Soerensen's company, mother and daughter took leave of each other in full, loving understanding.

v. *Master and Pupil*

Now Malli learned Ariel's part by heart, and Herr Soerensen took upon himself to perfect her in it. He did not leave her in peace either by day or night. He scolded and swore, with inspired cruelty sneered at her facial expression and her intonation, pinched her slim arms black and blue and even one day soundly boxed her ears.

The other members of the troupe, who had been

astonished witnesses of the bashful girl's sudden advancement and might well have been jealous of her for it, instead took pity on her. The company's leading lady, Mamzell Ihlen, a beauty with long black hair, who was to play Miranda, once or twice ventured to protest to the director on Malli's account. The *jeune premier*, a fair-haired young man with fine legs, more meekly waited in the wings to comfort the novice when she came reeling off the stage from a rehearsal. If none the less they did not, either on or off the stage, attempt to come nearer to Herr Soerensen's victim, and did not even talk much about her among themselves, it was not due to lack of sympathy; they were as uncertain in face of what went on before their eyes as are the people who follow the growth of a young tree under the fakir's spell. Such a relationship may awaken admiration or uneasiness; it baffles discussion or condemnation.

But Herr Soerensen himself grew happier from lesson to lesson, and Malli understood that he was fuming for her own good and that it was all love. It also came about that at one of her lines the old actor abruptly halted his berserk rage and looked hard and searchingly at his pupil. "Say that once more," he begged her gently and humbly. When Malli repeated:

> "*I have made you mad,*
> *And even with such like valor, men hang and drown*
> *their proper selves.*"

Herr Soerensen remained stock-still for a moment, like a person who finds it hard to believe his eyes and ears, until he at last drew a deep breath and found release in one of Prospero's own lines:

> *"Bravely the figure of this harpy hast thou*
> *Performed, my Ariel."*

He nodded to her and went on with the lesson.

He would also, in exuberant pride and joy, give her a few fatherly taps on her behind and then, more to himself than to her, develop his theories upon female beauty.

"How many women," he said, "have got their tails where they ought to be? In some of them—God help them—they are coming down to their heels! You, ducky," he added cheerfully, with his cigar in his mouth, "are long in the leg! Your trotters don't pull you downwards.—Nay, your two legs are straight and noble columns—which proudly carry, where you walk or stand, your whole nice little person heavenwards!"

One day he clapped his hands to his head and burst out: "And I meant to have a girl like that trip about in a pair of French silk slippers! Fool, fool that I was! Who did not know that it was a pair of seven-league boots that fitted those legs!"

VI. *A Tempest*

So day by day Malli grew more Ariel, just as, day by day, Herr Soerensen grew more Prospero, and the date of *The Tempest's* first performance in Christianssand was already fixed for March 15th, when an unexpected and fateful event overwhelmed both Herr Soerensen and Malli, and the whole theatrical company. This event was so sensational that it did not only become far and wide the one topic of conversation, but it also got into print on the first page of the *Christianssand Daily News* as follows:

A Heroine

During the hard weather which in the past week has supervened along the coast, there occurred in our neighborhood a calamity, which by all human reckoning must have led to a deplorable loss of life as well as of a good seaworthy coasting-steamer, had not at the very last moment, next to the mercy of providence, a brave girl's pluck brought about a happier solution. We present to our readers a short account of the drama.

On Wednesday, March 12th, the passenger boat *Sofie Hosewinckel* left Arendal for Christianssand. The visibility was poor, with snow and a stiff breeze from the southeast. Late in the afternoon the wind rose to gale force, and as all know, we experienced some of the worst weather which within the memory of man has ravaged our coast. *Sofie Hosewinckel* had aboard sixteen passengers, among whom was the well-known and respected theatre manager, Herr Valdemar Soerensen, with his company, on their way to give a performance in Christianssand.

Our steamer with difficulty had worked her way to Kvasefjord when the storm broke in all earnest. She was compelled to heave to, but was none the less driven in toward the skerries outside Randsund, without it being possible for those on board to make a landfall, owing to the snow-mist, and because the hull was ceaselessly awash from bow to stern from the heavy seas.

At eight o'clock in the evening sunken rocks were visible on both quarters, the roaring sea breaking over them house-high. *Sofie Hosewinckel* was lucky enough to slip over the outermost skerry into somewhat smoother water in the lee of a narrow islet, but here the ship ran head-on onto a sunken rock and immediately shipped a quantity of water. During the storm the captain himself, with two of his crew, had been injured, and it was now difficult for the mate to maintain order aboard. One of the steamer's lifeboats was found to be smashed by the seas, but our gallant seamen succeeded in launching the other boat, which could hold twenty. The passengers, with as many of the crew as were required to maneuver the boat, took their seats in it in order to row to the island. Only a nineteen-year-old girl, Mamzell Ross, of Herr Soerensen's theatrical company, made known her decision to remain on board, giving up with noble woman's courage her place in the boat to one of the injured sailors.

The intention was that the mate should return to the ship with the boat to take ashore those remaining on board. But during the landing on the island the fragile craft was completely shattered. The people who were in it came safe ashore, but it was now impossible to renew contact with the steamer, which those ashore could only glimpse through flying snow and spray. Soon after it became apparent to those on the island that a sea lifted her off her rocky bed, and one could only surmise that her last hour had come.

Also on board they were clear about the imminent danger that the vessel would fill with water and quickly go to the bottom. The ten men of the crew left on her became almost panic-stricken and came within an ace of giving up the struggle with the elements. As a last possibility of saving life they thought of running the *Sofie Hosewinckel* into the wind as close to shore as they could. This in all probability in the dense darkness would have brought about total loss.

It was at this moment that Mamzell Ross, as if at the summons of higher powers, lone woman on the ship in distress, by her very dauntlessness struck courage into the breasts of the crew. This quite young girl first of all went down into the stokehold and persuaded the chief engineer and the stokers to get up full steam again. She herself helped in the dangerous work of setting the pumps going, and after this achievement, right through the night while the ship lay hove-to under the breakers and with each hour sank deeper, she stood indefatigable by the side of the helmsmen of the changing watches.

It is understandable that a maiden's unconquerable spirit in the hour of need might prevail upon and strengthen our struggling seamen. But it is as good as inconceivable that a young female, unproved in seafaring life, should be found in possession of so great a strength. A young ordinary seaman, Ferdinand Skaeret by name, at this point deserves marked recognition. From the very first moment he stood shoulder to shoulder with Mamzell Ross, and through the stormy night carried out each of her orders. Above the weather's roaring din the girl could often be heard calling him aloud by name.

Toward the early hours of Thursday, March 13th, the storm abated somewhat. At daybreak it became possible to bring *Sofie Hosewinckel* in through Christianssand Fjord and run her aground in sinking condition by Odder Island, from where the steamer can be salvaged from shore without difficulty. And at the moment when this paper is going to press, the owner of the steamer, our honored townsman Jochum Hosewinckel, no less than the wives and mothers of our good seamen, from the bottom of their hearts will be thanking, after God, the heroic maiden for the rescue of the ship.

VII. *For Bravery*

During the night of storm described in the *Christianssand Daily News* lights were lit in all rooms on the first floor of the fine yellow wooden house in the market-square where lived the shipowner Jochum Hosewinckel.

The shipowner himself walked up and down the rooms, halted, listened to the storm, and walked again. His thoughts were with the ships he had at sea that night, most of all with *Sofie Hosewinckel* which was on her way from Arendal. This ship was named after his favorite sister, who a lifetime ago had died at the age of nineteen. Toward morning he fell asleep in the grandfather's chair by the table, and when he woke up he felt convinced that the ship had gone to the bottom and was lost.

At that moment his son Arndt, whose rooms were in a side wing of the house, came in, his hair and cloak all white with snow, straight from the harbor, and told his father that the *Sofie Hosewinckel* was saved and was off Odder Island. A fisherman had brought in the news at daybreak. Jochum Hosewinckel laid his head upon his folded hands on the table and wept.

Arndt next recounted how the ship's rescue had been brought about. Then was the old shipowner's joy so great that he had to talk over the event with his brethren of the shipping world. He took his son's arm and walked with him to the harbor, and from the harbor around the town. Everywhere the news was greeted with wonder and joy, all details were gone through time after time, and more than one glass was drunk to the rescue of the ship and to the health of Mamzell Ross. Jochum Hosewinckel after the terrible, endless night became as light of heart and head as he had not been for many a year. He sent word home to his wife that when the noble girl arrived in town they would take her into their own house and would have ready for her the room which had once been Sofie's.

When late in the afternoon the fishing boat from Odder Island, bringing the shipwrecked folk to the town, stood into the harbor, half Christianssand was there. People greeted the shipowner with happy faces; a particular circumstance, a tradition or legend in Jochum Hosewinckel's family, added something almost devotional to the salutations.

It was a wild, turbulent evening. It had ceased to snow, the sky was dark, only along the horizon ran a faint light. As the sun went down, a strange copper-colored gleam fell over the deeply disturbed waters, and the many faces on the quay became aglow with it.

The boat was received with an acclaim such as a seafaring nation accords to its sea heroes. All eyes searched for the maiden who had saved *Sofie Hosewinckel* and who to the imagination took the form of an angel. They did not find her at once, for she had changed her wet clothing for a fisherman's jersey, trousers and seaboots, and in this equipment, which was too big for her, looked like a ship's boy. For a few seconds disappointment and anxiety ran through the crowd. But a thick-set man in the boat lifted the girl up and shouted to those on shore: "Here is a treasure for you!" At the instant when the angel was revealed in the likeness of a young seaman, one of their very own, a hundred hearts melted as one. A tremendous cheering burst forth, caps were waved in the air, and the whole assembly laughed toward the boat. Yet there were many who wept at the same time.

The girl's sou'wester had fallen off as she was lifted up, her hair, tumbled and curly from salt water and snow, was turned by the evening sun into a halo behind her head. She was unsteady on her feet, a young man took her in his arms and carried her. It was Arndt Hosewinckel. Malli stared into his face, and thought that she had never seen so beautiful a human face. He looked into hers; it was very pale with black rings round the eyes and a trembling mouth. He felt her body in its coarse clothes against his own, a lock of her hair strayed into his mouth and tasted salt; it was as if she had been flung into his embrace by the sea itself.

One moment she was unaware of what the black mass in front of her meant; her light, wide-open eyes sought Arndt's. In the next instant she heard her own name shouted, so that the air vibrated with it. At that she surrendered herself—in the deep wave of blood which rose to her face, in a wide, dizzy glance and in one single movement—completely to the crowd about her, as delighted and wild with joy as the crowd itself. Arndt had her radiant face close to his; he gave her a kiss.

The people made room for the old shipowner, who with bared head and in a loud, deeply moved voice addressed a few words to the girl and the assembly. Arndt laughingly shielded her against being embraced by all Christianssand. When the crowd realized that the owner of the rescued ship was taking the girl to his own house, she and her host were accompanied to the gate with cheers.

The young sailor Ferdinand, who to the minds of the cheerers stood by the girl's side as the hero of the great happy drama, had his home in the town with his widowed mother. He was carried to it shoulder-high.

A little later in the evening the other shipwrecked folk, who had been set safely ashore on the island, were brought in, and people had an opportunity of remaining in their festive mood. Herr Soerensen with lightning speed conceived his position. He no longer thought of his own sufferings, but beamed in the reflection of his young disciple's glory, and by his authoritative and powerful attitude affirmed the fact that he had created her, and that she was his. Apart from this nothing was really clear to him, and particularly not what was up and what was down in the world around him. In the course of the day he had become very hoarse; now he lost his voice altogether and spent the first few days after the shipwreck with a number of woolen scarves round his throat, in complete silence. In the town the rumor went that during the storm, at the thought of the danger to Mamzell Ross, his hair had turned white. The truth was that his chestnut wig had been whirled away into the waves from the lifeboat. He bore the loss with fine, regal calm, conscious that in exchange for a temporal possession he had won an eternal experience, and also that he would have his loss replaced when his old carpetbag was brought ashore.

Soon also the other members of the theatrical company were landed, pale and semiconscious, but one and all proud and undaunted. In the boat Mamzell Ihlen let her long dark hair cover her like a cloak.

The troupe's fair-haired leading young man the day after the rescue wrote an Ode to the North Wind and had it accepted by the daily paper, the more weather-wise readers of which realized that a poet cannot be expected to have an insight both into versifying and the points of the compass.

The theatrical performances for the moment had to be postponed. Yet in the course of the week some of the actors, as a foretaste, gave extracts from their programme in the smaller hall of the Hotel Harmonien. The proprietor of the hotel under the particular, moving circumstances magnanimously allowed the company to stay at reduced prices. And when it became known that costumes and set-pieces on board *Sofie Hosewinckel* had been damaged by salt water, a collection was started on behalf of the sufferers. It brought in a fine return, and Herr Soerensen, in his bed and his dumbness, reflected upon the public's valuation of an artist's efforts in art and life respectively.

The stately house in the market-square had opened its doors to Malli, and shut them behind her, in generous heartfelt gratitude to the lonely young girl who had risked her life for one of its ships.

Among a people that lives by and from the sea, reality and fantasy become strangely interwoven. During the first days after the girl's arrival the faces of her housemates when turned toward her were stamped with a kind of awe. They could not tell whether the sea, that ever-present and ever-inscrutable supreme force, had really let go its grip of her.

Would not the next of the long rollers which lifted high the craft in the harbor suck her back with it, so that when they sought her in her room they would find it empty, with a dark streak of sea water and weed along the floor like the ones ghosts from the sea leave behind them? After some days, however, the house felt surer about her. She then became a symbol to it: half of the ship *Sofie Hosewinckel* which had been in distress at sea, half of young Sofie Hosewinckel herself, who had once blossomed in its rooms.

Malli never in her life had been inside such a magnificent house. She gazed at the crystal chandeliers in the ceiling, the lace curtains, the gold-framed family portraits on the walls and the camphor-wood chests, and felt that she ought to curtsey to them all. And in this house she was made much of; she was given coffee and buns in bed and violet-scented soap by her washbasin.

She was still shy and did not have much to say. Of her great exploit she related no more than she had to bring out as answers to the questions of the others. But she was happy; she walked, smiling, amid smiles. She felt that the house, the day after her arrival, was surprised to see that she was pretty. She had entered it pale and dirty of face and in ugly clothes; in its embrace she became, as she herself saw in the mirror, prettier day by day. Also at this fact, that it had thought her to be plain, while in reality she was a lovely girl, the old house smiled. So Malli, with the house's own approval, went a small step further and looked around among the people who lived in it.

She felt most at ease in the company of the old shipowner. It was, she thought, because for such a long time she had been longing for a father that she liked being with men, and herself felt that in glance, posture and voice she had much to give them. Toward the lady of the house she was more bashful. Mrs. Hosewinckel was a stately lady in a black silk gown, with a long gold watch-chain on her bosom. She had a large, delicately pink and white face, and Malli thought that she resembled Queen Thora in *Axel and Valborg*. Mrs. Hosewinckel did not say much, but Queen Thora in the tragedy has but one single line, addressed to her son, "May God forgive thee!," and yet the audience knows her to be kind and majestic, and to wish the noble characters well. Of Arndt, the son of the house, Malli only knew or thought that his face had been wondrously beautiful when he had lifted her ashore from the boat.

VIII. *The House in the Market Square*

Jochum Hosewinckel and his wife were God-fearing folk; their house was the most decorous in the town and the most charitable to the poor. They had married young and had lived together happily, but for a long time their marriage had been childless. In the Hosewinckel family it was a tradition that while paying one's respects to Providence in church on Sunday and in the daily morning and evening prayers, one did not push oneself forward with personal petitions. Only by a strict, righteous life had the couple brought themselves and their longing to the notice of the Almighty. A small, disturbing question was concealed beneath their silence: was not the Almighty in this matter standing somewhat in His own light? Eighteen years after their wedding their unexpressed prayer was heard, their son came into the world. And gratitude they felt free to show openly. At the christening of the child large endowments were made which bore Arndt Jochumsen Hosewinckel's name. From now on the house displayed a generous hospitality.

But the shipowner and his wife as years went by became almost uneasy about their good fortune.

For their son from his tenderest age was so radiantly lovely that people stood still and were stricken to silence when they saw him. And as he grew up he became intelligent, quick to learn, gallant and noble beyond other boys. When as a young man he was sent to Lübeck and Amsterdam to learn the shipping business, by his clear-headedness, his pleasant manner and his upright conduct he everywhere won the confidence and affection of those set in authority over him. At the age of twenty-one he became his father's partner in the shipping company and there displayed a remarkably good understanding of ships and shipping. Everything he set his hand to turned out well, and both seamen and clerks were happy to serve him. He had a special love of music, and himself played and sang well.

Within the last few years from time to time a particular shadow was cast over his parents' happiness: it did not look as if Arndt Hosewinckel thought of marrying. In the family many had died young and unmarried, as if they had been too good and fine to mingle the world's nature with their own. Was it going to turn out the same in the case of its last, late-born and precious child? The old people, however, were not going to worry themselves unnecessarily. After all, their son was honorable, straight and chivalrous to all young girls in Christianssand, and could make his choice from among them when he wished.

All those who now looked at Arndt Hosewinckel, with unconscious deep delight let their eyes dwell on the beauty, power and charm of his body, on the remarkable perfection of his features, and the peculiar expression of his face, at the same time frank and thoughtful, and reflected that this young man from Christianssand in his cradle had received everything that a human being can desire, and almost more than anyone can easily bear.

He had received even more than they knew of. He had a receptive and reflective nature and he had made his experiences in life.

When Arndt was fifteen years old a fisherman's daughter from Vatne, whose name was Guro, had come as maid to his parents' home. She was a year older than the son of the house, but the handsome boy, with wealth and the admiration of people surrounding his head like a halo, had awakened a mighty, irresistible emotion in the half-savage girl's breast. She was incapable of hiding her passion from him; they were lovers before they knew of it. He was so young that he felt no guilt. He had never in his life feared, nor had had reason to fear, that the things he wanted by nature might possibly conflict with noble conduct or ways of thinking. An unknown sweetness and desire, a game which was all the more delightful because it was secret, had grown up between him and Guro. They smiled at each other; they wished each other well from the bottom of their hearts. Of his father and mother—if at that time they ever came into his mind at all—the boy thought: "They would not understand this." They were so much older than he; as long as he had known them, while he had felt himself full of spirit and determination, they had been staid people. It hardly entered his head that they themselves might once have known the same game.

The secret love affair in the shipowner's house lasted six weeks. Then one spring night Guro threw her arms around her young lover's neck and cried out in a storm of tears: "I am a lost creature because I have met you and have looked at you, Arndt!" On the morrow she was gone, and two days later she was found floating in the fjord.

Arndt saw Guro again when she was carried into the house, white, ice-cold, with salt water running from her clothing and her hair. The reason for her desperate act was soon known: Guro was with child. Three days passed during which the boy believed himself to be the one who had caused the young woman's misfortune and death. But after that time her father and mother came to the town to fetch her body home, and the house got to know that things had been wrong with the girl before she entered it. She had a sweetheart in Vatne; he had deserted her, but had since thought better of it and had twice looked her up in town, asking her to marry him. But now Guro would have nothing to do with him. The master and mistress of the house were dismayed at the dark, sorrowful tale that had come to pass under their roof. They were loath to speak of it in their young son's hearing, but they felt it to be unavoidable, or even to be their duty, to tell him the truth quite briefly, adding a few solemn words on the wages of sin.

This truth which Arndt had from the lips of his father and mother did away with his own guilt. But it seemed at the same time to do away with everything else, so that he himself was left with empty hands. There was nothing there but a longing which for many a day sucked at his heart, and which was less for the girl herself or the happiness she had brought him than for his own faith in her and in it. A secret felicity in life had revealed itself to him and proved its existence, then immediately afterwards had denied itself and proved that it had never been. And Guro's farewell words rang in his ears like a fateful prophecy that it was a misfortune to meet him and to look at him, even to those for whom he wished the very best. "I am a lost creature because I have met you!" she had lamented with her tear-wet face against his own. The events had passed through his life in the course of a few months and without any living soul knowing about them. And so to him, the tenderly watched-over child, it was as if he had come to know most of what there is to know in the world in complete isolation.

All this had happened twelve years ago. Since then

he had looked around the world and had had to do
with many people and circumstances. He had had
friends in many countries, and had known girls who
were as pretty and devoted as the fisherman's daughter
from Vatne. He thought of her no longer, and hardly
remembered how it had first come about that he preferred to keep himself somewhat aloof from people,
lest through him they should be lost.

IX. *A Ball in Christianssand*

Now ladies and gentlemen from the town's best society came to the house in the square to see and pay
their respects to Mamzell Ross. They combined to
give a ball in her honor in the ballroom of Harmonien. Malli till that day had gone about in the rich
house in her one modest frock, and had not given it a
thought; a ball-frock she had never possessed. But for
the ball Mrs. Hosewinckel, in all haste, had her own
dressmaker make up a tulle gown with flounces and a
sash for the house's young guest. The elderly woman
on the evening of the ball was surprised to see how
easily and regally the milliner's daughter wore her
finery, and wondered a little whether she herself and
the whole town did not do wrong to treat, in return
for a heroic deed, the heroine like a toy. She might
have spared herself her worry. Such treatment might
have turned the head of another girl, but here one had
to deal with a young person who accepted being
treated as a toy with gratitude, and who could at the
same time treat a whole town with its harbor, streets,
town-hall and citizens as her own plaything.

So Malli went to the ball, but she could not take a full part in it, for she had never learned to dance. One of the ladies of the committee begged her instead to sing to the party. Malli did this gladly, and all listened with pleasure to her pure, clear voice, the old gentlemen at the card tables raising their punch glasses high to her as she gave them a sea chanty from their own young days. A young girl next suggested that she should sing something they could dance to. Malli held back a little, and then, like a bird in a tree, with a long-concealed, suddenly emerging delight broke into her own song, Ariel's song:

> *"Come unto these yellow sands,*
> *And then take hands:*
> *Curtsied when you have, and kiss'd,—*
> *The wild waves whist,—*
> *Foot it featly here and there,*
> *And, sweet sprites, the burden bear."*

The dance swept on in time with the song, and Malli stood in the midst of the glittering hall and watched it turning and swaying to the command of her beat.

Ferdinand had been invited to the ball, and Malli had been happily looking forward to seeing him and talking with him, for the two had not met since the night of the storm. But he had sent word that he could not come. Now the singer fixed her eyes on Arndt Hosewinckel.

Arndt had stood talking to some old merchants, but when Malli began to sing he listened, and when she sang for the dance he joined in the dancing. She saw how well he danced, and in one single glance realized what he meant in the ballroom and the town, and what the lovely young ladies at the ball, who had learned to dance, thought of him. But the simple girl, who had bought her entry to the only ball of her young life by risking that life itself, while watching the town's first young man dancing, realized even more. She thought: "God! what deep need!" And again: "I can help there. I can help him in his need and save him!"

Malli did not go to bed when she came home, but kept sitting for a long time in her filmy gown in front of her candle-lit mirror. Arndt Hosewinckel did not go to bed either, but went out of the house for a long night-walk. Not seldom did it happen that he went out at night like this to the harbor and to the warehouses there, or farther out, along the fjord.

x. *Exchange of Visits*

Malli wished to visit the sick Herr Soerensen, and Arndt Hosewinckel walked with her to show her the way to the hotel, and to pay his respects to the man who together with the girl had endured distress at sea on board the *Sofie Hosewinckel*.

Herr Soerensen was out of bed in an easy-chair, but he was still as good as dumb. The relationship between the old man and the girl was so much conditioned by the boards that Malli, once she had adjusted herself to the situation, immediately turned the whole meeting into pantomime, just as if her old teacher, because he had lost his voice, must of necessity also have become deaf. Master and pupil lighted up in each other's company, and Malli at once understood that Arndt's beauty strongly affected and moved the old director, and that he was thinking: "Ay, if one had only a first lover like that!" She did not know that he was at the same time wondering at her own appearance and asking himself: "How can this girl's bosom have grown so rounded in such a short time?" All her movements were thus rounded and soft while, in pantomime, she was explaining to him with how much friendliness she had met since the two had been together.

When the time came for her and Arndt to say goodbye, Herr Soerensen took her hand, pressed it to the best of his ability and feebly whispered or wheezed to her: "Why, that's my dainty Ariel! I shall miss thee!" At that Malli found her voice. "And I you!" she cried aloud, without remembering that there had been no talk of parting at all.

Herr Soerensen was left alone, and for several days remained deeply gripped and moved. He understood, or by glimpses caught, his young pupil's attitude, and was impressed. Here was a mighty undertaking: the whole world, the everyday common life, lifted onto the stage and being made one with it. Thy will be done, William Shakespeare, as on the stage so also in the drawing room! Here in very reality his Ariel did spread out a pair of wings and did rise into the air straight before his eyes. Suddenly and strangely it was brought back to him how once, in the exuberance of heart of a young actor, he himself had dreamed of

such an apotheosis. And it now also happened to him,
for the first two or three nights after Malli's visit, in
regular dreams in the narrow bed of his lodging, to
find himself a partner in her venture, one time as
Prospero on a father-in-law visit to the young King
and Queen of Naples, another time as the fool in the
Hosewinckel house. But when again awake he dismissed the idea. In the course of a long life he had
gained experience and insight, and to any person of
experience and insight, indeed to anyone but a young
actress in love, the project of lifting daily life onto
the stage was paradoxical, and in its essence blasphe-
mous. For it was more likely that daily life would
drag down the stage to its own level than that the
stage would succeed in maintaining it so highly elevated; and the whole world-order might well end up
pell-mell.

He next reflected that he was now to lose his Ariel,
and that the great enterprise of his life would never
materialize. At this he grieved. Why, he asked himself, must the hideous, wet tempest in Kvasefjord
break right into the middle of his William's *Tempest?*
Could it be that it had been brought about by the will
of that forceful, fearless, formidable child?

Yet as soon as the old director had to some extent
regained the modulated register of his voice, he paid
a return visit to the shipowner's house. For the occasion he had purchased a pair of lavender-colored
gloves, which stood out against his old frock coat and
frayed top hat, but was in harmony with his carriage
and tone of voice. His manner was so courteous and

obliging that Fru Hosewinckel, who was not accustomed to such self-effacing men of the world, became almost bashful. He made a bow each minute and was untiring in his praise of everything in the rooms. If he had overlooked any single object, he hastened to make good the neglect, as if he were making the lofty mirrors between the windows or the view over the marketplace the humblest apologies for his forgetfulness.

He burst out: "What glorious, magnificent possessions—collected in old Europe at what cost! What treasures brought from China and the Indies! Oh, what extremely charming chandeliers—and brilliant paintings of majestic ships!"

Herr Soerensen and Malli for a moment were alone in the drawing room. Herr Soerensen put a finger to his lips, blew Malli a little kiss, and solemnly announced: "My girl, you are Dame Fortune's favorite!" As Malli looked back at him in a clear, firm gaze, he himself looked aside, pulled an old silk handkerchief out of his coat pocket, mopped his forehead, and finished up, somewhat subdued and more to himself than to her:

> *"My Pegasus is slack,*
>   *Plays truant when he can!*
>   *But wait, thou ancient hack,*
>   *I am thy master man.*
>   *(I'll show thee who's the man.")*

When he had again taken his leave in a series of sweet bows, Malli kept standing by the window, letting her eyes follow his figure as it strode proudly across the square, grew smaller and disappeared.

XI. *The Story of an Engagement*

The thought or notion that Malli, instead of continuing the journey with Herr Soerensen and his company, might remain in the town and come to belong to it, first arose among the people who had cheered her when her boat came into the harbor. One might say that in the town community this thought or notion moved in a spiral; as its rings became narrower it constantly rose higher, both socially and emotionally. When in the end it reached those on whom it turned, it also reached its zenith of tension and destiny.

In a small community where not many things happen, as a rule there is much talk. There an engagement is the supreme topic of conversation and discussion, and the more interest beforehand existent in the young persons who are believed to become engaged, the more lively the talk. It may therefore be worth recording that in this case so little was said. Arndt Hosewinckel was the town's darling and its best match; Malli was its heroine. But as the two drew closer together and to the mind of the people became one, it was as if their figures eluded observation. A deep breath of comprehension passed through the town, but the names were spoken less often than before.

The plain people of the town took pleasure in the idea that Arndt Hosewinckel and Mamzell Ross might

become a pair. It was once again the happy ending,
both surprising and foreseen, to the old tale in which
Cinderella marries the Prince. Their town in reward
for a handsome deed handsomely gave the best it had
to give. That the yellow house in the marketplace
should come to open its door to a poor daughter-in-
law, a drowned skipper's child, rejoiced and moved the
sailors' wives, and there was in their joy no kind of
malice toward the shipowner or his lady. For had it
not been proclaimed in the very harbor that the bride
was a treasure? Inasmuch as she symbolized the sea,
the breadwinner and the fate of all, she united, even
as the sea itself, the town's humble folk with its
richest citizen.

The thought or notion climbed its spiral path to a
higher and narrower circle and gained access to the
houses of the best society. Then Malli's good name
for a day or two trembled on the brink of an abyss.
For up here one asked oneself whether the heroine
was not in reality an adventuress gambling on the
town's admiration and gratitude in order to make a
match above her station. But something in the picture
of the girl herself almost immediately tipped the balance in her favor. The old gentlemen of the ball were
the first to acquit her. Their wives, who were honest
folk and who had often trembled for ships and crews,
examined Malli's behavior in the night of the storm
and acknowledged that nothing in it could be inter-
preted as calculation.

Possibly each single one of the young burghers'
daughters, to whose dancing Malli had sung, reasoned

that if she could not herself have Arndt Hosewinckel, the girl from the wreck was the one to whom she could easiest renounce him. Or perhaps those girls, who had known one another from their days of curved combs and pantalets, knew too much of one another's shortcomings. Of one young beauty, who was specially admired for her small feet, they knew that she had her shoes made yet a size smaller and so had acquired a corn. Of another charmer they knew that her shining golden tresses did not all grow on her own head. Of the stranger the fair young girls knew that she was poor, badly dressed and too big to be elegant, and that she could not dance. But there was in her special shy manner so much trust in, and so much recognition of, all beauty round her that in her presence everyone thought herself more beautiful. It also happened that they suddenly felt the girl from the sea to have in her a laughter different from their own. It had rung out through a storm, or had accompanied it.

The thought or notion reached the house on the square. It found a foothold in the servants' hall before it rose to the first floor and was here felt to be of extreme importance. The servants' hall finished by accepting Malli; it even silently closed a ring round the house's young lady-to-be, who owned only one frock and three shifts, and who sang so sweetly.

The thought or notion came up the stairs and into the drawing room of the paintings of majestic ships, and filled it with pregnant silence. It had reached high in its course; in here it was the future itself.

It found the atmosphere in the drawing room prepared or expectant, like the tuned instrument for the melody. The old master of the house at this time was in high spirits, with a delicate pink in his cheeks; he put on chokers and brought home presents of lace for his lady and sugarplums for Malli. With his ship's miraculous rescue in the night of the storm something romantic and heroic had come into his precisely regulated life—a gale's breath, the song of the wind in the sails. It was very fitting that he himself as father-in-law should in the end be taken by storm by a heroine. It may be considered a dangerous thing to extend one's enthusiasm for a heroic deed to everyday life, and the experienced shipowner might well have been somewhat uneasy about a heroic daughter-in-law—had she been the Maid of Orleans herself—whose exploits had been carried out ashore. But Malli's halo had been won at sea, amid salt breakers and surf spray. Jochum Hosewinckel as a very young man had suffered shipwreck on one of his father's ships. He would not mind a daughter-in-law in whose presence he would once more be eighteen years.

Malli's obscure origin might have cast a shadow over her young figure as it moved about the house. But since the sea had once shown itself to be the girl's ally, it was taken for granted that the harmony between the two was perfect, and that Alexander Ross had gone down with his ship an honorable man. Indeed his daughter's steadfastness on the *Sofie Hosewinckel* in some mystic way became a proof of this fact. Jochum Hosewinckel called to mind the name of an old Swedish Commander Ross, a friend of his father's, who had also been of Scotch origin, and about whose figure some mystery had also rested. The Commander could well have been a relative of the lost ship's captain, and one might well here have to do with a family of heroes.

Fru Wencke Hosewinckel, ever a woman of few words, in silence wondered at the quickness with which all men seemed able to take up a standpoint in face of life's events. She watched her son's face, listened to his voice, and bided her time.

The thought or notion finally reached its close and its summit with the two young people themselves who were to be the happy pair. It took them both by surprise like an amazing, brilliant idea from an outside world which they had forgotten. For some weeks they had dwelt among immortal powers. As now the mortal world too gave them its blessing, they happily accepted that too, and from now on their eternity could become their everyday.

For Malli this came to be the completion and perfection of her own mighty rise. She had once been given wings; they had grown miraculously and had been able to carry her, ever upward, to this unspeakable glory. She stood on a dizzying height, but she could fearlessly cast herself out from it anywhere, because anywhere Arndt's arms would catch her and bear her. Now she was also to become his wife, to have his name and make his house her home, she was to

> "*share all that he doth possess,*
> *by having him making herself no less.*"

She had tremblingly dreamt of playing Juliet, now life had given her a role as fine as Juliet's. And she was the maid of Arendal who would not consent to be anybody's prize!

Arndt's happiness was of a different kind. Promises of long ago, which his own mind had rejected, now rose again and were fulfilled. The world had been restless, disorganized and empty. A young girl looked at it, and under her eyes it became united, became a cosmos.

He had received, at the harbor, the penniless, valiant girl who had saved one of his house's ships. Such a young maiden was the last human being he wanted to make unhappy; he was not going to become her destiny. He had kissed her, and to make up for the kiss had at first in his parents' house kept away from her. But one day Malli had looked at him with bright, candid eyes, openly enough to make him feel that neither he nor anyone else in the world could make this young lass unhappy. This struck the rich youth as a jest on the part of Fate; he looked back at the girl, approached her and spoke to her. And behold, he himself then had a destiny—clear-eyed, generous, without *arrière-pensées*.

Ay, she was a heroine, a lion-hearted maiden, as they all said. But she was so in a manner other than they knew of. She had no need to fear, for where she was, danger was not. There were still shipwrecks, distress and misfortune. But shipwrecks, distress and misfortune were changed, and became evidence of God's omnipotence and mercy.

Later in the night he saw, strangely, the picture of himself as he had been before she came. He thought: "She has power to wake the dead."

Just before daybreak came also the picture of Guro, of whom he had not thought for many years. And he remembered that they had been friends and happy together, rich in desire and tenderness in spring nights, in such nights as this one. He understood that in the very last spring night the sea had taken Guro in a mighty embrace wherein there was power and love, forgiveness and forgetfulness.

"And sweet sprites, the burden bear!" echoed around him in the dim house.

It is reasonable to assume that Arndt asked Malli to become his wife in a completely ordinary suitor's fashion and that she answered "yes" in the manner of an ordinary girl. But the question was put and answered as if it was to decide his and her eternal salvation.

They stood closely embraced, borne and elevated on the same wave. But they did not kiss; a kiss did not fit into this instant of eternity.

A while later as they were sitting together on the sofa by the window, she asked him lowly and gravely: "Are you happy?" He answered her slowly: "Yes, I am happy. But it is not happiness that you are, Malli. It is life. I was not sure that life was to be found anywhere in the world. People said: 'That is a matter of

life and death,' and I thought: 'What a small matter it
is.' I thought of myself that I knew about everything, and that I portended ruin. Oh, Malli, today I
am an enigma to myself, and a harbinger of joy to the
world."

Shortly after he had spoken she sank down before
him, and as he would raise her up she prevented him
by laying her clasped hands upon his knee.

"Nay, let me lie here," she said. "This is the most
fitting place of all."

Her gentle, enraptured and humble face shone up
toward him.

"Yes," she went on very slowly. "Yes. 'I am the
resurrection and the life,' said Malli. " 'He that believeth in me, though he were dead, yet shall he live.
And whosoever liveth and believeth in me, shall never
die, but have everlasting life.' "

Arndt had to go to Stavanger for the firm; owing
to a sudden bankruptcy a ship was for sale there. He
set out a few days later, early in the morning.

He had not known how much it would cost him to
part from Malli; now at the last moment he had to
force himself to leave. Malli too, on her side, had
taken this separation of a few days lightly; she almost
felt that she needed to draw her breath. It was only
when at his departure she saw him so pale that she herself became very pale. Something terrible might happen to him on the journey. She ought to have prevented him from going away, or she ought to have
gone with him in order to ward off the misfortune
that threatened him. In the chill spring morning she

stood on the front steps of the house, in the East Indian shawl her mother had given her, and watched his cariole depart.

"My God!" she thought. "If it goes with him as with Father! If he never comes back!"

XII. *Ferdinand*

It now happened, the day after Arndt had left, that a couple of ladies of the town were paying a call on Fru Hosewinckel, and that while they were sitting around the coffee table Malli came into the room in cloak and bonnet, radiant with happiness, ready to go out. Fru Hosewinckel asked her where she was going, and she answered that she was going to see Ferdinand. The ladies fell silent and looked at each other. Fru Hosewinckel got up from her chair, went toward Malli and took her hand.

"My dear girl," she said, "you cannot see Ferdinand any more."

"Why not?" ask Malli in amazement.

"Alas, Ferdinand is dead," said Fru Hosewinckel.

"Ferdinand!" Malli cried aloud.

"Yes, our poor, good Ferdinand," said Fru Hosewinckel.

"Ferdinand!" Malli cried again.

"Such was the will of God," said Fru Hosewinckel.

"Ferdinand!" Malli cried for the third time, as if to herself.

The two ladies of the town said that they were very sorry indeed, and then went on to report in de-

tail what had happened to Ferdinand. On board the
Sofie Hosewinckel he had, on the night of the tempest,
been struck by a falling piece of the yardarm and had
suffered severe internal injuries. These at first had not
appeared to be serious, but yesterday he had died.

"So after all it was the tempest," said one of the
ladies, "which brought on the death of the brave
young man."

"The tempest!" Malli exclaimed. "The tempest!
No, how can you think that? I must go to him. Then
will you see that you are utterly mistaken!"

"Unfortunately there can be no doubt about it,"
said another lady. "And it is such a very poor home.
How, now, is his poor mother to get along? Alas no,
Mamzell Ross, there is no doubt at all."

Malli stood for a while considering.

"Indeed yes," she then burst out forcefully. "He
stood on the deck with me, you know! We were together the whole night through. In the morning, in
the fisherman's hut, he was the one who helped me
change my clothes. And you have seen for yourselves," she went on, turning to face the ladies, "that
he came ashore in the boat with me. No, Ferdinand is
not dead!" Once more she was silent.

"I must go to him at once!" she cried. "God! To
think that I have not gone before!"

The ladies did not know what to do about this
wild, disturbed agitation, so remained silent and let
the girl go her way.

Malli came into Ferdinand's home just as the young
seaman was being laid in his coffin. His mother and

small brothers and sisters, and a few relatives who had assisted them, stood around and in their dark clothing filled up the small dark room. They all made way for the girl, and the dead boy's mother greeted her, took her by the hand and led her forward, so that she should see Ferdinand for the last time.

Malli had sped through the streets like a gale and was panting after her run; now she stood as if turned to stone. Ferdinand's young face on its pillow of shavings was as peaceful as if he were asleep. Suffering and agony had passed over it and again away, and had left behind, as it were, a deep, solemn experience. Malli had never before seen a corpse; neither had she ever seen Ferdinand so quiet.

The strangers in the room had been about to leave when she came; they now said good-bye to her and she shook hands with them one by one, with wide-open, dumb eyes. Ferdinand's mother saw the visitors out; Malli was alone with him.

She fell on her knees by the coffin.

"Ferdinand!" she called out very gently. And again: "Ferdinand! Dear Ferdinand!"

As he did not answer, she stretched out her hand and touched his face. Death's icy chill penetrated through her fingers; she felt it go right into her heart and withdrew her hand. But a little after she laid it back again, let it rest on the boy's cheek until she thought that her hand had become as cold as that cheek itself, and so began slowly to stroke the still face. She felt the cheekbones and the eyesockets against the tips of her fingers. Her own face the while took on the expression of the dead sailor boy's face; the two grew to resemble each other like brother and sister.

Ferdinand's mother came into the room again and made Malli sit down on a chair. She began to tell about Ferdinand and about what a good son he had always been to her. She went over his short life, relating small traits and incidents from his childhood and boyhood, and as she did so the tears ran down her cheeks. But when she began to tell of how Ferdinand had ever laid aside almost all his pay to give to his mother when he came home, she ceased to cry. She only sighed deeply and heavily over how hard life would now be for his small brothers and sisters, and for herself.

"Ferdinand," she said sorrowfully, "would have been so grieved to see it."

Malli listened, and deep in her heart recognized this subdued woman's wailing. It was her own mother's anxiety about bread for herself and her child. She looked about her, and now also recognized the needy, narrow room. This was the room of her own home; here she had grown up. The old familiar, bare world came back to her, so strangely gentle, and so inescapable.

It was as if a hand—and was it Ferdinand's own cold hand, on which hers had just now rested?—seized her by the throat, and she grew giddy and sank, or everything round her sank. The elder woman looked at her, and with the quiet tact of the poor changed the subject. She began to tell of Ferdinand's pride at being the young lady's friend. She had from Ferdinand's own lips heard more of the shipwreck than anyone else, and had followed Malli's steps from the deck to the engine room, and from the engine room to the helm. By her son's sickbed she had had to read aloud to him so many times the report of the *Christianssand Daily News* that she now knew it all by heart. A little smile broke out on her careworn face as she explained how, to please him, she herself had had to repeat the young lady's cry through the din and roaring of the tempest: "Ferdinand!"

At that Malli rose from her chair, pale as death. She looked at the simple bench and table, at the one poor flower pot in the window and at the woman's threadbare clothes. Lastly she turned toward the silent face in the coffin. But now she dared not go near it. She merely for an instant wrung her hands in its direction in a movement that was like a shriek. Then she gave Ferdinand's mother her hand and went away.

When she came home, she sought out Fru Hose-winckel and said to her:

"Ay, Ferdinand is dead. And it is such a poor home. How, now, is his mother to get along?"

Fru Hosewinckel felt sorry for the pale girl.

"Dear Malli," she said, "we will not forget Ferdinand's loyalty. We will stand by this poor mother."

Malli stared at her as if she had not understood what was said and was waiting to hear something she could better comprehend.

"My dear child," said Fru Hosewinckel. "That is the happiness of possessing wealth, that one may help where need is great."

When next morning Malli came downstairs, she was so changed that her housemates were frightened. She was once more the girl with the stiff white face and the dark rings under her eyes, paralyzed in all her joints, who had been brought in from the wreck. And she was now also dumb, as at that time Herr Soerensen himself. She would not go out, but also dreaded to stay in; she got up from one chair to sit down on another. Fru Hosewinckel proposed sending for the family doctor, but Malli begged her not to with such anguish that she again gave up the idea. The household then in perplexity left her in peace; only the lady of the house attentively followed the distressed expressions in the young face.

XIII. *The Altar Cloth*

As long as Arndt was in the house it had been difficult for Fru Hosewinckel, in the strong light with which her son's love surrounded Malli, really to catch sight of the girl. In her sober way she had almost looked forward to his absence, during which she would have time and peace to look at her. The sudden ominous change in Malli's face and manner frightened her, and she did not know what to think about it. For some days her son was still so close to her that she saw Malli with his eyes. The girl then was to her a precious possession, and she tried to the best of her ability to help and console her.

Now she also reproached herself, more seriously than on the evening of the ball, with having thoughtlessly allowed Malli to be the object of so many people's curiosity and homage. This very young girl had looked death in the face, had immediately after been taken up into new, rich surroundings, and there to all probability had had her life's course decided. Let good fortune be ever so sweet, the elderly woman reflected, it takes strength to bear even that. Now there must be an end to parties and gatherings, and Malli must remain unobserved and undisturbed under the protection of the house.

As Fru Hosewinckel spoke of her resolve to Malli herself, it was as if for the first time since Ferdinand's death the girl did really grasp what was said to her.

"Yes, unobserved," whispered Malli. "Be subject to no sight but thine and mine, invisible to every eyeball else! What lovely words."

But soon afterwards she was once more white and restless in the grip of her grief.

Arndt's mother knew Malli so little that she could not guess what she was grieving about. She noticed that least of all the girl could bear to hear her son's name mentioned; it was as if each time the sound of it struck her at the heart. A terrible thought for a while gained hold of Fru Hosewinckel's mind. Was it possible that this girl was not quite sane? Nobody had really known her father, and who could tell what ghosts of old forgotten times had been admitted to the house together with the valiant maiden? Yet till now no one had noticed any derangement in Malli, and she again dismissed her fear. There was something else weighing on the girl's mind, and what was it?

She called to mind that it was the news of Ferdinand's death which had brought Malli to despair. What could there have been between the girl and the young sailor? While pondering on this she called to mind that she herself, while her engagement to Jochum Hosewinckel was still a secret, had had another suitor applying for her hand and had been unhappy about it. Malli in the turbulence of the storm might have given Ferdinand a promise, and might now be grieving because she had not got herself released from it in time. Slowly Fru Hosewinckel groped her way further into the idea, at times amazed at the unwonted audacity of her own fantasy. Did the girl, she wondered, now imagine that the dead young ordinary seaman might rise from his grave and call her to account? Young girls have strange notions and may almost die of them. But a secret distress to be relieved must be brought into the light of day. She must persuade or force Malli to speak.

For a few days she cautiously questioned the girl on her childhood and her time with Herr Soerensen's troupe. Malli artlessly answered all her questions; in this past there were no secrets. Fru Hosewinckel went on to mention Ferdinand's name, and it seemed evident that Ferdinand had never caused Malli any sorrow but his death. The elder woman almost lost patience with the young one who suffered and would not let herself be helped. Then she bethought herself that in this world there are powers stronger than the human will, and decided to turn to them with regard to Malli's salvation.

As already mentioned, she was unaccustomed to

troubling heaven with direct petitions; this was perhaps the first time she approached it with a personal plea. But she did it for the sake of her only son, and because she had now gone so far into the matter that to her there was no retreat. Neither could she hand over her task to anyone else. Her husband was as pious as herself, and for more than forty years the two had said their evening prayers together. But just as Fru Hosewinckel—although she inwardly hoped that she might be wrong—could not quite believe that any man could attain to eternal life, she could not quite imagine that a person of the male sex could put a matter before God in the form of prayer.

So next Sunday she went to church and collected herself to submit her demand. She did not ask for strength or patience; what was required of these she must, she knew, herself supply. But she prayed for an inspiration to find clarity in the affair and help for the sorrowing girl, for she realized that she herself was not rich in inspiration. She walked home from church with hope in her heart.

Fru Hosewinckel, in her gratitude for the rescue of *Sofie Hosewinckel*, had wished to present her church with a new altar cloth, a fine piece of drawn-thread work fitted together in squares which could be embroidered separately and when ready joined together. She herself worked on one such piece and had asked Malli, who had been taught needlework by her mother, to do another, and this occupation, a return to days of old, was the only one in which the girl seemed to be at ease; she worked on steadily, almost without looking up. On Sunday evening the lady of the house and its young guest were sitting together by the drawing-room table sewing; in the large, dim room the linen shone a delicate white in the gleam of the paraffin lamp. Shortly after the master of the hous came into the room and sat down with them.

xiv. *Old Folk and Old Tales*

Old Jochum Hosewinckel during the last years had been living under the growing shadow of a fate hard to bear because to him it seemed to include some kind of guilt or shame; he had never spoken about it to anyone. Yet this was no personal or individual visitation, but a share in conditions common to all the human race: when men live long enough they come to know it. He had begun to feel the burden of old age. The people of his family were long-lived; he had watched his father and his grandfather grow old in a manner both expected and respected, becoming hard of hearing and in the end stone-deaf, stiff in the back as in mode of thought, walking about as honorable and honored memorials to a long row of years and experiences. With him himself, it seemed, old age was making itself known in a different way, and in his own mind he blamed his mother's mother, who had come from the far north of Norway, for the fact. He did not grow stiff or petrified, but the whole world, and he himself with it, day by day seemed to be losing in weight and dissolving. Matters and ideas changed color as the coat of paint on a boat that has been out in wind and weather will change color. The hues on the boat's planks may become almost prettier than before, there will be a new play in them, but all the same it is not as it should be, and one has one's boat painted afresh. It became difficult for him to keep his accounts and to determine whether things happening round him were of an advantageous or undesirable, of a gay or sad, nature, ay, whether in the books of his conscience they ought to be entered as credits or debits. At times it seemed to him that he could no longer rightly distinguish between past and present; his mind willingly let go its grasp of near things to run back to vanished times; childhood games and boy's pranks grew more alive to him than cargoes and rates of exchange. He was afraid lest his surroundings should discover the decay in him and became highly watchful in all communication with his skippers and clerks. He was least worried in front of his wife, who once for all had taken him for what he was, and now as a rule did not look much at him; but he sometimes shunned his son's company. In himself he might at times feel happy and even buoyant in an existence without accounts, but this fact to an old man of an old family, whose struggle throughout life had been to keep assets and liabilities apart, was disquieting, and he called himself to account. It went so far with him that the suspense in the days round *Sofie Hosewinckel's* shipwreck for a while had brought him a feeling of relief, because here one could clearly distinguish between good and bad luck.

Then Malli came into the house, a young being

whose idea of the universe could not be expected to include strict border lines, and who nonetheless, against the views of competent people, had headed straight for a goal and had saved his own good ship—a child who deserved to be spoiled and jested with. A joyous understanding and confidence sprang up between the old host and the young guest, as if within the whole household those two belonged to one another. She accompanied him on his early morning walks to the harbor and the warehouses, she took the trouble to recall songs of old days and sang them to him; one time when he brought her a bird in a cage she kissed him on both cheeks.

As now she grew ill or deeply melancholy and kept back from all other people, the understanding between the two was strengthened and found a particular expression. Malli was loath to hear about matters or events of the present day, but was pleased to listen to accounts of old times, even to plain nursery tales. And her old ally and protector, with his gentle bony face and his white whiskers, was pleased to recount to her childhood experiences and tales which more than sixty years ago had been told to him by the house's servants, by old skippers and fishermen and by his mother's mother. So it became a kind of tradition in the Hosewinckel house that when in the evening the ladies sat sewing by the table, its master would come in from his office, settle down in his grandfather's chair and bring out a story to them. At such hours he did not mind being heard by his wife to indulge in queer fancies. He might imagine himself and Malli to be running, hand in hand, into a twilight, a darkness of their own. But it was not barren; it was the mighty night of northern lights, and in it things lived: heavy, shaggy bears padded and puffed, wolves whirled in long trails through the blizzard over the plains, ancient Finns, who knew witchcraft, chuckled while selling fair winds to the seamen. Old Jochum Hosewinckel sat in his chair smiling, as if in a refuge from life, to which a bad conscience was not admitted.

On this Sunday evening he entered the room with a story for Malli ready at hand, and shortly after began to tell it.

"Tonight, Malli," he said, "I am going to tell you about a grave danger that once threatened the house in which you are sitting; God preserve it from another such. And also about my grandmother's grandfather, Jens Aabel. I myself had the story told me when I was a small boy."

xv. *Jens Aabel's Story and His Good Advice*

"This old Jens Guttormsen Aabel," he began his tale, the light from the lamp, which did not reach his face, falling upon his big old folded hands, "had come here from Saeterdalen, where the folk at that time were still half heathen, but he himself was a good Christian. He was a well-to-do man, held in respect by the whole town, and already getting on in years, when in the month of February, 1717, the great fire broke out in Christianssand.

"It was a grave disaster, in six hours more than thirty

houses were laid in ashes. It was reported that the mighty glow from the fire on the sky could be seen from Lillesand and from ships lying off Mandal. That night it blew a gale from the northwest, so that the fire, which first sprang up in Lillegade, ran straight toward my great-great-grandfather's house and warehouses in Vestergade, and it looked as if they were doomed.

"Already Jens Guttormsen's servants and shop-assistants had begun to bring out money chests and ledgers. Many people had gathered at the other end of the street, and some of them wept for the good man who was to see all that he had collected in life brought to nothing. So close was the fire, old people of the town have been telling, that in the midst of winter it was as hot in the street as in a bakehouse.

"Then, my girl," the old shipowner went on, "Jens Aabel came out of his gate with his scales in his right hand and his yardstick in his left. He took his stand in the street and spoke in a loud voice, so that all heard it. He said: 'Here stand I, Jens Guttormsen Aabel, merchant of this town, with my scales and my measure. If in my day I have made wrong use of any of them, then, wind and fire, proceed against my house! But if I have used these righteous things righteously, then you two wild servants of God will spare my house, so that in years to come it may serve men and women of Christianssand as before.'

"And at that moment," Jochum Hosewinckel recounted, "just when he had spoken, all people in the street saw the wind waver and for a moment cease altogether, so that smoke and sparks swept down over them. But immediately after it changed and shifted from northwest to due north, and the fire swerved off Vestergade and down toward the marketplace. Jens Aabel's house in this way was out of danger, and the things which had just been brought out could be brought in again."

The big clock in the room slowly struck eight, and the old narrator and the listening girl remained silent, absorbed in the story, as if they had stood together in Vestergade on that winter's night.

"You will have seen, Malli," Jochum Hosewinckel, who could not all at once bring himself to return to everyday life, took up the tale again, "you will have seen the big Bible lying on the table in my office. That is Jens Aabel's Bible, which has come into the family through my father's mother. And it has this quality to it, that if anyone in the house, uncertain as to what he ought to do, goes to it to ask advice from it, and lets it fall open where it chooses, he will get from it the right answer to what he is asking."

Fru Hosewinckel looked across the table at Malli, and at that moment it seemed to her that her prayer was being answered. She sat still on her sofa, but she followed the conversation closely.

"I can tell you," said her husband, "how I myself did once ask Jens Aabel's Bible for advice. But you must then take a candle and fetch it in here, so that I can find the right text. It is heavy, you will have to carry it on both arms and to leave the candle standing till you have laid the book back again."

Malli went away with the candle and came back

with the book, carrying it on both arms, and laid it on the table in front of the old gentleman who was waiting for it.

He took up his glasses, hesitated a moment, sat back in his chair and related:

"One time many years ago my cousin Jonas came to me to make me go halves with him in the purchase of a ship. For the sake of my good aunt, his mother, I was loath to say no, but when I considered the man himself I was even more unwilling to say yes, for he was an unsafe man in all his dealings and had duped me before. As now he sat on the sofa, impatient to get my answer, and I walked up and down the floor sadly uncertain about it, my eyes fell on our Bible.

" 'Why, yes,' I thought, 'give me your advice, Jens Aabel,' and I went and opened it, as if I were looking for something among the papers on the table.

"It was, that time, at the book of Ecclesiasticus that it fell open, the twenty-ninth chapter. And I shall read to you now what I read myself that evening, more than thirty years ago."

He put on his glasses and wetted his finger to turn the pages of the book, and when he found his place he read out slowly:

" 'Many have reckoned a loan as a windfall, and have given trouble to those that helped them.'

" 'Just so,' I thought, 'that fits cousin Jonas, here behind my back, well enough.' And then came further:

" 'And when payment is due he will prolong the time, and return words of heaviness, and complain of the times.' "

" 'Just so,' I thought again. I was about to close the

book and turn round to him, when the next verse came in as of its own accord, and it went:

" 'Howbeit with a man in poor estate be long suffering, and let him not wait for thine alms. Lose thy money for a brother and friend, and it shall profit thee more than gold.'

"Then for a moment I stood stock-still. 'Say you that? Say you that, Jens Aabel?' I asked.

"And now, my girl, I can finish off my tale by telling you that this good ship *The Attempt*, which Jonas and I bought together, on her very first trip made an exceptional catch of herring and paid me my money back then and there.

"But on her second journey," the old man concluded after a short silence, and with a new expression running over his face, or indeed with a new face, the story-teller's face, "it happened that cousin Jonas went overboard off Bodoe after a merry evening ashore. His mother in this way was spared any further distress on his account."

The old gentleman for a while sat lost in his recollections.

"You will bear the book back where it belongs, Malli," he said, "for Arndt, too, must be able to find advice in it one day, when somebody wants to trick him, and all the same with a person in poor estate he should be long-suffering."

Fru Hosewinckel's gaze again rose to Malli's young figure, as she stood up, and followed it through the door.

A few minutes later husband and wife in the drawing

room heard a heavy fall to the floor in the next room. They found the girl lying in front of the table as if she were dead, and the book open upon it.

Fru Hosewinckel never forgot that in that moment she seemed to hear her son's voice: "Is this what you wanted?"

They lifted up Malli and laid her on the horsehair-covered sofa. She opened her eyes, but appeared to see nothing. In a while she raised her hand and stroked the old man's face. "I felt dizzy, Arndt," she whispered.

Fru Hosewinckel rang for the maids and with their help supported Malli upstairs and had her put to bed.

When she came down into the office again her husband stood where she had left him, gazing into the candle by the open Bible on the table. He looked up at her and closed the book. She made a movement to stop him, but he went on to fasten the heavy clasp.

XVI. *Pupil and Master*

Early next morning, before the Hosewinckel household was awake, Malli got up quietly, dressed and went down the back-stairs, and through the back-door out into the side street. As late as the day before she would have had to look round for the way to Herr Soerensen's hotel, now she steered straight to it like a homing-pigeon to its cote.

For many long hours of the night she had longed for dawn. As now she hurried along she saw the world about her slowly regain light and color. Scents met her, and a gentle breeze, and she thought: "Everything here is different to what it was when I first came; that is because spring has come. Later comes summer." She suddenly called to mind, almost word for word, Arndt's plan of how in the summer, in one of his father's ships, he and she would go north to where the sun never sets.

While her thoughts ran thus, she had come through the gateway of the hotel and up Herr Soerensen's small staircase, and without knocking, as if she had known she was expected, had opened the door.

Herr Soerensen as usual was up before other people and busy with his meticulous morning toilet. When he saw Malli enter he withdrew behind a screen and from there instructed her to sit down on a chair by the window. She did not, however, settle down at once, but looked round the room, at a picture of the coronation of King Carl Johan and at Herr Soerensen's old carpet-bag propped against a wardrobe. Then she slowly took off her hat and coat as if to show that she had come to stay, and sank down on the chair pointed out to her.

Herr Soerensen popped his head over the screen three times in various stages of lathering and shaving, observing her attentively. But he said not a word.

In the end he came out into the room freshly shaved and with his wig on, in a dressing-gown of which the wadding stuck out here and there. Malli got up and threw herself in his arms; she was trembling so violently that she could not speak. Herr Soerensen made no attempt to calm her and did not even put his arms round her, but let her cling to him like a drowning person to a piece of timber.

During the conversation that followed she in turn drew back from him in order to watch his face, and again pressed against him as if she sought a dark shelter where she did not need to see anything.

She first of all cried out lowly and hoarsely at his breast: "Ferdinand is dead!"

"Yes," Herr Soerensen said gently and gravely. "Yes, he is dead."

"Did you know?" she cried out as before. "Had you heard of it? Did you believe it?"

"Yes," he answered. "I did so."

She steadied herself and regained control of her voice, let go of him and stood back a step.

"Arndt Hosewinckel loves me!" she cried in full, ringing tones.

Herr Soerensen's glance followed the change in her face.

"And do you love him too?" he asked. Because the question lay close to a line in a beloved tragedy, he repeated it, this second time in the tragedy's own words:

"And lovest thou him too, pure maiden?"

The tragedy's cues were also retained in Malli's heart, she immediately cried back to him with great force:

"—sun and moon,
The starry host, the angels, God himself and men
may hear it: I am steadfast in my love for him!"

"Well," said Herr Soerensen.

"Well," he said again after a silence. "And what now, Malli?"

"Now?" Malli wailed in a cry of distress like a sea-
bird in the breakers. "Now I must go away. God, I
must go away before I make them all unhappy."

She wrung her hands hanging down before her.

"I will not make people unhappy," she said. "I will
not! I will not! God himself knows that I was not
aware I was doing so! I thought, Herr Soerensen, that
I had told no lies, and made no mistakes!

"Now I must go away; I cannot stay here any
longer," she cried again, abruptly, as if it were some
quite new decision of which she was informing him. "I
cannot, you know that I cannot, go back into that
house on the square, unless I know that soon, as soon
as I can, I shall be leaving it again. For I have been
shown the door of it, Herr Soerensen. A righteous
man, who has never made wrong use of his scales or
his measure, showed me the door yesterday evening.
Righteous people can halt a gale, so that it changes
from northwest to due north. But I!" she lamented.
"Our gale of Kvasefjord came straight to where I
was. Yet I never prayed God to send it, I swear that I
never did.

"My old grandmother's sister," she suddenly began,
as if she was seeking a fresh course of thought, but
once more found herself up against the misery of the
preceding one, "was so angry with Mother for marrying Father, she would not set foot in her house. But
one day she met me in the street, made me come into
her room, and spoke to me of Father. She said: 'Your
father, Malli, did not come from Scotland, and was no
normal seaman. He was one of whom many people

have heard, and for whom they have a name. He was The Flying Dutchman.'—Do you think that is true, Herr Soerensen?"

After some consideration Herr Soerensen answered: "No, I don't."

Malli for a moment seemed to find consolation in his assurance, then a returning wave of despair again engulfed her.

"All the same," she cried, "I betray them all, as Father betrayed Mother!"

Again Herr Soerensen considered for a while, then said: "Whom have you betrayed, Malli?"

"Ferdinand!" cried Malli. "Arndt!

"When I am far away," she said, "then I shall have the courage to write to Arndt how matters stand with me. But I cannot, I dare not tell him to his face."

At the thought of this face she grew silent for a while. Then she once more wrung her hands.

"I must go away," she said. "If I do not go away I shall bring misfortune upon him. Oh, misfortune and misery, Herr Soerensen!"

Here she took one of her short steps backwards and looked him in the face with clear, wide-open eyes.

"You may well believe me, Herr Soerensen," she said, "for I speak as one that has a familiar spirit, out of the ground."

There was a long silence in the room.

"Well, yes," said Herr Soerensen. "I can believe you all right, Malli. For see you, little Malli, I have been married myself."

"Married?" Malli repeated in surprise.

"Yes," he said. "In Denmark. To a good, lovable woman."

"Where is she now?" Malli asked and looked around bewildered, as if the lost Madam Soerensen could be found in the small room.

"Thanks be to God," said Herr Soerensen. "Thanks be to God, she is married now. To a good man. In Denmark. They have children together. She and I had no children.

"I went away," he continued, "without letting her know, in secret. The last evening we sat together in our little home—we had a beautiful little home, Malli, with curtains and a carpet—she said to me: 'Everything you do in life, Valdemar, you do to make me happy. That is so sweet of you.'"

"Oh, yes," the girl cried out, as if struck to the heart. "That is how they talk to us, that is what they believe about us."

Herr Soerensen for the third time stood deep in thought, then took Malli's hand, said: "My girl," and was silent as before.

"Let us sit down and talk together," he at last said, and led her to a small sofa with broken webbing. They sat down side by side without it coming to any talk between them. But after a while Malli in her need of human sympathy and as if to appease a judge, or as in an attempt to comfort another unhappy person under the same sentence as herself, began to fumble over Herr Soerensen's shoulders, neck and head. She let her fingers run through his wig, so that a lock or two of it stood right on end. And as, while beseeching or caressing him, she did not look up at him, in order to avoid getting the imploring fingers in his eyes or his mouth he had to take aim with his head and butt it gently in the air to the right and left.

Herr Soerensen, who was accustomed to being obeyed and admired, but not to being caressed, allowed the situation to prolong itself for several minutes, and remained sitting as before, even after Malli had let fall her hands. He at first felt that their group was taking form like that of the old unhappy king and his loving daughter. But presently the center of gravity was shifted and he became fully conscious of his authority and responsibility: he was no fugitive, it was his young disciple who had fled to him for help. He once more became the man powerful above others: Prospero. And with Prospero's mantle round his shoulders, without lessening his pity of the despairing girl by his side, he was aware of a growing, happy consciousness of fulfillment and reunion. He was not to abandon his precious possession, but she was still his and would remain with him, and he was to see his life's great project realized.

At long last he spoke:

> "*. . . now I arise.*
> *Sit still, and hear the last of our sea-sorrow.*"

He rose, and erect and with firm steps walked to a small rickety table by the other window in the room, which served him as writing-table. He took papers out of the drawer and buried himself in them, sorting them, making notes, putting some of them back and taking out others. It lasted a long time, and when Malli stirred, he beckoned her off without turning his head. In the end he pushed his papers and pencils aside, but remained sitting with his back to her.

"I shall," he said, "give up my performances in Christianssand."

There was no answer from Malli.

"Ay," he continued in a firm voice. "Ay. I shall have it announced to the town that I cancel the performances and am moving on to Bergen. Why, of course," he declared as if she had been raising objections, "it will be at a cost. We might have had a big, a singular success in this town. On your account, my poor girl. It will be a loss. But not so big a loss as I had feared. The collection of the townsfolk will make up for it not a little. And in life, Malli, one must keep one's profit-and-loss account open.

"I myself, and you," he said, "will go away from here first, secretly. The others, on my instructions, will follow later."

He heard Malli get up, take a step toward him and stop.

"When will you be going?" her trembling voice asked behind his back.

Herr Soerensen answered: "I am fairly sure there is a ship on Wednesday." And briefly, with the authority of an admiral on his deck, he repeated: "On Wednesday."

"On Wednesday," came from Malli like a long sorrowful echo in the fells.

"Yes," said Herr Soerensen.

"The day after tomorrow!" came in the same manner from her.

"The day after tomorrow," from him.

As he gave his orders he still felt his own figure to be expanding, but he was at the same time sensitive to her deep silence behind him, and silence was ever a difficult thing for him to bear. As if he had had a pair of keen eyes at the back of his head he saw her standing in the middle of the small room, deathly pale from long hardships, as on the evening after the shipwreck, in the boat. Within this conflict between his consciousness of power and his compassion, he for some moments wavered in spirit, and also rocked a little in his chair. Finally he spun right round, and laid his arms on the back of the chair and his chin on his arms, ready to face the sight of the whole world's distress.

Malli stepped away from the spot on the floor where she was standing, and came toward him, tardily but with great strength, like a wave running toward the coast. Everything in the following conversation came from her very slowly, with each sentence slower, not loudly but with the clear, profound ring of a bell. She said:

> "*I prithee*
> *Remember, I have done thee worthy service;*
> *Told thee no lies, made no mistakings, serv'd*
> *Without or grudge or grumblings:*"

Herr Soerensen sat perfectly still, he thought: "God preserve me, how that girl's eyes shine. She is not looking at me, perhaps she does not see me at all. But her eyes shine!"

There was a short pause, then she slowly continued:

> *"All hail, great master! grave sir, hail! I come*
> *To answer thy best pleasure; be't to fly,*
> *To swim, to dive into the fire, to ride*
> *On the curl'd clouds: to thy strong bidding task*
> *Ariel and all his quality."*

Another pause. And then again:

> *"the elements*
> *Of whom your swords are temper'd, may as well*
> *Wound the loud winds, or with bemock'd-at stabs*
> *Kill the still-closing waters, as diminish*
> *One dowle that's in my plume."*

Herr Soerensen was in no way taken aback by Malli skipping from one place in the text of the drama to another; he was as much at home in the text as she and could skip in it himself.

Now she looked straight at him, altogether collected in glance and voice, and again spoke, so sweetly, meekly and straightforwardly that Herr Soerensen's heart melted in his breast and came into his eyes as clear tears:

> *"Full fathom five my body lies,*
> *Of my bones are coral made,*
> *Those are pearls that were my eyes,*
> *Nothing of me that doth fade,*
> *But doth suffer a sea-change*
> *Into something rich and strange.*
> *Sea-nymphs hourly ring my knell.*
> *Hark! now I hear them—ding dong bell."*

There was a last and very long silence.

But Herr Soerensen could not let himself be beaten in the exchange like this. He raised his head, stretched his right arm straight toward her above the back of the chair and, slowly as she herself, spoke:

> *"My Ariel, chick, then to the elements*
> *be free, and fare thou well!"*

Malli stood on awhile, then looked about her for her cloak and put it on, and he noticed that it was her old cloak from home. When she had buttoned it she turned toward him.

"But why," she asked him, "must things go with us like that?"

"Why?" Herr Soerensen repeated.

"Why must things go with us so disastrously, Herr Soerensen?" she said.

Herr Soerensen was mightily exalted and inspired after Prospero's last words; he was conscious that he must now answer her out of his experience of a long life, and said:

"O girl, be silent. We must never question—it is the others shall come questioning us—it is our noble privilege to answer—o answers fine and clear, o wondrous answers!—the questions of a baffled and divided— humanity. And ne'er ourselves to ask."

"Yes," said Malli after a moment or two. "And what do we get for it?"

"What do we get for it?" he repeated.

"Yes," she said again. "What do we get in return, Herr Soerensen?"

Herr Soerensen looked back over their conversation, then looked further back over that long life out of which he was to answer her.

"In return? Alas, my little Malli," he said, in an altogether changed voice, and this time he was not aware that he continued in his chosen, sacred tongue: "And in return we get the world's distrust—and our dire loneliness. And nothing else."

XVII. *The Last Letter*

When on Friday evening Arndt Hosewinckel came home from Stavanger they handed him a letter with a gold coin in it. The letter ran as follows:

Dear beloved Arndt,

I am writing to you with streaming tears. When you read this, I shall be far away, and we shall never see each other again. I am not the one for you, for I have deceived you and been unfaithful to you.

Yes, I had deceived you before I saw you for the first time, and you lifted me from the boat. But yet I swear to you that I did not know of it and did not understand how things were with me. And one more thing I swear to you, and this too you must believe. That as long as I live I shall love you.

I have a secret to tell you in this letter. I know, Arndt, that you love me, and maybe when I have told this secret to you, you will forgive me and tell me that it shall be as it was between you and me. But it cannot be so. For I carry my unfaithfulness toward you within myself, and wherever I am there it is too. I believed that nothing in the world was stronger than our love. But my unfaithfulness to you is stronger.

The very first time I understood this was when I heard that Ferdinand had died. For he has died, but of that you do not know in Stavanger. And when I saw him lying in his coffin and heard his poor mother's sorrowing words, then I guessed, as if somebody had spoken it from far away, that his death would come to part you and me. Still I did not yet fully understand that things were as they were, but it seemed to me that perhaps even now everything could turn out lovely for me as before, alas, how lovely!

But there was more to it, as I went about in great sadness and uneasiness and knew not in my heart what to believe. For on Sunday evening, as we sat in the drawing room, your father to please me told me the story of Jens Aabel and the fire. Your father afterwards told me that if some person in despair wanted good advice, he must let Jens Aabel's Bible fall open on its own, and he would then find it there. In my sorrow I betook myself to do this. But what I read was terrible.

I have tonight brought the Bible into my room here, and it is lying before me. And I have looked up the text to write it to you. In this way it is to me as if I were writing in the presence of that good, deserving man, Jens Aabel. And when you read, you must also imagine that he has been sitting by me while I wrote.

What I came upon was the Book of Isaiah, the twenty-ninth chapter, which starts thus:

"Woe to Ariel, to Ariel! . . . And thou shalt be brought down, and thou shalt speak out of the ground, . . . and thy voice shall be as of one that hath a familiar spirit, out of the ground, and thy speech shall whisper out of the dust!"

These words of the Prophet Isaiah filled me with great fear. Yet it was not until I read further that I fully understood how to me all hope was gone. For I read then the eighth verse:

"It shall even be as when an hungry man dreameth, and behold, he eateth; but he awaketh, and his soul is empty; or as when a thirsty man dreameth, and behold, he drinketh; but he awaketh, and behold, he is faint, and his soul **hath** appetite."

Yes, Arndt, this is as it would come to be with you if you kept me, and no otherwise. Therefore I tell you that you shall not think of forgiving me, because that is such a thing as cannot be done.

We are both young, and I am the younger of us two. But in what I now write I speak to you as if I were as old as the Prophet Isaiah, for that I am at this hour. And as if I were as wise as he, for that I am at this hour. And it seems to me as if, in my bottomless unhappiness, I shall yet find words that will console you a little. It shall never come to be of no avail to you, Arndt, that you have met me. And it shall never come to be of no avail to me that you grieve over me.

I will write to you too that tonight I have made a poem. I have never before made a poem, so that this one is not as it should be. Still you shall read it, and have it in your thoughts when you remember me. For it goes like this:

I have made you poor, my sweetheart dear.
I am far from you when I am near.
I have made you rich, my dearest heart.
I am near when we are far apart.

And now I have gained courage, and I will write to you the secret of which you know nothing.

You are to know then, Arndt, that when I was in the midst of the storm in Kvasefjord, on *Sofie Hosewinckel*, then *I was not in the least afraid.*

People in Christianssand call me a heroine. But a heroine is such a girl as sees the danger and is afraid of it, but defies it. But I, I saw it not, and understood not that there was danger.

Alas, Arndt, in that same hour your good father went about in great fear for *Sofie Hosewinckel*, and Ferdinand's mother was in deep fear and dread for her son. And I understand now, and see well, that in a human being it is beautiful to fear, and also I see clearly that the one who does not fear is all alone, and is rejected, an outcast from among people. But I, I was not in the least afraid.

For I thought or believed something that you can never imagine on your own, but that I shall now explain to you. I thought that the storm was the storm in the play *The Tempest* in which I was then soon to play a part, and which I had read more than a hundred times. Therein I myself am Ariel, a spirit of the air, and a mighty magician, Prospero, is my master. And in that night I thought that if *Sofie Hosewinckel* went down, I could fly off and wing my way from her.

When I heard the crew shout, "All lost!" then I recognized the words, and thought our shipwreck was the wreck in the first scene. And when in great distress they cried out, "Mercy on us," I recognized these words also. And may God have mercy on me myself, I laughed aloud at them in the storm.

They tell me that in that night I called out many times for poor Ferdinand. But that too was for the same reason, and because the hero in the play is called Prince Ferdinand. And so on board the *Sofie Hosewinckel* it was Ariel who in the roaring gale called Prince Ferdinand to him in a loud voice.

In this play there is also a lovely island full of tones, sounds and music sweet, on it in the end all the shipwrecked folk are rescued unharmed. And I thought, in the midst of the snowstorm, that this island was not far away.

Yes, now you know all. And it is for such a reason that you cannot keep me, for I belong elsewhere and must now go there. For it is possible, I know, that you might forget what had once happened. But it would ever be the same in all that happened between you and me. Ay, that the hungry man dreameth, and behold, he eateth; and he awaketh, and his soul is empty. And that the thirsty man dreameth, and behold, he drinketh; but he awaketh, and he is faint, and his soul hath appetite.

I am putting a gold coin for you in this letter, by which you shall remember me. It comes from my father, but it is pure gold.

Now I will sit quite still and wait an hour before I close my letter. So I have got one hour more in which I have disclosed nothing to you, and in which nothing is over between you and me. But I am your sweetheart, who am to be wedded to you.

Now the hour is at an end. Within it I have thought of two things.

The first of the two is this: That when soon I sail from here, I may again run into such a storm as the one in Kvasefjord. But that this time I shall clearly understand that it is not a play in the theatre, but it is death. And it seems to me that then, in the last moment before we go down, I can in all truth be yours. And I am thinking that it will be fine and great to let wave-beat cover heart-beat. And in that hour to say: "I have been saved, because I have met you and have looked at you, Arndt!"

But the other of the two is this: If now I heard your steps on the stairs from the office, and you came into the room to me! It seems to me now that those moments in which I did so hear your steps on the stairs were the happiest in my whole life. Then my arms ached so badly in their longing to lie round your neck that I could have cried out for pain. Ay, how they ache!

Farewell then. Farewell. Farewell, Arndt.

Yours upon earth faithless and rejected, but in death, in the resurrection, in eternity faithful,

Malli

The Immortal Story

1. *Mr. Clay*

In the sixties of the last century there lived in Canton an immensely rich tea-trader, whose name was Mr. Clay.

He was a tall, dry and close old man. He had a magnificent house and a splendid equipage, and he sat in the midst of both, erect, silent and alone.

Amongst the other Europeans of Canton Mr. Clay had the name of an iron-hard man and a miser. People kept away from him. His looks, voice and manner, more than anything actually known against him, had made him this reputation. All the same two or three stories about him, many times repeated, seemed to bear out the general opinion of the man. One of the stories ran as follows:

Fifteen years ago a French merchant, who at one time had been Mr. Clay's partner but later, after a quarrel between them, had started on his own, was ruined by unlucky speculations. As a last chance he tried to get a consignment of tea on board the clipper *Thermopylae*, which lay in the harbor ready to go under way. But he owed Mr. Clay the sum of three hundred guineas, and his creditor laid hands on the tea, got his own shipment of tea off with the *Thermopylae*, and by this move finally ruined his rival. The Frenchman lost all, his house was sold, and he was thrown upon the streets with his family. When he saw no way out of his misfortune he committed suicide.

The French merchant had been a talented, genial man; he had had a lovely wife and a big family. Now that, in the eyes of his friends, he was contrasted with the stony figure of Mr. Clay, he began to shine with a halo of gay and gentle rays, and they started a collection of money for his widow. But owing to the rivalry between the French and English communities of Canton it did not come to much, and after a short time the French lady and her children disappeared from the horizon of their acquaintances.

Mr. Clay took over the dead man's house, a big beautiful villa with a large garden in which peacocks strutted on the lawns. He was living in it today.

In the course of time this story had taken the character of a myth. Monsieur Dupont, it was told, on the last day of his life had called together his pretty, gentle wife and his bright young children. Since all their misery, he declared, had risen from the moment when he first set eyes on the face of Mr. Clay, he now bound them by a solemn vow never, in any place or under any circumstance, to look into that face again. It was also told that when he had been about to leave his house, of which he was very proud, he had burnt or smashed up every object of art in it, asserting that no thing made for the embellishment of life would ever consent to live with the new master of the house. But he had left in all the rooms the tall gilt-framed looking-glasses brought out from France, which till now had reflected only gay and affectionate scenes, with the words that it should be his murderer's punishment to meet, wherever he went, a portrait of the hangman.

Mr. Clay settled in the house, and sat down to dine in solitude, face to face with his portrait. It is doubt-

ful whether he was ever aware of the lack of friendliness in his surroundings, for the idea of friendliness
had never entered into his scheme of life. If things had
been left entirely to himself, he would have arranged
them in the same way; it was only natural that he
should believe them to be as they were because he had
willed them to be so. Slowly, in his career as a nabob,
Mr. Clay had come to have faith in his own omnipotence. Other great merchants of Canton held the
same faith in regard to themselves and, like Mr. Clay,
kept it up by ignoring that part of the world which lay
outside the sphere of their power.

By the time that Mr. Clay was seventy years old
he fell ill with the gout, and for a long time was almost
paralyzed. The pain was so severe that he could not
sleep at nights, and his nights then seemed infinitely
long.

Late one night it happened that one of Mr. Clay's
young clerks came to his house with a pile of accounts
that he had been revising. The old man in his bed heard
him talk to the servants, he sent for him and made him
go through the account books with him. When the
morning came he found that this night had passed less
slowly than the others. So the next evening he again
sent for the young clerk, and again made him read out
his books to him.

From this time it became an established rule that the
young man should make his appearance in the huge,
richly furnished bedroom by nine o'clock, to sit by his
old employer's bedside and read out, by the light of a
candle, the bills, contracts and estimates of Mr. Clay's

business. He had a sonorous voice, but toward morning it would grow a little hoarse. This vexed Mr. Clay, who in his young days had had sharp ears, but was now getting hard of hearing. He told his clerk that he was paying him to do this work and that, if he could not do it well, he would dismiss him and take on another reader.

When the two had come to the end of the books now in use at the office, the old man sighed and turned his head on the pillow. The clerk thought the matter over; he went to the lockers and took out books five, ten and fifteen years old, and these he read out, word for word, during the hours of the night. Mr. Clay listened attentively; the reading brought back to him schemes and triumphs of the past. But the nights were long; in the course of time the reader ran short even of such old books and had to read the same things over again.

One morning when the young man had for the third time gone through a deal of twenty years ago, and was about to go home to bed himself, Mr. Clay held him back, and seemed to have something on his mind. The workings of his master's mind were always of great moment to the clerk; he stayed on a little to give the old man time to find words for what he wanted.

After a while Mr. Clay asked him, reluctantly and as if himself uneasy and doubtful, whether he had not heard of other kinds of books. The clerk answered no, he had no knowledge of other kinds of books, but he would find them if Mr. Clay would explain to him what he meant. Mr. Clay in the same hesitating manner told him that he had in mind books and accounts, not of deals or bargains, but of other things which people at times had put down, and which other people did at times read. The clerk reflected upon the matter and repeated, no, he had never heard of such books. Here the talk ended, and the clerk took his leave. On his way home the young man turned Mr. Clay's question over in his mind. He felt that it had been uttered out of some deep need, half against the speaker's own will, with bashfulness and even with shame. If the clerk had himself had any sense of shame in his nature he might have left his old employer at that, and have wiped his one slip from dignity off his memory. But since he had nothing of this quality in him he began to ponder the matter. The demand, surely, was a symptom of weakness in the old man; it might even be a foreboding of death. What would be, he reflected, the consequence to him himself of such a state of things?

II. *Elishama*

The young clerk who had been reading to Mr. Clay was known to the other accountants of the office as Ellis Lewis, but this was not his real name. He was named Elishama Levinsky. He had given himself a new name, not—like some other people in those days emigrating to China—in order to cover up any trespass or crime of his own, he had done it to obliterate crimes committed against himself, and a past of hard trials.

He was a Jew and had been born in Poland. His

people had all been killed in the big Pogrom of 1848, at a time when he himself had been, he believed, six years old. Other Polish Jews, who had managed to escape, had happened to carry him with them among other sad and ragged bundles. Since that time, like some little parcel of goods in small demand, he had been carried and dropped, set against a wall and forgotten, and after a while once more flung about.

A lost and lonely child, wholly in the hands of chance, he had gone through strange sufferings in Frankfort, Amsterdam, London and Lisbon. Things not to be recounted and hardly to be recalled still moved, like big deep-water fish, in the depths of his dark mind. In London chance had put him in the hands of an ingenious old Italian bookkeeper, who had taught him to read and write, and who had, before he died, in one year implanted in him as much knowledge of book-keeping by double entry as other people will acquire in ten years. Later the boy was lifted up and shifted eastward, where in the end he was set down in Mr. Clay's office in Canton. Here he sat by his desk, like a tool ground upon the grindstone of life to an exceedingly sharp edge, with eyes and ears like a lynx, and without any illusions whatever of the world or of humanity.

With this equipment Elishama might have made a career for himself, and might have been a highly dangerous person to meet and deal with. But it was not so, and the reason for the apparently illogical state of things was the total lack of ambition in the boy's own soul. Desire, in any form, had been washed, bleached and burnt out of him before he had learned to read. To look at, he was a fairly ordinary young man, small, slim and very dark, with veiled brown eyes, and might have passed as a citizen of any nation. Mentally he had nothing of a youth, but all of a precocious child or a very old man. He had no softness or fullness in him, no yearning for love or adventure, no sense of competition, no fear and no wish to fight. Outwardly and inwardly he was like some kind of insect, an ant hard to crush even to the heel of a boot.

One passion he had, if passion it may be called—a fanatical craving for security and for being left alone. In its nature this feeling was akin to homesickness or to the instinct of the homing-pigeon. His soul was concentrated upon this one request: that he might enter his closet and shut his door, with the certainty that here no one could possibly follow or disturb him.

The closet which he entered, and to which he shut the door, was a modest place, a small dark room in a narrow street. Here he slept on an old sofa rented from his landlady. But in the room there were a few objects which did really belong to him—a painted, ink-stained table, two chairs and a chest. These objects to their owner were of great significance. Sometimes, in the night, he would light a small candle to lie and gaze at them, as if they proved to him that the world was still fairly safe. He would also, at night, draw comfort from the idea of the numeral series. He went over its figures—10, 20, 7000. They were all there, and he went to sleep.

Elishama, who despised the goods of this world,

passed his time from morning till night amongst greedy and covetous people, and had done so all his life. This to him was as it should be. He understood to a nicety the feelings of his surroundings, and he approved of them. For out of those feelings came, in the end, his closet with the door to it. If the world's desperate struggle for gold and power were ever to cease, it was not certain that this room or this door would remain. So he used his talents to fan and stir up the fire of ambition and greed in people round him. He particularly fanned the fire of Mr. Clay's ambition and greed, and watched it with an attentive eye.

Even before the time of their nocturnal readings there had existed between Mr. Clay and Elishama a kind of relation, a rare thing to both of them. It had first begun when Elishama had drawn Mr. Clay's attention to the fact that he was being cheated by the people who bought his horses for him. Some unknown ancestor of Elishama's had been a horse-dealer to Polish princes and magnates, and the young bookkeeper in Canton had all this old Jew's knowledge of horses in his blood. He would not for anything in the world have been the owner of a horse himself, but he encouraged Mr. Clay's vanity about his carriage and pair, from which, in the end, his own security might benefit. Mr. Clay on his side had been struck by the young man's insight and judgment; he had left the superintendence of his stable to him and never been disappointed. They had had no other direct dealings, but Mr. Clay had become aware of Elishama's exist-

ence, as Elishama had for a long time been aware of
Mr. Clay's.

The relationship showed itself in a particular way.
It might have been observed that neither of the two
ever spoke about the other to anybody else. In both
the old and the young man this was a breach of habit.
For Mr. Clay constantly fretted over his young staff
to his overseers, and Elishama had such a sharp tongue
that his remarks about the great and small merchants
of Canton had become proverbial in the storehouses
and the offices. In this way the master and the servant
seemed to be standing back to back, facing the rest of
the world, and did indeed, unknowingly, behave exactly as they would have behaved had they been
father and son.

In his own room Elishama now thought of Mr. Clay,
and put him down as a greater fool than he had held
him to be. But after a time he rose to make a cup of
tea—a luxury which he permitted himself when he
came back from his nightly readings—and while he
drank it, his mind began to move in a different way.
He took up Mr. Clay's question for serious consideration. It was possible, he reflected, that such books as
Mr. Clay had asked about did really exist. He was accustomed to getting Mr. Clay the things he wanted. If
these books existed, he must look out for them, and
even if they were rare he would find them in the end.

Elishama sat for a long time with his chin in his hand,
then stood up and went to the chest in the corner of
the room. Out of it he took a smaller, red-painted

box which, when he first came to Canton, had contained all that he owned in the world. He looked it through carefully and came upon an old yellow piece of paper folded up and preserved in a small silk bag. He read it by the candle on the table.

III. *The Prophecy of Isaiah*

In the party of Jews who in their flight from Poland had taken Elishama with them, there had been a very old man who had died on the way. Before he died he gave the child the piece of paper in the red bag. Elishama tied it round his neck, and managed to keep it there for many years, mainly because during this time he rarely undressed. He could not read, and did not know what was written on it.

But when in London he learned to read, and was told that people set a value on written matter; he took his paper out and found it to be written in letters different from those he had been taught. His master from time to time sent him on an errand to a dark and dirty little pawnshop, the owner of which was an unfrocked clergyman. Elishama took the paper to this man and asked him if it meant anything. When he was informed that it was written in Hebrew, he suggested that the pawnbroker should translate it to him for a fee of three pence. The old man read the paper through and recognized its contents; he looked them up in their own place, copied them out in English and gravely accepted the three pence. The boy, from now on, kept both the original and the translation in his small red bag.

In order to help Mr. Clay, Elishama now took the bag from his box. Under other circumstances he would not have done so, for it brought with it notions of darkness and horror and the dim picture of a friend. Elishama did not want friends any more than Mr. Clay did. They were, to him, people who suffered and perished—the word itself meant separation and loss, tears and blood dripped from it.

Thus it came about that a few nights later, when Elishama had finished reading the accounts to Mr. Clay, and the old man growled and prepared to send him off, the clerk took from his pocket a small dirty sheet of paper and said: "Here, Mr. Clay, is something that I shall read to you." Mr. Clay turned his pale eyes to the reader's face. Elishama read out:

"The wilderness and the solitary places shall be glad for them. And the desert shall rejoice, and blossom as the rose. It shall blossom abundantly. And sing even with joy and singing. The glory of Lebanon shall be given to it . . ."

"What is that?" Mr. Clay asked angrily.

Elishama laid down his paper. "That, Mr. Clay," he said, "is what you have asked for. Something besides the account books, which people have put together and written down." He continued:

"The excellency of Carmel and Sharon. They shall see the glory of the Lord. And the excellency of our God. Strengthen ye the weak hands. And confirm the feeble knees. Say to them . . ."

"What is it? Where did you get it?" Mr. Clay again asked.

Elishama held up his hand to impose silence, and read:

"Say to them that are of a fearful heart: be strong, fear not. Behold, your God will come with a vengeance. Even God with a recompense. He will come and save you. Then the eyes of the blind shall be opened and the ears of the deaf shall be unstopped. Then shall the lame man leap as a hart, and the tongue of the dumb sing. For in the wilderness shall waters break out. And streams in the desert. And the parched ground shall become a pool, and the thirsty land springs of water, and the habitation of dragons, where each lay, shall be grass with reeds and rushes."

When Elishama had got so far, he laid down his paper and looked straight in front of him.

Mr. Clay drew in his breath asthmatically. "What was all that?" he asked.

"I have told you, Mr. Clay," said Elishama. "You have heard it. This is a thing which a man has put together and written down."

"Has it happened?" asked Mr. Clay.

"No," answered Elishama with deep scorn.

"Is it happening now?" said Mr. Clay.

"No," said Elishama in the same way.

After a moment Mr. Clay asked: "Who on earth has put it together?"

Elishama looked at Mr. Clay and said: "The Prophet Isaiah."

"Who was that?" Mr. Clay asked sharply. "The Prophet—pooh! What is a prophet?"

Elishama said: "A man who foretells things."

"Then all these things should come to happen!" Mr. Clay remarked disdainfully.

Elishama did not want to disavow the Prophet Isaiah; he said: "Yes. But not now."

After a while Mr. Clay ordered: "Read again that of the lame man."

Elishama read: " 'Then the lame man shall leap as a hart.' "

Again after a moment Mr. Clay ordered: "And that of the feeble knees."

" 'And confirm the feeble knees,' " Elishama read.

"And of the deaf," said Mr. Clay.

" 'And the ears of the deaf,' " said Elishama, " 'shall be unstopped.' "

There was a long pause. "Is anybody doing anything to make these things happen?" asked Mr. Clay.

"No," said Elishama with even deeper contempt than before.

When after another pause Mr. Clay took up the matter, Elishama by the tone of his voice realized that he was now wide-awake.

"Read the whole thing over again," he commanded.

Elishama did as he was told. When he had finished, Mr. Clay asked: "When did the Prophet Isaiah live?"

"I do not know, Mr. Clay," said Elishama. "I think that it will have been about a thousand years ago."

Mr. Clay's knees were at this moment hurting badly, and he was painfully aware of his lameness and infirmity.

"It is a foolish thing," he declared, "to foretell things which do not begin to take place within a thousand years. People," he added slowly, "should record things which have already happened."

"Do you want me," Elishama asked, "to take out the books of accounts once more?"

There was a very long pause.

"No," Mr. Clay said. "No. People can record things which have already happened, outside of account books. I know what such a record is called. A story. I once heard a story myself. Do not disturb me, and I shall remember it.

"When I was twenty years old," he said after another long silence, "I sailed from England to China. And I heard this story on the night before we touched the Cape of Good Hope. Now I remember it all well. It was a warm night, the sea was calm, and there was a full moon. I had been sitting for some time by myself on the afterbody, when three sailors came up and sat down on the deck. They were so close to me that I could hear all that they said, but they did not see me. One of the sailors told the others a story. He recorded to them things which had happened to him himself. I heard the story from the beginning to the end, I shall tell it to you."

IV. *The Story*

"The sailor," Mr. Clay began, "had once come ashore in a big town. I do not remember which, but it does not matter. He was walking by himself in a street near the harbor, when a fine costly carriage drove up to him, and an old gentleman descended from it. This gentleman said to the sailor: 'You are a fine-looking sailor. Do you want to earn five guineas tonight?' "

Mr. Clay was so completely unaccustomed to telling a story, that it is doubtful whether he could have gone on with this one except in the dark. He continued with an effort and repeated: " 'Do you want to earn five guineas tonight?' "

Elishama, here, put the prophecy of Isaiah back into its bag and into his pocket.

"The sailor," Mr. Clay related, "naturally answered yes. The rich gentleman then told him to come with him, and drove him in his carriage to a big and splendid house just outside the town. Within the house everything was equally grand and sumptuous. The sailor had never believed that such riches existed in the world, for how would a poor boy like him ever have come inside a really great man's house? The gentleman gave him a fine meal and expensive wine, and the sailor recounted all that he had had to eat and drink, but I have forgotten the names of the courses and the wines. When they had finished this meal, the master of the house said to the sailor: 'I am, as you see, a very rich man, the richest man in this town. But I am old. I have not many years left, and I dislike and distrust the people who will inherit what I have collected and saved up in life. Three years ago I married a young wife. But she has been no good to me, for I have no child.' "

Here Mr. Clay made a pause to collect his thoughts.

"With your permission," said Elishama, "I, too, can tell that story."

"What is that?" exclaimed Mr. Clay, very angry at the interruption.

"I shall tell you the rest of that story, with your permission, if you will listen, Mr. Clay," said Elishama.

Mr. Clay did not find a word to say, and Elishama went on.

"The old gentleman," he recounted, "led the sailor to a bedroom which was lighted by candlesticks of pure gold, five on the right side and five on the left. Was it not so, Mr. Clay? On the walls were carved pictures of palm-trees. In the room there was a bed, and a partition was made by chains of gold before the bed, and in the bed lay a lady. The old man said to this lady: 'You know my wish. Now do your best to have it carried out.' Then from his purse he took a piece of gold—a five-guinea piece, Mr. Clay—and handed it to the sailor, and after that he left the room. The sailor stayed with the lady all night. But when the day began to spring, the door of the house was opened to him by the old man's servant, and he left the house and went back to his ship. Was it not so, Mr. Clay?"

Mr. Clay for a minute stared at Elishama, then asked: "How do you come to know this story? Have you too met the sailor from my ship near the Cape of Good Hope? He will be an old man by now, and these things happened to him many years ago."

"That story, Mr. Clay," said Elishama, "which you believe to have happened to the sailor on your ship, has never happened to anyone. All sailors know it. All sailors tell it, and each of them, because he wishes that it had happened to him himself, tells it as if it were so.

But it is not so. All sailors, when they listen to the story, like to have it told in that way, and expect to have it told in that way. The sailor who tells it may vary it a little, and add a few things of his own, as when he explains how the lady was made, and how in the night he made love to her. But otherwise the story is always the same."

The old man in the bed at first did not say a word, then in a voice hoarse with anger and disappointment he asked: "How do you know?"

"I shall tell you, Mr. Clay," said Elishama. "You have traveled on one ship only, out here to China, so you have heard this story only once. But I have sailed with many ships. First I sailed from Gravesend to Lisbon, and on the ship a sailor told the story which to-night you have told me. I was very young then, so I almost believed it, but not quite. Then I sailed from Lisbon to the Cape of Good Hope, and on the ship there was a sailor who told it. Then I sailed to Singapore, and on my way I again heard a sailor tell the story. It is the story of all sailors in the world. Even the phrases and the words are the same. But all sailors are pleased when, once more, one of them begins to tell it."

"Why should they tell it," said Mr. Clay, "if it were not true?"

Elishama thought the question over. "I shall explain that to you," he said, "if you will listen. All people, Mr. Clay, in one respect are the same.

"When a new financial scheme is offered for subscription, it is proved on paper that the shareholders will make on it a hundred per cent, or two hundred per cent, as the case may be. Such a profit is never made, and everybody knows that it is never made, still people must see these figures on paper in the issue of stocks, or they will have nothing to do with the scheme.

"It is the same, Mr. Clay, with the prophecy which I have read to you. The Prophet Isaiah, who told it, will, I believe, have been living in a country where it rained too little. Therefore he tells you that the parched ground becomes a pool. In England, where the ground is almost always a pool, people do not care to write it down or to read about it.

"The sailors who tell this story, Mr. Clay, are poor men and lead a lonely life on the sea. That is why they tell about that rich house and that beautiful lady. But the story which they tell has never happened."

Mr. Clay said: "The sailor told the others that he held a five-guinea piece on his hand, and that he felt the weight and the cold of gold upon it."

"Yes, Mr. Clay," said Elishama, "and do you know why he told them so? It was because he knew, and because the other sailors knew, that such a thing could never happen. If they had believed that it could ever happen, they would not have told it. A sailor goes ashore from his ship, and pays a woman in the street to let him come with her. Sometimes he pays her ten shillings, sometimes five, and sometimes only two, and none of these women are young, or beautiful, or rich. It might possibly happen—although I myself doubt it

—that a woman would let a sailor come with her for nothing, but if she did so, Mr. Clay, the sailor would never tell. Here a sailor will tell you that a young, beautiful and rich lady—such a lady as he may have seen at a distance, but has never spoken to—has been paying him, for the same thing, five guineas. In the story, Mr. Clay, it is always five guineas. That is contrary to the law of demand and supply, Mr. Clay, and it never has happened, and it never will happen, and that is why it is told."

Mr. Clay at this moment was so upset, puzzled and angry that he could not speak. He was angry with Elishama, because he felt that his clerk was taking advantage of his weakness, and was defying his authority. But he was upset and puzzled by the Prophet Isaiah, who was about to annihilate his whole world, and him himself with it. The two of them, he felt, were holding together against him. After a while he spoke.

His voice was harsh and grating, but as firm as when he was giving an order in his office.

"If this story," he said, "has never happened before, I shall make it happen now. I do not like pretense, I do not like prophecies. It is insane and immoral to occupy oneself with unreal things. I like facts. I shall turn this piece of make-believe into solid fact."

The old man when he had spoken was a little easier at heart. He felt that he was getting the better of Elishama and the Prophet Isaiah. He was still going to prove to them his omnipotence.

"The story shall become reality," he said very

slowly. "One sailor in the world shall tell it, from beginning to end with everything that is in it, as it has actually, from beginning to end, happened to him."

When Elishama walked home in the morning he said to himself: "Either this old man is going mad, and nearing his end. Or otherwise he will tomorrow be ashamed of his project of tonight, he will want to forget it, and it will be the safest thing not to mention it to him again."

v. *The Mission of Elishama*

Mr. Clay, however, was not ashamed. His project of the night had seized hold of him; the matter had become a trial of strength between him and the insurgents. Next midnight, as the clock struck, he took up the theme and said to Elishama: "Do you think that I can no longer do what I want to do?"

This time Elishama did not contradict Mr. Clay with a word; he answered: "No, Mr. Clay. I think you can do whatever you want."

Mr. Clay said: "I want the story which I told you last night to happen in real life, to real people."

"I shall see to it, Mr. Clay," said Elishama. "Where do you want it to happen?"

"I want it to happen here," said Mr. Clay, and proudly looked round his big, richly furnished bedroom. "In my house. I want to be present myself, and to see it all with my own eyes. I want to pick up the sailor myself, in the street by the harbor. I want to dine with him myself, in my dining room."

"Yes, Mr. Clay," said Elishama. "And when do you want the story to happen, to real people?"

"It ought to be done quickly," said Mr. Clay after a pause. "It will have to be done quickly. But I am feeling better tonight; in a week's time I shall be strong enough."

"Then," Elishama said, "I shall have everything ready within a week."

After a while Mr. Clay said: "It will involve expenses. I do not mind what the expenses may come to."

These words gave Elishama such an impression of cold and loneliness in the old man, that it was as if they had been spoken from the grave. But since he himself did feel at home in the grave, he and his employer were at this moment brought closer together.

"Yes," he said, "it is going to cost us some money. For you will remember that there is a young woman in the story."

"Yes, a woman," said Mr. Clay. "The world is full of women. A young woman one can always buy, and that will be the cheapest thing in the story."

"No, Mr. Clay," said Elishama, "it will not be the cheapest thing in this story. For if I bring you a woman of the town, the sailor will know her for what she is. And he will lose his faith in the story."

Mr. Clay growled a little.

"And a young miss I shall not be able to get you," said Elishama.

"I am paying you to do this work," said Mr. Clay. "It will be part of your work to find me a woman."

"I shall have to think it over," said Elishama.

But he had already, while they talked together, been thinking it over.

Elishama, as has been told, was well versed in book-keeping by double entry. He saw Mr. Clay with the eyes of the world, and to the eyes of the world—had the world known of his scheme—the old man was undoubtedly mad. At the same time he saw Mr. Clay with his own eyes, and to his own eyes his employer, with his colleagues in the tea-trade and in other trades, had always been mad. And indeed he was not sure whether, to a man with one foot in the grave, the pursuit of a story was not a sounder undertaking than the pursuit of profit. Elishama at any time would side with the individual against the world, since, however mad the individual might be, the world in general was sure to be still more hopelessly and wickedly idiotic. As, once more, he walked away from Mr. Clay's house, he realized that from this moment he was indispensable to his master, and could get out of him whatever he wanted. He did not intend to derive any advantage from the circumstance, but the idea pleased him.

In Mr. Clay's office there was a young accountant whose name was Charley Simpson. He was an ambitious young man and had resolved to become, in his own time, a millionaire and nabob like Mr. Clay himself. The big ruddy young gentleman considered himself to be Elishama's only friend, treated him with patronizing joviality, and had lately honored him with his confidence.

Charley kept a mistress in town; her name was

Virginie. She was, he told his protégé, a French-woman of very good family, but she had been ruined by her amorous temperament and now lived only for passion. Virginie wanted a French shawl. Her lover meant to make her a present of one, but he was afraid to go into a shop to buy it, as somebody might spot him there and report to his father in England. If Elishama would take a collection of shawls to Virginie's house, Charley would show his gratitude by introducing him to the lady herself.

The lovers had had a row immediately before Elishama's arrival with the shawls. But the sight of these somewhat appeased Virginie. She draped one shawl after another round her fine figure before the looking-glass, as if the men had not been in the room, and even lifted her skirts neatly over her knee and made a couple of *pas-de-basque's*. Over her shoulder she told her lover that he must now, surely, be able to see for himself that her real calling was the theatre. If she could only raise the money, the wisest thing she could do was to go back to France. There comedy, drama and tragedy still existed, and the great actresses were the idols of a nation!

Elishama was not familiar with the words comedy, drama or tragedy, but an instinct now told him that there was a connection between these phenomena and Mr. Clay's story. The day after his last conversation with Mr. Clay he turned his steps toward Virginie's house.

Within his nature Elishama had a trait which few people would have expected to find there. He felt a deep innate sympathy or compassion toward all women of this world, and particularly toward all young women.

Although, as has already been told, he did not himself want a horse, he could fix to a penny the price of any horse shown him. And although he did not himself in the least want a woman, he could view a woman with the eyes of other young men, and accurately determine her value. Only in the latter case he considered the eyes of other young men to be short-sighted or blind, the price to be erroneous, and the article itself in some sad way underestimated and wronged.

Mysteriously, he felt the same sympathy and compassion toward birds. The quadrupeds all left him indifferent, and horses—in spite of his knowledge and understanding of them—he disliked. But he would take a roundabout way to his office in order to pass the Chinese birdsellers' shops, and to stand for a long time in front of their piled-up birdcages, and he knew the individual birds within them and followed their fate with concern.

Walking along to Virginie's house he might well feel a twofold sympathy. For she was a young woman who reminded him of a bird. As in his thoughts he compared her to other young women of Canton, she there took on the aspect of a golden pheasant or a peacock in a poultry yard. She was bigger than her sisters, nobler and more pompous of gait and feather, strutting somewhat lonely amongst the smaller domestic fowl. At their one meeting she had been a little downcast and fretful, like a golden pheasant in the moulting season. But she was always a golden pheasant.

VI. *The Heroine of the Story*

Virginie lived in a small neat Chinese house with a little garden to it and green shutters to the window. The old Chinese woman who owned the house, kept it in order and cooked for her tenant, was out today. Elishama found the door open and went straight in.

Virginie was playing patience on her table by the window. She looked up and said: "God, is it you? What are you bringing? Shawls?"

"No, Miss Virginie, I am bringing nothing today," said he.

"What is the use of you then?" she asked. "Sit down and keep me company, in God's name, now that you are here."

Upon this invitation he sat down.

Virginie, in spite of her venturesome past, was still young and fresh, with a flowerlike quality in her, as if there had been a large rose in water in the room. She was dressed in a white muslin negligee with flounces and a train to it, but had not yet done up her rich brown hair, which floated down to the pink sash round her waist. The golden afternoon sun fell between the shutters into her lap.

She went on with her patience, but spoke the while. "Are you still with the old devil?" she asked.

Elishama said: "He is ill and cannot go out."

"Good," said Virginie, "is he going to die?"

"No, Miss Virginie," said Elishama. "He is even strong enough to make up new schemes. With your permission, I am now going to tell you one of them. I shall begin at the beginning."

"Well, so long as he is too ill to go out, I can stand hearing about him," said Virginie.

"Mr. Clay," said Elishama, "has heard a story told. Fifty years ago—on a ship, one night off the Cape— he heard a story told. Now that he is ill and cannot sleep at night, he has been pondering this story. He dislikes pretense, he dislikes prophecies, he likes facts. He has made up his mind to have the story happen in real life, to real people. I have been in his service for seven years; whom would he get to carry out his wish if not me? He is the richest man in Canton, Miss Virginie, he must have what he wants. Now I shall tell you the story.

"There was a sailor," he began, "who went ashore from his ship in the harbor of a big town. As he was walking by himself in a street near the harbor, a carriage with two fine, well-paired bay horses drove up to him, and an old gentleman stepped out of the carriage and said to him: 'You are a fine-looking sailor. Do you want to earn five guineas tonight?' When the sailor said yes, the old gentleman drove him to his house and gave him food and wine. He then, Miss Virginie, said to him: 'I am a merchant of immense wealth, as you will have seen for yourself, but I am all alone in the world. The people who, when I die, are to inherit my fortune are all silly people, con-

tinually disturbing and distressing me. I have taken
to myself a young wife, but . . .' "

Here Virginie cut short Elishama's tale. "I know
that story," she said. "It happened in Singapore to an
English merchant-captain, a friend of mine. Has he
been telling it to you as well?"

"No, Miss Virginie," said Elishama. "He has not
told it to me, but other sailors have told it. This is a
story that lives on the ships; all sailors have heard it,
and all sailors have told it. It might have been left at
sea and never come ashore, if it had not been that
Mr. Clay cannot sleep. He is now going to make it
happen here in Canton, in order that one sailor in the
world may be able to tell it from beginning to end,
exactly as, from beginning to end, it has happened
to him."

"He was sure to go mad in the end, with his sins,"
said Virginie. "If now he wants to play a comedy
with the Devil, it is a matter between the two of
them."

"Yes, a comedy," said Elishama. "I had forgotten
the word. People play in comedies and make money
by it; they become the idols of nations. Now there
are three people in Mr. Clay's comedy. The old gentleman he will play himself, and the young sailor he
will himself find in a street by the harbor, where sailors come ashore from their ships. But if an English
merchant-captain has told you this story, Miss Virginie, he will have told you that besides these two
there is also a beautiful young lady in it. On Mr.
Clay's behalf I am now looking for this beautiful

young lady. If she will come into this story, and finish it for him, Mr. Clay will pay her one hundred guineas."

Virginie, in her chair, turned her rich young torso all round toward Elishama, folded her arms upon her bosom and laughed to his face. "What is all this?" she inquired.

"It is a comedy, Miss Virginie," said he. "A drama or a tragedy. It is a story."

"The old man has got strange ideas of a comedy," said Virginie. "In a comedy the actors pretend to do things, to kill one another or to die, or to go to bed with their lovers. But they do not really do any of these things. Indeed your master is like the Emperor Nero of Rome, who, to amuse himself, had people eaten up by lions. But since then it has not been done, and that is a long time ago."

"Was the Emperor Nero very rich?" asked Elishama.

"Oh, he owned all the world," said Virginie.

"And were his comedies good?" he again asked.

"He liked them himself, I suppose," said Virginie. "But who would he nowadays get to play in them?"

"If he owned all the world, he would get people to play in them," said he.

Virginie looked hard at Elishama, her dark eyes shining. "I suppose that nobody could insult *you*, even if they tried hard?"

Elishama thought her remark over. "No," he said, "they could not. Why should I let them?"

"And if I told you," she said, "to go out of my house, you would just go?"

"Yes, I should go," he said. "It is your house. But when I had gone you would sit and think of the things for which you had turned me out. It is when people are told their own thoughts that they think they are being insulted. But why should not their own thoughts be good enough for other people to tell them?"

Virginie kept looking at him. Early that same day she had been so furious with her destiny that she had been planning to throw herself into the harbor. The patience had calmed her a little. Now she suddenly felt that she and Elishama were alone in the house, and that he had it not in him to repeat their conversation to anybody. Under the circumstances she might go on with it.

"What does Mr. Clay pay you for coming here and proposing this thing to me?" she asked. "*Trente pièces d'argent, n'est-ce pas? C'est le prix!*" When Virginie's mind moved in high spheres she thought, and expressed herself, in French.

Elishama, who spoke French well, did not recognize her quotation, but imagined that she was mocking him for being poorly paid in Mr. Clay's service. "No," he said. "I am not being paid for this. I am in Mr. Clay's employ; I cannot take on work anywhere but with him. But you, Miss Virginie, you can go wherever you like."

"Yes, I presume so," said Virginie.

"Yes, you presume so," said Elishama, "and you have been able to go wherever you liked all your life. And you have come here, Miss Virginie, to this house."

Virginie blushed deeply with anger, but at the same time she once more felt, and more deeply than before, that the two were alone in the house, with the rest of the world shut out.

VII. *Virginie*

Virginie's father had been a merchant in Canton. His motto in life, engraved in his signet ring, had been "*Pourquoi pas?*" All through his twenty years in China his heart had still been in France, and the great things going on there had filled and moved it.

At the time of his death Virginie had been twelve years old. She was his eldest child and his favorite. As a little girl she was as lovely as an angel; the proud father amused himself taking her round and showing her off to his friends, and in a few years she had seen and learned much. She had a talent for mimicry; at home she gave pretty little performances, imitating the scenes she had witnessed and repeating the remarks and the gay songs she had listened to. Her mother, who came from an old seafaring family of Brittany and was well aware that a wife ought to bear with her man's exuberant spirit, would still at times gently reprove her husband for spoiling his pretty daughter. She would get but a kiss in return, and the laughing comment: "*Ah, Virginie est fine! Elle s'y comprend, en ironie!*"

In his young days the handsome and winning gentleman had traveled much. In Spain he had done business with, and been on friendly terms with, a very great lady, the Countess de Montijo. When later, out in China, he learned that this lady's daughter had married the Emperor Napoleon III and become Empress of the French, he was as proud and pleased as if he himself had arranged the match. With him Virginie had for many years lived in the grand world of the French Court, in the vast radiant ballrooms of the Tuileries, among receptions of foreign majesties, court cabals, romantic love affairs, duels and the waltzes of Strauss.

After her father's death, during long years of poverty and hardship, and while she herself lost the angelic grace of her childhood and grew up too big, Virginie had secretly turned to this glorious world for consolation. She still walked up marble stairs lighted by a thousand candles, herself all sparkling with diamonds, to dance with princes and dukes; and her companions of a lonely, monotonous existence in dreary rooms wondered at the girl's pluck. In the end, however, the Tuileries themselves had faded and vanished round her.

Even when the father had endeavored to engraft moral principles in the daughter's young mind he had illustrated them with little anecdotes from the Imperial Court. One of them had impressed itself deeply in the little girl's heart. The lovely Mademoiselle de Montijo had informed the Emperor Napoleon that the only way to her bedroom ran through the Cathedral of Notre Dame. Virginie was familiar with the Cathedral of Notre Dame; a big engraving of it hung in her parents' drawing room. She had pictured to herself a bedroom of corresponding dimensions, and in the middle of it the lovely Mademoiselle Virginie, all in lace. The vision many times had warmed and cheered her heart.

Alas, the way to her bedroom had not run through the Cathedral of Notre Dame! It had not even run through the little gray French Church of Canton. Lately it had run, without much of a detour, from the offices and counting-houses of the town. For this reason Virginie despised the men that had come by it.

One triumph she had had in her career of disappointments, but nobody but herself knew of it.

Her first lover had been an English merchant-captain, who had made her run away with him to Japan, just then opened to foreign trade. On the couple's very first night in Japan there was an earthquake. All round their little hotel houses cracked and tumbled down and more than a hundred people were killed. Virginie that night had experienced something besides terror; she had lived through the great moment of her life. The thundering roar from heaven was directed against her personally; the earth shook and trembled at the loss of her innocence; the mighty breakers of the sea bewailed Virginie's fall! Frivolous human beings only—her lover with them—within this hour ignored the law of cause and effect and failed to realize the extent of her ruin.

Virginie had a good deal of kindness in her nature. In her present sad situation, after she had definitely come down from the Tuileries, she would have liked her lovers better had they left her free to love them in her own way, as poor pitiful people in need of sympathy. She might have put up with her present lover, Elishama's friend, if she could have made him see their liaison such as she herself saw it—as two lonely people's attempt to make, in an unpretentious bourgeois way and by means of a little mutual gentleness, the best of a sorry world. But Charley was an ambitious young man who liked to see himself as a man of fashion and his mistress as a great demimondaine. His mistress, who knew the real meaning of the word, in their daily life together was tried hard by this vanity of his, and it lay at the root of most of their quarrels.

Now she sat and listened to Elishama, with her arms folded, and her lustrous eyes half closed, like a cat watching a mouse. If at this moment he had wanted to run away she would not have let him go.

"Mr. Clay," said the young man, "is prepared to pay you a hundred guineas if, on a night appointed by him, you will come to his house. This, Miss Virginie . . ."

"To his house!" cried Virginie and looked up quite bewildered.

"Yes," said he. "To his house. And this, Miss Virginie . . ."

Virginie rose from her chair so violently that it tumbled over, and she struck Elishama in the face with all her might.

"Jesus!" she cried. "His house! Do you know what house that is? It is my father's house! I played in it when I was a little girl!"

She had a ring on her finger; when she struck him

it scratched Elishama's face. He wiped off a drop of
blood and looked at his fingers. The sight of blood
shed by her hand put Virginie into a fury beyond
words, she walked to and fro in the room so that her
white gown swished on the floor, and Elishama got
an idea of the drama. She sat down on a chair, got
up, and sat down on another.

VIII. *Virginie and Elishama*

"That house," she said at last, "was the only thing
left me from the time when I was a rich, pretty and
innocent girl. Every time that I have since then
walked past it I have dreamed of how I would enter
it once more!" She caught at her breath as she spoke;
white spots sprang out on her face.

"So you are to enter it now, Miss Virginie," said
Elishama. "So is, Miss Virginie, the young lady of
Mr. Clay's story rich, pretty and innocent."

Virginie stared at him as if she did not see him at
all, or as if she sat gazing at a doll.

"God," she said. "My God! Yes—'*Virginie est fine,
elle s'y comprend, en ironie!*'" She looked away, then
back at him. "You may hear it all now," she said.
"My father said that to me!"

She stopped her ears with her fingers for a moment, again let her hands drop and turned straight
toward him.

"You can have it all now," she cried, "you can
have it all! My father and I used to talk—in that
house—of great, splendid, noble things! The Empress

Eugenie of France wore her white satin shoes one single time only, then made a present of them to the convent schools for the little girls there to wear at their first communion! I was to have done the same thing—for Papa was proud of my small feet!" She lifted her skirt a little and looked down at her feet, in a pair of old slippers. "The Empress of France made a great, unexampled career for herself, and I was to have done the same. And the way to her bedroom—you can have it all now, you can have it all—the way to her bedroom ran through the Cathedral of Notre Dame! Virginie," she added slowly, "*s'y comprend, en ironie!*"

Now there was a long silence.

"Listen, Miss Virginie," said Elishama. "In the shawls . . ."

"Shawls?" she repeated, amazed.

"Yes, in the shawls that I brought you," he continued, "there was a pattern. You told your friend Mr. Simpson that you liked one pattern better than another. But there was a pattern in all of them."

Virginie had a taste for patterns; one of the things for which she despised the English was that to her mind they had no pattern in their lives. She frowned a little, but let Elishama go on.

"Only," he went on, "sometimes the lines of a pattern will run the other way of what you expect. As in a looking-glass."

"As in a looking-glass," she repeated slowly.

"Yes," he said. "But for all that it is still a pattern." This time she looked at him in silence.

"You told me," he said, "that the Emperor of Rome owned all the world. So does Mr. Clay own Canton and all the people of Canton"—all except myself, he thought. "Mr. Clay, and other rich merchants like him, own it. If you look out into the street you will see many hundred people going north and south, east and west. How many of them would be going at all, if they had not been told to do so by other people? And the people who have told them, Miss Virginie, are Mr. Clay and other rich merchants like him. Now he has told you to go to his house, and you will have to go."

"No," said Virginie.

Elishama waited a moment, but as Virginie said no more he went on.

"What Mr. Clay tells people to do," he said, "that is what matters. You struck me a little while ago; you tremble now, because of what he told you to do. It matters very little in comparison whether you do go or not."

"It was you who told me," she said.

"Yes, because he told me to do so," said Elishama. There was another pause.

"Let down your hair over your face, Miss Virginie," said he. "If one must sit in darkness, one should sit in one's own darkness. I can wait for as long as you like."

Virginie, in her very refusal to do as he advised her, furiously shook her head. Her long hair from which, when she rushed up and down the room, the ribbon had fallen, floated round her like a dark cloud, and as she let her head drop, it tumbled forward and hid her face. She sat for a while immovable in this chiaroscuro.

"That way of which you spoke," said Elishama, "which ran through the Cathedral of Notre Dame —it is in this pattern. Only in this pattern it is reversed."

From behind her veil of hair Virginie said: "Reversed?"

"Yes," said Elishama. "Reversed. In this pattern the road runs the other way. And runs on."

The strange sweetness of his voice, against her own will, caught Virginie's ear.

"You will make a career for yourself, Miss Virginie," said Elishama, "no less than the Empress of France. Only it runs the other way. And why not, Miss Virginie?"

Virginie, after a minute, asked: "Did you know my father?"

"No, I did not know him," said Elishama.

"Then," she asked again, "from where do you know that the pattern of which you speak does run in my family, and that there it is called a tradition?"

Elishama did not answer her, because he did not know the meaning of the word.

After another minute she said very slowly: "And *pourquoi pas?*"

She flung back her hair, raised her head, and sat behind her table like a saleswoman behind her desk. To Elishama her face looked broader and flatter than before, as if a roller had passed over it.

"Tell Mr. Clay from me," she said, "that I will not come for the price which he has offered me. But that I shall come for the price of three hundred guineas. That, if you like, is a pattern. Or—in such terms as Mr. Clay will understand—it is an old debt."

"Is that your last word, Miss Virginie?" he asked.

"Yes," said Virginie.

"Your very last word?" he asked again.

"Yes," she said.

"Then, if it is so," he said, "I shall now hand you over three hundred guineas." He took up his wallet and laid the notes on the table.

"Do you want a receipt?" she asked.

"No," he said, reflecting that this bargain would be safer without a receipt.

Virginie swept the notes and the playing cards, all together, into the drawer of the table. She was not going to play any more patience today.

"How do you know," she said and looked Elishama in the face, "that I shall not set fire to the house in the morning, before I leave it again, and burn your master in it?"

Elishama had been about to go; now he stood still.

"I shall tell you one thing before I go," said he. "This story is the end of Mr. Clay."

"Do you believe that he is going to die with malice?" asked Virginie.

"No," said he. "No, I cannot tell. But one way or another, it will be the end of him. No man in the world, not the richest man within it, can take a story which people have invented and told and make it happen."

"How do you know?" she asked.

He waited a moment. "If you add up a column of figures," he said slowly so as to make the matter clear to her, "you begin from your right-hand side, with the lowest figure, and move left, to the tens, the hundreds, the thousands and the ten thousands. But if a man took into his head to add up a column the other way, from the left, what would he find? He would find that his total would come out wrong, and that his account-books would be worth nothing. Mr. Clay's total will come out wrong, and his books will be worth nothing. And what will Mr. Clay do without his books? It is not a good thing for me myself, Miss Virginie. I have been in his employ for seven years, and I shall now lose my situation. But there is no getting away from it." This was the first time that Elishama ever spoke confidentially about his master to a third party.

"Where are you going now?" Virginie asked him.

"Me?" he said, surprised that anybody should take an interest in his movements. "I am going home now to my own room."

"I wonder," said she with a kind of awe in her voice, "where that will be. And what it will be like. Had you a home when you were a child?"

"No," said he.

"Had you brothers and sisters?" she asked again.

"No," said he.

"No, I thought so," said Virginie. "For I see now who you are. When you came in, I thought that you were a small rat, out of Mr. Clay's storehouses. *Mais toi—tu es le Juif Errant!*"

Elishama gave her a quick deep glance from his veiled eyes and walked away.

IX. *The Hero of the Story*

On the night which Mr. Clay had destined for his story to materialize, the full moon shone down upon the city of Canton and the China Sea. It was an April night, the air was warm and sweet, and already innumerable bats were soundlessly swishing to and fro in it. The oleander bushes in Mr. Clay's garden looked almost colorless in the moonlight; the wheels of his victoria made but a low whisper on the gravel of his drive.

Mr. Clay with much trouble had been dressed and got into his carriage. Now he sat in it gravely, erect against the silk upholstering, in a black cloak and with a London top hat on his head. On the smaller seat opposite to him Elishama, cutting a less magnificent figure, silently watched his master's face. This dying man was driving out to manifest his omnipotence, and to do the thing that could not be done.

They passed from the rich quarters of the town, with its villas and gardens, down into the streets by the harbor, where many people were about and the air was filled with noises and smells. At this time of day nobody was in a hurry; people walked about leisurely or stood still and talked together; the carriage had to drive along slowly. Here and there lamps in many colors were hung out from the houses like bright jewels in the pale evening air.

Mr. Clay from his seat looked sharply at the men on the pavement. He had never before watched the faces of men in the street; the situation was new to him and would not be repeated.

A lonely sailor came walking up the street, gazing about him, and Mr. Clay ordered Elishama to stop the carriage and accost him. So the clerk got out and under his master's eye addressed the stranger.

"Good evening," he said. "My master, in this carriage, requests me to tell you that you are a fine-looking sailor. He asks you whether you would like to earn five guineas tonight."

"What is that?" said the sailor. Elishama repeated his phrase.

The sailor took a step toward the carriage to have a better look at the old man in it, then turned to Elishama. "Say that again, will you?" he said.

As Elishama spoke the words for the third time, the sailor's mouth fell open. Suddenly he turned round and walked off as fast as he could, took the first turning into a side street and disappeared.

Upon a sign from Mr. Clay, Elishama got back into the carriage, and ordered the coachman to drive on.

A little farther on, a square-built young man with the look of a seaman was about to cross the street, and had to stop before the carriage; he and Mr. Clay looked each other in the face even before it halted. Elishama once more got out, and spoke to him in the same words as to the first sailor. This young man obviously came from a public house, and was somewhat unsteady on his legs. He too made the clerk repeat the sentence to him, but before Elishama had finished it the second time he burst out laughing and beat his thigh.

"Why, God help me!" he cried out. "This, I know, is what happens to a good-looking sailor when he visits the landlubbers. You need not say any more! I am coming with you, old master, and you have hit on the right man, too. Jesus Christ!"

He vaulted into the carriage by Mr. Clay's side, stared at him, at Elishama and at the coachman, and let his hand run along the seat.

"All silk!" he cried out, laughing. "All silk and softness! And more to come!"

As they drove on he began to whistle, then took off his cap to cool his head. All at once he clapped both hands to his face and sat like that for a moment, then without a word jumped out of the carriage, began to run, and disappeared into a side street just as the first sailor had done.

Mr. Clay made the carriage turn and go back along the same street, then turn once more and drive back slowly. But he did not stop it again. He said nothing during the drive, and Elishama, who now kept his eyes off him, began to wonder if they were to drive like this all night. Then suddenly Mr. Clay ordered the coachman to return to the house.

They had already got out of the narrow streets near the harbor and on to the road leading to Mr. Clay's house, when three young sailors came straight toward them, arm in arm. As the carriage approached, the two at the sides let go their hold of the one in the middle and ran on leaving the last one in front of it.

Mr. Clay stopped the carriage and held up his hand to Elishama.

"I will get out myself this time," he said.

Slowly and laboriously he descended upon the arm of his clerk, took a step toward the sailor, stood still before him as straight as a pillar, and poked his stick at him. When he spoke, his voice was hard and cracked, with a little deadly note to it.

"Good evening," he said. "You are a fine-looking sailor. Do you want to earn five guineas tonight?"

The young sailor was tall, broad and large-limbed, with very big hands. His hair was so fair and stood out so long and thick round his head, that at first Elishama believed him to have on a white fur cap. He did not speak or move, but looked at Mr. Clay quietly and dully, somewhat in the manner of a young bull. In his right hand he carried a big bundle; he now shifted it over to the left and began to rub his free hand up and down his thigh as if at the next moment he meant to strike out a blow. But instead he reached out and took hold of Mr. Clay's hand.

The old man swallowed, and repeated his proposal. "You are a fine-looking sailor, my young friend," he said. "Do you want to earn five guineas tonight?"

The boy for a moment thought the question over.

"Yes," he said. "I want to earn five guineas. I was thinking about it just now, in what way I was to earn five guineas. I shall come with you, old gentleman."

He spoke slowly, with a stop between each of his phrases and with a quaint, strong accent.

"Then," said Mr. Clay, "you will get into my carriage. And when we arrive at my house I shall tell you more."

The sailor set down his bundle on the bottom of the carriage, but did not get in himself. "No," he said, "your carriage is too fine. My clothes are all dirty and tarred. I shall run beside, and I can go as fast as you."

He placed his big hand on the mudguard, and as the carriage started he began to run. He kept pace with the two tall English horses all the way, and when they stopped at the front door of Mr. Clay's house he did not seem to be much out of breath.

Mr. Clay's Chinese servants came out to receive their master and to help him out of his carriage and his cloak, and the butler of the house, a fat and bald Chinaman all dressed in green silk, appeared on the verandah and held up a lantern on a long pole. In the golden light of the lamp Elishama took a look at the host and the guest.

Mr. Clay had strangely come to life. It was as if the young runner by his carriage had made his own old blood run freer; he even had a faint pink in his cheeks, like that of a painted woman. He was satisfied with his catch out of the harbor of Canton. And very likely there was not another fish of just that kind to be caught there.

The sailor was little more than a boy. He had a broad tanned face and clear light blue eyes. He was so very lean, his big bones showing wherever his clothes did not cover him, and his young face was so grave, that there was something uncanny about him, as about a man come from a dungeon. He was poorly dressed, in a blue shirt and a pair of canvas trousers, with bare feet in his old shoes. He lifted his bundle from the carriage and slowly followed the butler with the lantern into Mr. Clay's house.

x. *The Supper of the Story*

The lighted candles on the dinner table, in heavy silver candlesticks, were manifoldly reflected in the gilt-framed glasses on the walls, so that the whole long room glittered with a hundred little bright flames. The table was laid, the food ready and the bottles drawn.

To Elishama, who had come into the room last and had sat down silently on a chair at one end of it, the two diners and the servants going to and fro noiselessly, waiting on them, all looked like human figures in a picture seen at a great distance.

Mr. Clay had been helped into his pillow-filled armchair by the table, and here sat as erect as in the carriage. But the young sailor, slowly gazing round him, seemed afraid to touch anything in the room, and had had to be invited two or three times to sit down before he did so.

The old man by a movement of his hand told his butler to pour out wine for his companion, watched him as he drank, and all through the meal had his glass refilled. To keep him company he did even, against his habit, sip a little wine himself.

The first glass of wine had a quick and strong effect on the boy. As he put down the empty glass he suddenly blushed so deeply that his eyes seemed to water with the heat from his burning cheeks.

Mr. Clay in his armchair drew one profound sigh and coughed twice. When he began to speak his voice was low and a little hoarse; as he spoke, it became shriller and stronger. But all the time he spoke very slowly.

"Now, my young friend," he said, "I am going to tell why I have fetched you, a poor sailor-boy, from a street by the harbor. I am going to tell you why I have brought you to this house of mine, into which few people, even amongst the richest merchants of Canton, are ever allowed. Wait, and you shall hear all. For I have many things to tell you."

He paused a little, drew in his breath, and continued:

"I am a rich man. I am the richest man in Canton. Some of the wealth which in the course of a long life I have made, is here in my house; more is in my storehouses, and more even is on the rivers and on the sea. My name in China is worth more money than you have ever heard of. When, in China or in England, they name me, they name a million pounds."

Again there was a short pause.

Elishama reflected that so far Mr. Clay had recorded only such facts as had been long stored up in his mind, and he wondered how he would get on when he should have to move from the world of reality into that of imagination. For the old man, who in his long life had heard one story told, in his long life had never himself told a story, and had never pretended or dissimulated to anybody. When, however, Mr. Clay again took up his account, the clerk understood that he had on his mind more things of which he meant to clear it. Deep down within it there were ideas, perceptions, emotions even, of which he had never spoken and of which he could never have spoken, to any human being except to the nameless, barefooted boy before him. Elishama began to realize the value of what is named a comedy, in which a man may at last speak the truth.

"A million pounds," Mr. Clay repeated. "That million pounds is me myself. It is my days and my years, it is my brain and my heart, it is my life. I am alone with it in this house. I have been alone with it for many years, and I have been happy that it should be so. For the human beings whom in my life I have met and dealt with I have always disliked and despised. I have allowed few of them to touch my hand; I have allowed none of them to touch my money.

"And I have never," he added thoughtfully, "like other rich merchants, dreaded that my fortune should not last as long as myself. For I have always known how to keep it tight, and how to make it multiply.

"But then lately," he went on, "I have comprehended that I myself shall not last as long as my fortune. The moment will come, it is approaching, when we two shall have to part, when one half of me must go and the other half live on. Where and with whom, then, will it live on? Am I to let it fall into the hands which till now I have managed to keep off it, to be fingered and meddled with by those greedy and offensive hands? I would as soon let my body be fingered and meddled with by them. When at night I think of it I cannot sleep.

"I have not troubled," he said, "to look for a hand into which I might like to deliver my possessions, for I know that no such hand exists in the world. But it has, in the end, occurred to me that it might give me pleasure to leave them in a hand which I myself had caused to exist.

"Had caused to exist," he repeated slowly. "Caused to exist, and called forth. As I have begotten my fortune, my million pounds.

"For it was not my limbs that ached in the tea fields, in the mist of morning and the burning heat of midday. It was not my hand that was scorched on the hot iron-plates upon which the tea-leaves are dried. Not my hands that were torn in hauling taut the braces of the clipper, pressing her to her utmost speed. The starving coolies in the tea-fields, the dog-tired seamen on the middle watch, never knew that they were contributing to the making of a million pounds. To them the minutes only, the pain in their hands, the hail-showers in their faces, and the poor copper coins of their wages had real existence. It was in my brain and by my will that this multitude of little things were combined and set to co-operate to make up one single thing: a million pounds. Have I not, then, legally begotten it?

"Thus, in combining the things of life and by making them co-operate according to my will, I may legally beget the hand into which I can with some pleasure leave my fortune, the lasting part of me."

He was silent for a long time. Then he dipped his own old, skinny hand deep into his pocket, drew it out and looked at it. "Have you ever seen gold?" he asked the sailor.

"No," said the boy. "I have heard of it from captains and supercargoes, who have seen it. But I have not seen it myself."

"Hold out your hand," said Mr. Clay.

The boy held out his big hand. On the back of it a cross, a heart and an anchor were tattooed.

"This," said Mr. Clay, "is a five-guinea piece. The five guineas which you are to earn. It is gold."

The sailor kept the coin on the flat of his hand, and for a while both looked at it concernedly. When Mr. Clay took his eyes off it he drank a little wine.

"I myself," he said, "am hard, I am dry. I have always been so, and I would not have it otherwise. I have a distaste for the juices of the body. I do not like the sight of blood, I cannot drink milk, sweat is offensive to me, tears disgust me. In such things a man's bones are dissolved. And in those relationships between people which they name fellowship, friendship or love, a man's bones themselves are likewise dissolved. I did away with a partner of mine because I would not allow him to become my friend and dissolve my bones. But gold, my young sailor, is solid. It is hard, it is proof against dissolution. Gold," he repeated, a shadow of a smile passing over his face, "is solvency.

"You," he went on after a pause, "are full of the juices of life. You have blood in you, you have, I suppose, tears. You long and yearn for the things which dissolve people, for friendship and fellowship, for love. Gold you have tonight seen for the first time. I can use you.

"To you, tonight, the minutes only, the pleasure of your body and the five guineas in your pocket will have real existence. You will not be aware that you are contributing to a worthy piece of work of mine. To the fine bafflement of my relations in England, who were once pleased to get rid of me, but who have now for twenty years been on the lookout for the legacy from China. May they sleep well on that."

The sailor stuck the piece of gold into his pocket. He was by now flushed with food and wine. Big and bony, with his shaggy hair and shining eyes, he looked as strong, greedy and lusty as a bear just out of his winter lair.

"Say no more, old master," he broke out. "I know what you are going to tell me. I have, before now, heard it told on the ships, every word. This, I know, is what happens to a sailor when he comes ashore. And you, old gentleman, are in luck tonight. If you want a strong, hearty sailor, you are in luck. You will find none stronger on any ship. Who stood by the pumps in the blizzard off Lofoten for eleven hours? It is hard on you being so old and dry. As for me, I shall know well enough what I am doing."

Once more the boy suddenly and violently blushed crimson. He broke off his bragging and was silent for a minute.

"I am not," he said, "in the habit of talking to rich old people. To tell you the truth, old master, I am not just now in the habit of talking to anybody at all. I shall tell you the whole story. A fortnight ago, when the schooner *Barracuda* picked me up and took me on board, I had not spoken a word for a whole year. For a year ago, by the middle of March, my own ship, the bark *Amelia Scott*, went down in a storm, and of all her crew I alone was cast ashore on an island. There was nobody but me there. It is not, tonight, more than three weeks since I walked there, on the beach of my island. There were many sounds on my island, but no one ever spoke. I myself sang a song there sometimes—you may sing to yourself. But I never spoke."

xi. *The Boat*

The unexpected strain of adventure in his sailor, and in his story, was agreeable to Mr. Clay. He turned his half-closed eyes to the boy's face and for a moment let them rest there with approval, almost with kindness.

"Ah," he said, "so you have starved, slept on the ground, and dressed in rags, for a year?" He looked proudly round the rich room. "Then all this must be a change to you?"

The sailor looked round too. "Yes," he said. "This house is very different from my island." As he looked back at the old man, he stuck his hand into his hair. "And that is why my hair is so long," he said. "I meant to have it cut tonight. The other two promised to take me to a barber's shop, but they changed their mind and were going to take me to the girls instead. It was good luck to me that I did not get there, for then I should not have met you. I shall soon get used to talking to people again. I have talked before; I am not such a fool as I look."

"A pleasant thing," said Mr. Clay, as if to himself. "A highly pleasant thing, I should say, to be all by yourself on an island, where nobody can possibly intrude upon you."

"It was good in many ways," said the boy gravely. "There were birds' eggs on the beach, and I fished there too. I had my knife with me, a good knife; I cut a mark with it in the bark of a big tree each time that I saw the new moon. I had cut nine marks, then I forgot about it, and there were two or three more new moons before the *Barracuda* came along."

"You are young," said Mr. Clay. "I presume that you were pleased when the ship came and took you back to people."

"I was pleased," said the sailor, "for one reason. But I had got used to the island; I had come to think that I would remain there all my life. I told you there were many sounds on the island. All night I heard the waves, and when the wind rose I would hear it round me on all sides. I heard when the seabirds woke in the morning. One time it rained for a whole month and another time for a fortnight. Both times there were great thunderstorms. The rain came from the sky like a song, and the thunder like a man's voice, like my old captain's voice. I was surprised; I had not heard a voice for many months."

"Were the nights long?" asked Mr. Clay.

"They were as long as the days," answered the sailor. "The day came, then the night, then the day. The one was as long as the other. Not like in my own country, where the nights are short in summer and long in winter."

"What did you think of at night?" asked Mr. Clay.

"I thought mostly of one thing," said the sailor. "I thought of a boat. Many times I also dreamed that I had got her, that I launched her and steered her. She was to be a good, strong, seaworthy boat. But she need not be big, not more than five lastages. A sloop would be the thing for me, with tall bulwarks. The stern should be blue, and I should carve stars round the cabin windows. My own home is in Marstal in Denmark. The old shipbuilder Lars Jensen Bager was a friend of my father's; he might help me to build the boat. I should make her trade with corn from Bandholm and Skelskor to Copenhagen. I did not want to die before I had got my boat. When I was taken up by the *Barracuda*, I thought that this was the first bit of my way to her, and that was the reason why I was pleased, then. And when I met you, old gentleman, and you asked me if I would earn five guineas, I knew that I had been right to come away from the island. And that was why I went with you."

"You are young," said Mr. Clay again. "Surely on the island you also thought about women?"

The boy sat silent for a long time and looked straight in front of him, as if he had in reality forgotten to speak.

"Yes," he said. "On the *Amelia Scott*, and on the *Barracuda* too, the others talked about their girls. I know, I know very well what you are paying me to do tonight. I am as good as any sailor. You will have no reason to complain of me, Master. Your lady here, waiting for me, will have no reason to complain of me."

Suddenly, for a third time, the blood rushed to his face; it sank back, mounted again and kept glowing darkly through the tan of his cheeks. He stood up from his chair, tall and broad and very grave.

"All the same," he said in a new, deep voice, "I may as well now go back to my ship. And you, my old gentleman, will take on another sailor for your job." He stuck his hand into his pocket.

The faint rosy tinge disappeared from Mr. Clay's cheeks. "No," he said. "No, I do not want you to go back to your ship. You have been cast on a desert island, you have not spoken to a human being for a year. I like to think of that. I can use you. I shall take on no other sailor for my job."

Mr. Clay's guest took one step forward and there looked so big that the old man suddenly clenched the arms of the chair with his hands. He had before now been threatened by desperate men, and had beaten them off by the weight of his wealth, or by the force of his cool, sharp brain. But the irate creature before him was too simple to give in to any of those arguments. He might have stuck his hand in his pocket to draw out the good knife of which he had just spoken. Was it, then, a matter of life and death to make a story come true?

The sailor took from his pocket the gold coin which Mr. Clay had given him, and held it toward the old man.

"You had better not try to hold me back," he said. "You are very old, you have but little strength to stand up against me. Thank you, old master, for the food and the wine. I shall now go back to my ship. Good night, old gentleman."

Mr. Clay in his state of surprise and alarm could speak only lowly and hoarsely, but he spoke.

"And your boat, my fine young seaman," he said. "The boat which is to be all your own? The seaworthy smack of five lastages, which is to trade with corn from your own place to Copenhagen? What will she be, now that you are paying back your five guineas and going away? A story only, which you have been telling me—which will never come to be launched, which will never come to sail!"

After a moment the boy put the coin back in his pocket.

XII. *The Speech of the Old Gentleman in the Story*

While the nabob and the sailor-boy were entertaining one another in the brilliantly lighted dining room, Virginie in the bedroom, where tonight all candles had been softly shaded by rose-colored screens, was preparing herself for her own part, the heroine's part, in Mr. Clay's story.

She had sent away the little Chinese maid, who had helped her to arrange the room and adorn it with such objects as would make it seem an elegant lady's bedroom. Two or three times she had suddenly stopped the work and informed the girl that they were both immediately going to leave the house. Now that she was alone, she no longer thought of leaving.

The room in which she found herself had been her parents' bedroom, where on Sunday mornings the children were let in to play in the big bed. Her father and mother, who for a long time had seemed far away, were with her tonight; she had entered their old house with their consent. To them as to her, this night would bring about the final judgment of their old deadly enemy; the disgrace and humiliation of their daughter provided the conclusive evidence against him. The daughter, according to her vow of long ago, would not see his face at the verdict, but the dead father and mother were there to watch it.

The ornaments with which Virginie had embellished her bedroom of one night—the figurines, Chinese fans and Maquart bouquets—were all similar to those she remembered from her childhood, and which had been so sadly burnt or smashed up by her father before Mr. Clay ever entered the house. A few bibelots had come from her own house. In this way Virginie had joined her gloomy existence of the last ten years with her gay and guiltless past of long ago, and had had it recognized by Monsieur and Madame Dupont.

She set to dress and adorn her own person. She started on the task solemnly and darkly, the way Judith in the tent of the Babylonians adorned her face and body for the meeting with Holofernes. But she immediately and inevitably became absorbed in the process—as, very likely, Judith herself did.

Virginie was an honest person in money matters; out of Mr. Clay's three hundred guineas she had conscientiously and generously purchased everything belonging to her role. She had a weakness for lace, and was at this moment floating in a cloud of Valenciennes, with a coral necklace round her throat, pearls in her ears and a pair of pink satin slippers on her feet. She powdered and rouged her face, blackened her eyebrows and painted her full lips; she let down her hair in rich silky ringlets over her smooth shoulders, and scented her neck, arms and bosom. When all was done, she gravely went up to one after another of the long looking-glasses in the room.

These glasses had reflected her figure as a little girl, and had told her, then, that she was pretty and graceful. As she looked into them she remembered how, at the age of twelve, she had entreated them to show her what she would be like in years to come, as a lady. The child, she felt, could never have hoped to be shown, in a sweeter or rosier light, a lovelier, a more elegant and bewitching lady. Virginie's love of the dramatic art, inherited from her father and encouraged by him, came to her aid in the hour of need. If she was not what she appeared to be, neither had her father's business transactions always been quite what they appeared to be.

During these reflections she had stepped out of her small silk slippers and stretched her fair, slim, strong body between the smooth sheets rich with lace, her dark silken tresses spread over the pillowcase.

She had been engrossed in the thought of her enemy, and she had become engrossed in the vision of herself. It was not till she heard steps in the corridor outside that she gave any thought to the third party in the story, her unknown guest of the night. Then for a second a little cold draft of contempt for Mr. Clay's hired and bribed puppet ran through her mind.

When the doorknob turned she cast down her eyes, and till the door was once more opened and shut she kept her glance fixed upon the sheet. But in this withdrawal there was as much energy and vigor as in any direct glance of deadly, uncompromising enmity.

Mr. Clay, in his long dressing-gown of heavy Chinese silk, came into the room leaning on his stick. Two respectful steps behind him a big, blurred shadow slowly crossed the threshold.

The one glass of wine he had taken with his guest had acted upon the invalid of many sleepless nights. He had also, a few minutes ago, been frightened a little, and although in the course of his life he had frightened many people, fear to himself was a rare experience and might well stir his blood in a new way. But the old man was drunk with a still stronger liquor. For tonight he was moving in a world created by his will and at his word.

His triumph had aged him; in a few hours his hair seemed to have grown whiter. But at the same time it had strangely rejuvenated him.

He was at this hour conquering and subjugating; he was indeed, in absorbing them into his own being, annihilating the forces which unexpectedly had bid defiance to him. He was materializing a fantasy and changing a fable into fact. Dimly he felt that he was about to triumph over the person who had attempted to upset his own idea of the world—the Prophet Isaiah.

He smiled a little; he was a little bit unsteady on his legs. For the first time in his life he was impressed by a woman's beauty. He gazed almost happily at the girl in the bed, whom his command had called to life, and for a second the vague picture of a child long ago shown to him by a proud father appeared before him, and disappeared. He nodded his head in approval. His dolls were behaving well. The heroine of his story was pink and white, and her downcast eyes bore witness to alarmed modesty. The story was fetching headway.

This was the moment, Mr. Clay knew, for the speech of the old gentleman in the story. He remembered it word for word from the night fifty years ago, but the consciousness of his power was somehow going to the head of the nabob of Canton. The Prophet Isaiah is crafty; behind a pious mien he has knowledge of many ways and measures. Mr. Clay had been a child only a very short time, until he had learned to speak and to understand the speech of other people. Now, as he was about to enter the heaven of his omnipotence, the Prophet laid his hand on his head and turned him into a child—in other words, the old stone-man was quietly entering his second childhood. He began to play with his story; he could not let go the theme of the dinner table.

"You," he began, poking his forefinger at the girl in the bed, "and you"—without looking at him he poked it at the boy—"are young. You are in fine health, your limbs do not ache, you sleep at night. And because you can walk and move without pain, you believe that you are walking and moving according to your own will. But it is not so. You walk and move at my bidding. You are, in reality, two young, strong and lusty jumping-jacks within this old hand of mine."

He paused, the little hard smile still on his face.

"So," he went on, "so are, as I have told you, all people jumping-jacks in a hand stronger than their own. So are, as I have told you, the poor jumping-jacks in the hands of the rich, the fools of this earth in the hands of the shrewd. They dance and drop as these hands pull the strings.

"When I am gone," he finished, "and when you two are left to yourselves, and believe that you are following the command of your own young blood only, you will still be doing nothing, nothing at all, but what I have willed you to do. You will be conforming to the plot of my story. For tonight this room, this bed, you yourselves with this same young hot blood in you—it is all nothing but a story turned, at my word, into reality."

It came hard for him to tear himself from the room. He remained standing by the end of the bed for another minute, hung on his stick. Then with fine dignity he turned his back on the small actors on the stage of his omnipotence.

As he opened the door Virginie raised her eyes.

She looked straight at the figure of her father's murderer, and saw a withdrawing and disappearing figure. Mr. Clay's long Chinese dressing-gown trailed on the floor, and as he closed the door behind him it was caught in it; he had to open and close the door a second time.

XIII. *The Meeting*

The room remained without a sound or a stir till, in the very same instant, the boy took two long steps forward and Virginie, in the bed, turned her head and looked at him.

At that she was so mortally frightened that she forgot her high mission, and for a moment wished herself back in her own house, and even under the patronage, such as it was, of Charlie Simpson. For the figure by the end of the bed was not a casual sailor out of the streets of Canton. It was a huge wild animal brought in to crush her beneath him.

The boy stared at her, immovable except for his broad chest slowly going up and down with his deep regular breath. At last he said: "I believe that you are the most beautiful girl in the world." Virginie then saw that she had to do with a child.

He asked her: "How old are you?"

She could not find a word to say. Was it possible, now, that her great dark tragedy was to be turned into a comedy?

The boy waited for an answer, then asked her again: "Are you seventeen?"

"Yes," said Virginie. And as she heard her own voice pronounce the word her face, turned toward him, softened a little.

"Then you and I are the same age," said the boy.

He took another slow step and sat down on the bed.

"What is your name?" he asked.

"Virginie," she answered.

He repeated the name twice and sat for some time looking at her. Then he lay down gently beside her on top of the quilt. In spite of his size he was light and easy in all his movements. She heard his deep breathing quicken, break off, and start again with a faint moan, as if something was giving way within him. They lay like this for a while.

"I have got something to tell you," he suddenly broke out in a low voice. "I have never till tonight slept with a girl. I have thought of it, often. I have meant to do it, many times. But I have never done it."

He was silent once more, waiting to hear what she would say to this. As she said nothing he went on.

"It was not all my own fault," he said. "I have been away for a long time, in a place a long way off, where there were no girls."

Again he stopped, and again spoke. "I have never told the others on the boat," he said. "Nor my friends with whom I came ashore tonight. But I thought that I had better tell you."

Against her will Virginie turned her face toward him. His own face, quite close to hers, was all aglow.

"When I was in the place, far away from here, that I told you about," he went on, "I sometimes fancied that I had a girl with me, who was mine. I brought her bird's eggs and fish, and some big sweet fruits that grew there, but of which I do not know the name, and she was kind to me. We slept together in a cave that I had found when I had been in the place for three months. When the full moon rose it shone into it. But I could not think of a name for her. I did not remember any girl's name—Virginie," he added very slowly. "Virginie." And once more: "Virginie."

All at once he lifted the quilt and the sheet, and slid in beneath them. Although he still kept a little away from her she sensed his body there, big, supple, and very young. After a time he stretched out his hand and touched her. Her lace nightgown had slipped up on her leg; as now slowly the boy put out his hand it met her round naked knee. He started a little, let his fingers run gently over it, then withdrew his hand and felt his own lean and hard knee over.

A moment later Virginie cried out in fear of her life. "God!" she screamed. "For God's sake! Get up, we must get up. There is an earthquake—do you not feel the earthquake!"

"No," the boy panted lowly into her face. "No. It is not an earthquake. It is me."

xiv. *The Parting*

When at last he fell asleep he held her close to him as in a vise, with his face bored into her shoulder, breathing deeply and peacefully.

Virginie, who had lately thought of so many things, lay awake but could think of nothing in the world. She had never in her life felt such a strength. It would be useless and hopeless for her, here, to try to act on her own. She felt his mighty grip round her as a hitherto-unknown kind of reality, which made everything else seem hollow and falsified.

In the middle of the night she suddenly remembered things which her mother had told her about her own people, the seafaring men of Brittany. Old French songs of the sailor's dangers, and of his homecoming, came back to her as on their own. In the end, from far away, came the sailor-wife's cradlesong.

When in the course of the night the boy woke up, he behaved with the girl in his bed like a bear with a honeycomb, growling over her in a wild state of greed and ecstasy. A couple of times they talked together.

"On the ships," he said, "I sometimes made a song."

"What were your songs about?" she asked.

"About the sea," he answered. "And the life of the sailors. And their death."

"Say a little of them to me," said she.

After a moment he slowly recited:

> *"As I was keeping the middle watch,*
> *and the night was cold,*
> *three swans flew across the moon,*
> *over her round face of gold."*

"Gold," he repeated, somewhat uneasily. And after a pause: "A five-guinea piece is like the moon. And then not at all like her."

"Did you make other songs?" asked Virginie, who did not understand what he meant, but somehow did not want him to be worried.

"Yes, I made other songs," he said. "About my boat."

"Say a little of them to me, then," she again asked. Again he recited slowly:

"When the sky is brown,
and the sea yawns, three thousand fathoms down,
and the boat runs downward like a whale,
still Povl Velling will not turn pale."

"Is your name Paul, then?" she asked.

"Yes, Povl," he answered. "It is not a bad name. My father was named Povl, and his father too. It is the name of good seamen, faithful to their ship. My father was drowned six months before I was born. He is down there, in the sea."

"But you are not going to drown, Paul?" she said.

"No," said he. "Maybe not. But I have many times wondered what my father thought of, when the sea took him at last, altogether."

"Do you like to think of that sort of thing?" she asked, somewhat alarmed.

He thought her question over. "Yes," he said. "It is good to think of the storms and the high sea. It is not bad to think of death."

A little while after he called out, in a sudden, low cry: "I shall have to go back to my ship as soon as it grows light. She sails in the morning."

At these words a long, sad pain ran through Virginie's whole body. But the next moment it was again swallowed up in his strength. Soon after they both fell asleep in each other's arms.

Virginie woke up when the morning showed in gray stripes between the window curtains. The boy had loosened his grasp of her, but was still, in his deep sleep, holding on to her hand.

The moment she woke she was gripped, as in a strangle hold, by one single thought. Never before had one thought filled her so entirely, to the exclusion of everything else. "When he sees my face in the daylight," she reflected, "it will be old, powdered and rouged. An aged, wicked woman's face!"

She watched the light growing stronger. She had ten minutes yet, she had five minutes yet, she thought—her heart heavy, heavy in her breast. Time was up, and she called his name twice.

When he woke she told him that he must get up in order to be back on his ship before she sailed. He did not answer her, but clung to her hand, and in a while pressed it to his face, moaning.

She heard a bird singing in the garden and said: "Listen, Paul, there is a bird singing. The candles are burnt out, the night is over."

Suddenly, without a sound, like an animal springing, he flung himself out of the bed, seized her, and lifted her up with him.

"Come!" he cried. "Come with me, away from here!"

His voice was like a song, like a storm; it lifted her higher than his arms.

"I shall take you with me," he cried again, "to my ship. I shall hide you there, in the hold. I shall take you home with me!"

She thrust her hands against his chest to get away from him, and felt it going up and down like a pair of bellows, but she only made him, and herself within his embrace, sway a little, like a tree in the wind. He tightened his hold of her, raising her as if to throw her over his shoulder.

"I am not going to leave you!" he sang out. "I am not going to let anybody in the world part us. What! Now that you are mine! Never! never! never!"

Virginie at this moment caught sight of their two dim figures in one of the looking-glasses. She could not have asked for a more dramatic scene. The boy looked superhumanly big, formidable now, like an enraged bear, risen on his hind legs, and swinging his right forelimb in the air—and she herself, with her long hair hanging down, was the limp, defenseless prey in his left arm. Writhing, she managed to get one foot to the ground. The boy felt her tremble; he let her down, but still held her close.

"What are you afraid of?" he asked, forcing her face up toward his own. "You do not believe that I shall let anybody take you away from me! You are coming home with me. You will not be afraid of the storms, or the blizzards, or the big waves, when I am with you. You will never be afraid in Denmark. There we shall sleep together every night. Like tonight! Like tonight!"

Virginie's deadly terror had nothing to do with storms, blizzards or big waves; she did not even, at this moment, dread death. She dreaded that he should see her face in the light of day. At first she dared not speak, for she did not feel sure of herself, and might say anything. But when she had stood on both feet for a minute she collected her whole being to find a way of escape.

"You cannot do that," she said. "He has paid you."

"What?" he cried out, bewildered.

"That old man has paid you!" she repeated. "He has paid you to go away at dawn. You have taken his money!"

When he grasped the meaning of her words his face grew white and he let go his hold of her so suddenly that she swayed on her feet.

"Yes," he said slowly. "He has paid me. And I took his money.—But at that time," he cried, "I did not know!"

He stared into the air before him, above her head. "I have promised him!" he said heavily. Letting his head drop upon her shoulder he buried his face in her hair and her flesh. "Oh! oh! oh!" he wailed.

He lifted her, carried her back onto the bed and sat down on it beside her, his eyes closed. Time after time he raised her and pressed her body to his own, then laid her down again. Virginie was calmer as long as he kept his eyes closed. She looked back over their short acquaintance to find a word to say to him.

"You will have your boat," she said at last.

After a long silence he said: "Yes, I shall have the boat." And again after a while: "Was that what you said: that I shall have the boat?"

Once more he lifted her and held her for a long time in his arms. "But you!" he said.

"But you?" he repeated, slowly, after a moment. "What is going to happen to you, my girl?"

Virginie did not say a word.

"Then I must go," he said, "I must go back to my ship." He listened and added: "There is a bird singing. The candles are burnt out. The night is over. I must go." But he did not go till a little later.

"Good-bye, Virginie," he said. "That is your name —Virginie. I shall name the boat after you. I shall give her both our names—Povl and Virginie. She will sail with both our names on her, up through the Storstroem and the Bay of Koege."

"Will you remember me?" Virginie asked.

"Yes," the sailor said. "Always, all my life." He rose.

"I shall think of you all my life," he said. "How would I not think of you in my boat? I shall think of you when I hoist the sails and when I weigh anchor. And when I cast anchor. I shall think of you in the mornings when I hear the birds singing. Of your body, of your smell. I shall never think of any other girl, of any girl at all. Because you are the most beautiful girl in the world."

She followed him to the door and put her arms round his neck. Here, away from the window, the room was still dark. Here she suddenly heard herself weeping. "But I have got one minute more," she thought, as she held him in her arms and they kissed.

"Look at me," she begged him. "Look at me, Paul."

Gravely, he looked her in the face.

"Remember my face," she said. "Look at my face well, and remember it. Remember that I am seventeen. Remember that I have never loved anybody till I met you."

"I shall remember it all," he said. "I shall never for-get your face."

Clinging to him, her wet face lifted, she felt that he was freeing himself of her arms.

"Now you must go," she said.

xv. *The Shell*

By the light of that same dawn Elishama walked up Mr. Clay's graveled drive and entered the house, in order to be, in his quiet way, the full stop, or the epilogue, to the story.

In the long dining room the table was still laid, and there was still a little wine in the glasses. The candles were burnt out, only one last flame flickered on its candlestick.

Mr. Clay, too, was still there, propped up with cushions in his deep armchair, his feet on a stool. He had been sitting up, waiting for the morning, to drink off at sunrise the cup of his triumph. But the cup of his triumph had been too strong for him.

Elishama stood for a long time, immovable as the old man himself, looking at him. He had never till now seen his master asleep and from his complaints and laments had concluded that he should never see him so. Well, he thought, Mr. Clay had been right, he had struck on the one effective remedy against his suffering. The realization of a story was the thing to set a man at rest.

The old man's eyes were slightly open—pale, like pebbles—but his thin lips were closed in a little wry smile. His face was gray like the bony hands upon his knees. His dressing-gown hung in such deep folds that there hardly seemed to be a body in it to connect this face and head with these hands. The whole proud and rigid figure, envied and feared by thousands, this morning looked like a jumping-jack when the hand which has pulled the strings has suddenly let them go.

His servant and confidant sat down on a chair, listening for the usual whining and snarling in the old man's chest. But there was not a sound in the room. Elishama repeated to himself the words of his Prophet:

"And sorrow and sighing shall flee away."

For a long time Mr. Clay's clerk sat with him, meditating upon the events of the night, and upon human conditions in general. What had happened, he asked himself, to the three people who, each of them, had had his or her role in Mr. Clay's story? Could they not have done without it? It was hard, he reflected, as he had often done before, it was very hard on people who wanted things so badly that they could not do without them. If they could not get these things it was hard, and when they did get them, surely it was very hard.

After a while he wondered whether he should touch the sunken, immovable body before him, to demonstrate, in a gesture, his intention to wake up Mr. Clay to the triumphal end of his story. But again he made up his mind to wait a little, and to watch this end himself first. He silently left the silent room.

He went to the bedroom door, and as he waited

outside it he heard voices. Two people were talking at the same time. What had happened to those two in the night, and what was happening to them now? Could they not have done without it? Someone was weeping inside the room, the voice came to the listener's ear—broken, stifled by tears. Again Elishama quoted to himself the words of Isaiah:

"In the wilderness shall waters break out, and streams in the desert. And the parched ground shall become a pool."

A little later the door was opened; two figures were embracing and clinging to one another in the doorway. Then they severed, the one sliding back and disappearing, the other advancing and closing the door behind him. The sailor of last night for a few seconds stood still outside the door and gazed round him, then moved on.

Elishama took a step forward. He was loyal to his master and felt that he ought to get the attestation of Mr. Clay's victory from the boy's own lips.

The sailor looked at him gravely and said: "I am going away. I am going back to my ship. You will tell the old man that I have gone."

Elishama now saw that he had been mistaken the evening before; the boy was not so young as he had taken him to be. It made but little difference; it was still a long time till he would be as old as Mr. Clay, peacefully at rest in his armchair. For a long time yet he would be unsafe, in the hands of the elements, and of his own wants.

The clerk took upon himself to settle and balance up his master's concern.

"Now you can tell the story," he said to the boy.

"What story?" the boy asked.

"The whole story," Elishama answered. "When you tell what has happened to you, what you have seen and done, from yesterday evening till now, you will be telling the whole story. You are the one sailor in the world who can tell it truthfully, from beginning to end, with everything that is in it, as it has actually, from beginning to end, happened to you."

The boy looked at Elishama for a long time.

"What has happened to me?" he said at last. "What I have seen and done from yesterday evening till now?" And again after a while: "Why do you call it a story?"

"Because," said Elishama, "you yourself have heard it told as a story. About a sailor who comes ashore from his ship in a big town. And he is walking by himself in a street near the harbor, when a carriage drives up, and an old gentleman steps out of it and says to him: 'You are a fine-looking sailor. Do you want to earn five guineas tonight?'"

The boy did not move. But he had a curious capacity of collecting, suddenly and imperceptibly, his great strength, and of turning it toward the person with whom he spoke, like some threatening, like some formidable weight, which might well make the other feel in danger of his life. So he had puzzled Mr. Clay at their first meeting in the street, and had downright scared him later in the evening, in the dining room. Elishama, who had no fear in him, for a second was moved and stirred—so that he even drew back a little from the gigantic creature before him—not, however, with fright, but with the same strange kind of sympathy and compassion as all his life he had felt toward women and birds.

But the gigantic creature before him proved to be a peaceful beast. He waited a moment, then very quietly stated: "But that story is not in the least like what happened to me."

Again he waited a little.

"Tell it?" he said lowly. "To whom would I tell it? Who in the world would believe it if I told it?"

He laid his collected, concentrated strength and weight into a last sentence:

"I would not tell it," he said, "for a hundred times five guineas."

Elishama opened the door of the house to its guest of the night. Outside, the trees and flowers of Mr. Clay's garden were wet with dew, in the morning light they looked new and fresh, as if they had just this hour been created. The sky was red as a rose and there was not a cloud in it. One of Mr. Clay's peacocks screeched on the lawn, dragging its tail after it; it made a dark stripe in the silvery grass. From far away came the faint noises of the awakening town.

The sailor's eyes fell upon the bundle which last night he had left on a lacquered table in the verandah. He took it up to carry it away with him, then thought better of it, laid it down again and undid the knots.

"Will you remember to do something for me?" he asked Elishama.

"Yes, I shall remember," answered Elishama.

"A long time ago," said the boy, "I was on an island where there were many thousand shells along the shore. Some of them were beautiful, perhaps they were rare, perhaps they were only to be found on that same island. I picked up a few every day, in the morning. I took some of them, the most beautiful of them, with me. I meant to take them home to Denmark. They are the only things I have got, to take home with me."

He spread his collection of shells over the table, looked them over thoughtfully, and in the end picked out one big shining pink shell. He handed it to Elishama.

"I shall not give her them all," he said. "She has got so many fine things, she would not care to have a lot of shells lying about. But this one is rare, I think. I think that perhaps there is not another one just like it in all the world."

He slowly felt the shell over with his fingers. "It is as smooth and silky as a knee," he said. "And when you hold it to your ear there is a sound in it, a song. Will you give it to her from me? And will you tell her to hold it to her ear?"

He held it to his own ear, and immediately his face took on an attentive, peaceful look. Elishama reflected that after all he had been right last night, and that the boy was very young.

"Yes," he said. "I shall remember to give it to her."

"And will you remember to tell her to hold it to her ear?" asked the boy.

"Yes," said Elishama.

"Thank you. And good-bye," said the sailor, and gave Elishama his big hand.

He went down the verandah steps and along the drive with the bundle in his hand, and disappeared.

Elishama stood and looked after him. When the big young figure was no longer in sight, he himself lifted the shell to his ear. There was a deep, low surge in it, like the distant roar of great breakers. Elishama's face took on exactly the same expression as the sailor's face a few moments ago. He had a strange, gentle, profound shock, from the sound of a new voice in the house, and in the story. "I have heard it before," he thought, "long ago. Long, long ago. But where?"

He let his hand sink.

The Ring

On a summer morning a hundred and fifty years ago a young Danish squire and his wife went out for a walk on their land. They had been married a week. It had not been easy for them to get married, for the wife's family was higher in rank and wealthier than the husband's. But the two young people, now twenty-four and nineteen years old, had been set on their purpose for ten years; in the end her haughty parents had had to give in to them.

They were wonderfully happy. The stolen meetings and secret, tearful love letters were now things of the past. To God and man they were one; they could walk arm in arm in broad daylight and drive in the same carriage, and they would walk and drive so till the end of their days. Their distant paradise had descended to earth and had proved, surprisingly, to be filled with the things of everyday life: with jesting and railleries, with breakfasts and suppers, with dogs, haymaking and sheep. Sigismund, the young husband, had promised himself that from now there should be no stone in his bride's path, nor should any shadow fall across it. Lovisa, the wife, felt that now, every day and for the first time in her young life, she moved and breathed in perfect freedom because she could never have any secret from her husband.

To Lovisa—whom her husband called Lise—the rustic atmosphere of her new life was a matter of wonder and delight. Her husband's fear that the existence he could offer her might not be good enough for her filled her heart with laughter. It was not a long time since she had played with dolls; as now she dressed her own hair, looked over her linen press and arranged her flowers she again lived through an enchanting and cherished experience: one was doing everything gravely and solicitously, and all the time one knew one was playing.

It was a lovely July morning. Little woolly clouds drifted high up in the sky, the air was full of sweet scents. Lise had on a white muslin frock and a large Italian straw hat. She and her husband took a path through the park; it wound on across the meadows, between small groves and groups of trees, to the sheep field. Sigismund was going to show his wife his sheep. For this reason she had not brought her small white dog, Bijou, with her, for he would yap at the lambs and frighten them, or he would annoy the sheep dogs. Sigismund prided himself on his sheep; he had studied sheep-breeding in Mecklenburg and England, and had brought back with him Cotswold rams by which to improve his Danish stock. While they walked he explained to Lise the great possibilities and difficulties of the plan.

She thought: "How clever he is, what a lot of things he knows!" and at the same time: "What an absurd person he is, with his sheep! What a baby he is! I am a hundred years older than he."

But when they arrived at the sheepfold the old sheepmaster Mathias met them with the sad news that one of the English lambs was dead and two were sick. Lise saw that her husband was grieved by the tidings; while he questioned Mathias on the matter she

kept silent and only gently pressed his arm. A couple
of boys were sent off to fetch the sick lambs, while the
master and servant went into the details of the case. It
took some time.

Lise began to gaze about her and to think of other
things. Twice her own thoughts made her blush
deeply and happily, like a red rose, then slowly her
blush died away, and the two men were still talking
about sheep. A little while after their conversation
caught her attention. It had turned to a sheep thief.

This thief during the last months had broken into
the sheepfolds of the neighborhood like a wolf, had
killed and dragged away his prey like a wolf and like
a wolf had left no trace after him. Three nights ago
the shepherd and his son on an estate ten miles away
had caught him in the act. The thief had killed the
man and knocked the boy senseless, and had managed
to escape. There were men sent out to all sides to
catch him, but nobody had seen him.

Lise wanted to hear more about the horrible event,
and for her benefit old Mathias went through it once
more. There had been a long fight in the sheep house,
in many places the earthen floor was soaked with
blood. In the fight the thief's left arm was broken; all
the same, he had climbed a tall fence with a lamb on
his back. Mathias added that he would like to string
up the murderer with these two hands of his, and Lise
nodded her head at him gravely in approval. She remembered Red Ridinghood's wolf, and felt a pleasant
little thrill running down her spine.

Sigismund had his own lambs in his mind, but he was too happy in himself to wish anything in the universe ill. After a minute he said: "Poor devil."

Lise said: "How can you pity such a terrible man? Indeed Grandmamma was right when she said that you were a revolutionary and a danger to society!" The thought of Grandmamma, and of the tears of past days, again turned her mind away from the gruesome tale she had just heard.

The boys brought the sick lambs and the men began to examine them carefully, lifting them up and trying to set them on their legs; they squeezed them here and there and made the little creatures whimper. Lise shrank from the show and her husband noticed her distress.

"You go home, my darling," he said, "this will take some time. But just walk ahead slowly, and I shall catch up with you."

So she was turned away by an impatient husband to whom his sheep meant more than his wife. If any experience could be sweeter than to be dragged out by him to look at those same sheep, it would be this. She dropped her large summer hat with its blue ribbons on the grass and told him to carry it back for her, for she wanted to feel the summer air on her forehead and in her hair. She walked on very slowly, as he had told her to do, for she wished to obey him in everything. As she walked she felt a great new happiness in being altogether alone, even without Bijou. She could not remember that she had ever before in all her life been altogether alone. The landscape around her was still, as if full of promise, and it was hers. Even the swallows cruising in the air were hers, for they belonged to him, and he was hers.

She followed the curving edge of the grove and after a minute or two found that she was out of sight to the men by the sheep house. What could now, she wondered, be sweeter than to walk along the path in the long flowering meadow grass, slowly, slowly, and to let her husband overtake her there? It would be sweeter still, she reflected, to steal into the grove and to be gone, to have vanished from the surface of the earth from him when, tired of the sheep and longing for her company, he should turn the bend of the path to catch up with her.

An idea struck her; she stood still to think it over.

A few days ago her husband had gone for a ride and she had not wanted to go with him, but had strolled about with Bijou in order to explore her domain. Bijou then, gamboling, had led her straight into the grove. As she had followed him, gently forcing her way into the shrubbery, she had suddenly come upon a glade in the midst of it, a narrow space like a small alcove with hangings of thick green and golden brocade, big enough to hold two or three people in it. She had felt at that moment that she had come into the very heart of her new home. If today she could find the spot again she would stand perfectly still there, hidden from all the world. Sigismund would look for her in all directions; he would be unable to understand what had become of her and for a minute, for a short minute—or, perhaps, if she was firm and cruel enough, for five—he would realize what a void, what an unendurably sad and horrible place the universe would be when she was no longer in it. She gravely scrutinized the grove to find the right entrance to her hiding-place, then went in.

She took great care to make no noise at all, therefore advanced exceedingly slowly. When a twig caught the flounces of her ample skirt she loosened it softly from the muslin, so as not to crack it. Once a branch took hold of one of her long golden curls; she stood still, with her arms lifted, to free it. A little way into the grove the soil became moist; her light steps no longer made any sound upon it. With one hand she held her small handkerchief to her lips, as if to emphasize the secretness of her course. She found the spot she sought and bent down to divide the foliage and make a door to her sylvan closet. At this the hem of her dress caught her foot and she stopped to loosen it. As she rose she looked into the face of a man who was already in the shelter.

He stood up erect, two steps off. He must have watched her as she made her way straight toward him.

She took him in in one single glance. His face was bruised and scratched, his hands and wrists stained with dark filth. He was dressed in rags, barefooted, with tatters wound round his naked ankles. His arms hung down to his sides, his right hand clasped the hilt of a knife. He was about her own age. The man and the woman looked at each other.

This meeting in the wood from beginning to end

passed without a word; what happened could only be rendered by pantomime. To the two actors in the pantomime it was timeless; according to a clock it lasted four minutes.

She had never in her life been exposed to danger. It did not occur to her to sum up her position, or to work out the length of time it would take to call her husband or Mathias, whom at this moment she could hear shouting to his dogs. She beheld the man before her as she would have beheld a forest ghost: the apparition itself, not the sequels of it, changes the world to the human who faces it.

Although she did not take her eyes off the face before her she sensed that the alcove had been turned into a covert. On the ground a couple of sacks formed a couch; there were some gnawed bones by it. A fire must have been made here in the night, for there were cinders strewn on the forest floor.

After a while she realized that he was observing her just as she was observing him. He was no longer just run to earth and crouching for a spring, but he was wondering, trying to know. At that she seemed to see herself with the eyes of the wild animal at bay in his dark hiding-place: her silently approaching white figure, which might mean death.

He moved his right arm till it hung down straight before him between his legs. Without lifting the hand he bent the wrist and slowly raised the point of the knife till it pointed at her throat. The gesture was mad, unbelievable. He did not smile as he made it, but his nostrils distended, the corners of his mouth quivered a little. Then slowly he put the knife back in the sheath by his belt.

She had no object of value about her, only the wedding ring which her husband had set on her finger in church, a week ago. She drew it off, and in this movement dropped her handkerchief. She reached out her hand with the ring toward him. She did not bargain for her life. She was fearless by nature, and the horror with which he inspired her was not fear of what he might do to her. She commanded him, she besought him to vanish as he had come, to take a dreadful figure out of her life, so that it should never have been there. In the dumb movement her young form had the grave authoritativeness of a priestess conjuring down some monstrous being by a sacred sign.

He slowly reached out his hand to hers, his finger touched hers, and her hand was steady at the touch. But he did not take the ring. As she let it go it dropped to the ground as her handkerchief had done.

For a second the eyes of both followed it. It rolled a few inches toward him and stopped before his bare foot. In a hardly perceivable movement he kicked it away and again looked into her face. They remained like that, she knew not how long, but she felt that during that time something happened, things were changed.

He bent down and picked up her handkerchief. All the time gazing at her, he again drew his knife and wrapped the tiny bit of cambric round the blade. This was difficult for him to do because his left arm was broken. While he did it his face under the dirt and sun-tan slowly grew whiter till it was almost phosphorescent. Fumbling with both hands, he once more stuck the knife into the sheath. Either the sheath was too big and had never fitted the knife, or the blade was much worn—it went in. For two or three more seconds his gaze rested on her face; then he lifted his own face a little, the strange radiance still upon it, and closed his eyes.

The movement was definitive and unconditional. In this one motion he did what she had begged him to do: he vanished and was gone. She was free.

She took a step backward, the immovable, blind face before her, then bent as she had done to enter the hiding-place, and glided away as noiselessly as she had come. Once outside the grove she stood still and looked round for the meadow path, found it and began to walk home.

Her husband had not yet rounded the edge of the grove. Now he saw her and helloed to her gaily; he came up quickly and joined her.

The path here was so narrow that he kept half behind her and did not touch her. He began to explain to her what had been the matter with the lambs. She walked a step before him and thought: All is over.

After a while he noticed her silence, came up beside her to look at her face and asked, "What is the matter?"

She searched her mind for something to say, and at last said: "I have lost my ring."

"What ring?" he asked her.

She answered, "My wedding ring."

As she heard her own voice pronounce the words she conceived their meaning.

Her wedding ring. "With this ring"—dropped by one and kicked away by another—"with this ring I thee wed." With this lost ring she had wedded herself to something. To what? To poverty, persecution, total loneliness. To the sorrows and the sinfulness of this earth. "And what therefore God has joined together let man not put asunder."

"I will find you another ring," her husband said. "You and I are the same as we were on our wedding day; it will do as well. We are husband and wife today too, as much as yesterday, I suppose."

Her face was so still that he did not know if she had heard what he said. It touched him that she should take the loss of his ring so to heart. He took her hand and kissed it. It was cold, not quite the same hand as he had last kissed. He stopped to make her stop with him.

"Do you remember where you had the ring on last?" he asked.

"No," she answered.

"Have you any idea," he asked, "where you may have lost it?"

"No," she answered. "I have no idea at all."

Isak Dinesen is the pseudonym of Karen Blixen, born in Denmark in 1885. After her marriage in 1914 to Baron Bror Blixen, she and her husband went to live in British East Africa, where they established a coffee plantation. She was divorced from her husband in 1921 but continued to manage the plantation for another ten years, until the collapse of the coffee market forced her to sell the property and return to Denmark in 1931. There she began to write in English under the *nom de plume* Isak Dinesen. Her first book, and literary success, was *Seven Gothic Tales* (available in Vintage Books). It was followed by *Out of Africa* (also available in Vintage Books in a facsimile edition of the first printing); *The Angelic Avengers* (written under the pseudonym Pierre Andrézel); *Winter's Tales* (available in Vintage Book); *Last Tales; Anecdotes of Destiny;* and *Ehrengard*. Isak Dinesen died in 1962.

VINTAGE BELLES—LETTRES

V-418 **AUDEN, W. H.** / The Dyer's Hand
V-887 **AUDEN, W. H.** / Forewords and Afterwords
V-271 **BEDIER, JOSEPH** / Tristan and Iseult
V-512 **BLOCH, MARC** / The Historian's Craft
V-572 **BRIDGEHAMPTON** / Bridgehampton Works & Days
V-161 **BROWN, NORMAN O.** / Closing Time
V-544 **BROWN, NORMAN O.** / Hermes the Thief
V-419 **BROWN, NORMAN O.** / Love's Body
V-75 **CAMUS, ALBERT** / The Myth of Sisyphus and Other Essays
V-30 **CAMUS, ALBERT** / The Rebel
V-608 **CARR, JOHN DICKSON** / The Life of Sir Arthur Conan Doyle: The Man Who Was Sherlock Holmes
V-407 **HARDWICK, ELIZABETH** / Seduction and Betrayal: Women and Literature
V-244 **HERRIGEL, EUGEN** / The Method of Zen
V-663 **HERRIGEL, EUGEN** / Zen in the Art of Archery
V-201 **HUGHES, H. STUART** / Consciousness & Society
V-235 **KAPLAN, ABRAHAM** / New World of Philosophy
V-337 **KAUFMANN, WALTER (trans.) AND FRIEDRICH NIETZSCHE** / Beyond Good and Evil
V-369 **KAUFMANN, WALTER (trans.) AND FRIEDRICH NIETZSCHE** / The Birth of Tragedy and the Case of Wagner
V-985 **KAUFMANN, WALTER (trans.) AND FRIEDRICH NIETZSCHE** / The Gay Science
V-401 **KAUFMANN, WALTER (trans.) AND FRIEDRICH NIETZSCHE** / On the Genealogy of Morals and Ecce Homo
V-437 **KAUFMANN, WALTER (trans.) AND FRIEDRICH NIETZSCHE** / The Will to Power
V-995 **KOTT, JAN** / The Eating of the Gods: An Interpretation of Greek Tragedy
V-685 **LESSING, DORIS** / A Small Personal Voice: Essays, Reviews, Interviews
V-329 **LINDBERGH, ANNE MORROW** / Gift from the Sea
V-479 **MALRAUX, ANDRE** / Man's Fate
V-406 **MARCUS, STEVEN** / Engels, Manchester and the Working Class
V-58 **MENCKEN, H. L.** / Prejudices (Selected by James T. Farrell)
V-25 **MENCKEN, H. L.** / The Vintage Mencken (Gathered by Alistair Cooke)
V-151 **MOFFAT, MARY JANE AND CHARLOTTE PAINTER (eds.)** / Revelations: Diaries of Women
V-926 **MUSTARD, HELEN (trans.)** / Heinrich Heine: Selected Works
V-337 **NIETZSCHE, FRIEDRICH AND WALTER KAUFMANN (trans.)** / Beyond Good and Evil
V-369 **NIETZSCHE, FRIEDRICH AND WALTER KAUFMANN (trans.)** / The Birth of Tragedy and the Case of Wagner
V-985 **NIETZSCHE, FRIEDRICH AND WALTER KAUFMANN (trans.)** / The Gay Science
V-401 **NIETZSCHE, FRIEDRICH AND WALTER KAUFMANN (trans.)** / On the Genealogy of Morals and Ecce Homo

V-437   **NIETZSCHE, FRIEDRICH AND WALTER KAUFMANN (trans.)** / The Will to Power
V-672   **OUSPENSKY, P. D.** / The Fourth Way
V-524   **OUSPENSKY, P. D.** / A New Model of the Universe
V-943   **OUSPENSKY, P. D.** / The Psychology of Man's Possible Evolution
V-639   **OUSPENSKY, P. D.** / Tertium Organum
V-151   **PAINTER, CHARLOTTE AND MARY JANE MOFFAT (eds.)** / Revelations: Diaries of Women
V-986   **PAUL, DAVID (trans.)** / Poison & Vision: Poems & Prose of Baudelaire, Mallarme and Rimbaud
V-598   **PROUST, MARCEL** / The Captive
V-597   **PROUST, MARCEL** / Cities of the Plain
V-596   **PROUST, MARCEL** / The Guermantes Way
V-594   **PROUST, MARCEL** / Swann's Way
V-599   **PROUST, MARCEL** / The Sweet Cheat Gone
V-595   **PROUST, MARCEL** / Within a Budding Grove
V-899   **SAMUEL, MAURICE** / The World of Sholom Aleichem
V-415   **SHATTUCK, ROGER** / The Banquet Years (revised)
V-278   **STEVENS, WALLACE** / The Necessary Angel
V-761   **WATTS, ALAN** / Behold the Spirit
V-923   **WATTS, ALAN** / Beyond Theology: The Art of Godmanship
V-853   **WATTS, ALAN** / The Book: the Taboo Against Knowing Who You Are
V-999   **WATTS, ALAN** / Cloud-Hidden, Whereabouts Unknown: A Mountain Journal
V-665   **WATTS, ALAN** / Does it Matter?
V-951   **WATTS, ALAN** / In My Own Way
V-299   **WATTS, ALAN** / The Joyous Cosmology
V-592   **WATTS, ALAN** / Nature, Man and Woman
V-609   **WATTS, ALAN** / Psychotherapy East & West
V-835   **WATTS, ALAN** / The Supreme Identity
V-298   **WATTS, ALAN** / The Way of Zen
V-870   **WIESEL, ELIE** / Souls on Fire

Ehrengard

ISAK DINESEN

Ehrengard

VINTAGE BOOKS
A Division of Random House, New York

Library of Congress Cataloging-in-Publication Data
Dinesen, Isak, 1885–1962.
  Anecdotes of destiny; Ehrengard.
  I. Dinesen, Isak, 1885–1962. Ehrengard. 1985.
II. Title. III. Title: Anecdotes of destiny. IV. Title:
Ehrengard.
PR6003.L545A6 1985   839.8′ 1372   85-13591
ISBN 0-394-74215-X (pbk.)

Ehrengard

An old lady told this story.

A hundred and twenty years ago, she began, my story told itself, at greater length of time than you or I can give to it, and with a throng of details and particulars which we can never hope to know. The men and women who then gradually built it up, and to whom it was a matter of life and death, are all long gone. They may be, by this time and before the throne of the Lamb, occasionally exchanging a smile and a remark: "O yes! And do you remember . . . ?" The roads and paths on which it moved are overgrown with grass, or are no more to be found.

The very country in which it began, developed and came to an end, may be said to have faded out of existence. For it was, in those good days, a fair, free and flourishing small principality of old Germany, and its sovereign was responsible to no one but God in Heaven. But later on, when times and men grew harder, it was silently and sadly swallowed up into the great new German Empire.

I am not going to give you the real name of this country, nor of the ladies and gentlemen within my tale. These latter would not have liked me to do so. To them a name was a sacred thing, and with both pride and humility each of them held his or her name to be the noblest and most important—and the lasting—part of his or her person and existence. Moreover, these names are all well known, most of them appearing and reappearing in the history of their country. The family upon which my story turns was indeed no mere family but a house, and its good or bad luck, its honor and disgrace, were no ordinary family matters, but dynastic concerns.

So to begin with, my dearest, I shall inform you that the stage of our little comedy or tragedy was the lovely country and the fine city of Babenhausen, and that you will be devoting your attention to a chronicle of the Grand Ducal house of Fugger-Babenhausen. And as in the course of my narrative new gentlemen and ladies make their appearance in it, I shall endeavor to find a new noble name for each of them.

The story may be said to fall into three parts, the first of which—although I fear that it may seem to you a bit lengthy—is in reality only a kind of prelude to the second and third.

And so we begin.

❧

The Grand Duke and Grand Duchess of Babenhausen for a long time were childless and grieved over their lot. Particular circumstances made the misfortune more fatal. For the Grand Duke was the last of his line, and should he leave no son after him, the ducal crown would pass to a lateral branch of the dynasty, of doubtful legitimacy and principles. Great disturbance in the state might be the consequence.

It was therefore a great joy and relief to the loyal subjects of Babenhausen as well as to the Grand Ducal couple themselves when, after a waiting time of fifteen years, an heir was born. His cousins of the lateral branch bit their fingers and now, the sweet hope before them gone, took no trouble at all about their reputation, but openly surrounded themselves with the malcontents of the country.

Young Prince Lothar grew up graceful and wise. His proud parents appointed the best teachers in the nation for him, and took care to keep the wickedness and vulgarity of the world from him. For sixteen or seventeen years things were as happy as possible. Then a curious and unexpected anxiety began to stir in the heart of the Grand Duchess.

Very old families will sometimes feel upon them the shadow of annihilation. The plant loses contact with the soil, and while it may still put forth a single flower of exquisite loveliness, the root withers. The Grand Duchess came to wonder whether her son were not all too perfect for this world.

There was in Prince Lothar's ethereal and serene beauty a strain of aloofness which set him alone amongst the youths of his court and his generation. While he was devoted to the arts, and was himself a distinguished dilettante in music and painting and a skilled botanist and astronomer, the actual human world around him seemed incapable of captivating or holding him. He was never known of his own accord to touch any human being, he even shrank a little from the caresses of his mother. The time arrived when the Grand Duchess thought it her duty to form plans for his marriage, and she found that to this youth, whom any princess might be happy to call husband, the idea of marriage was as remote as the idea of death.

All women in their heart feel that through

the toils of pregnancy and the pangs of child-
birth they have become entitled to an everlasting
life in the flesh and on the earth. The Grand
Duchess might claim this reward before other
ladies of Babenhausen inasmuch as she had entered into matrimony with the sole idea of maintaining an ancient noble house, and loyally had
given herself over to her mission. She had been
brought to understand that, by law of nature, a
more ardent initiative was required by her partner in the task, and earlier in life the fact had
vexed and upset her, and had even cost her tears.
By now she had become fully reconciled to it.
She watched the angelic face and figure of her
son and was seized by a cruel apprehension. Had
her loyalty, her exertions and pain, served to
postpone by one generation only the extinction
of the dynasty of Fugger-Babenhausen?

Till this time the Grand Duchess had preferred for the ducal household ladies of a certain
age and of homely appearance. Now she gradually appointed more attractive representatives of
the sex to her staff. She gave a number of court
balls and she encouraged her son to frequent the

opera and the ballet. The Prince danced at the balls and came back from the theater delighted. He admired beauty in women as he admired it in flowers and was ever courteous to the ladies. But *la belle passion* as his young companions knew it, to him seemed to remain alien. His mother became impatient with her ladies and with the stars of the stage. What were they about, she indignantly asked herself, to be such bunglers in their *métier de femme?*

It so happened that at this time the Grand Duchess was having her portrait painted by that great artist the Geheimrat Wolfgang Cazotte.

Herr Cazotte at the age of forty-five had painted the portraits of most queens and princesses of Europe and was persona grata at a dozen courts. His fresh and pure nudes were bought at fancy prices by the galleries. At the same time he was on easy and friendly terms with street hawkers, circus performers and flower girls. He had velvety brown eyes, a red mouth and a remarkably sweet voice.

Although more than twice the age of Prince Lothar, Herr Cazotte for some time had been his closest friend and most constant companion. The young Prince felt a sincere admiration for the artist's extraordinary gifts, and the two had long talks together on elevated matters.

The Grand Duchess so far had not favored the friendship, for if Herr Cazotte was famous as a portraitist of fair ladies, he was no less celebrated and talked about as their conqueror and seducer, the irresistible Don Juan of his age.

My great-grandmother, Countess von Gassner, was Herr Cazotte's friend. A long time ago, when he had been a very poor young boy of Babenhausen and she a very great lady and a *bel-esprit* of the city, she had discovered his genius, had seen to it that he got a painting master and leisure for his studies, and had even for a while adopted him into her own house. Herr Cazotte had a gift for gratitude, and she on her side remembered him as the very last of the row of pretty youths whom she had helped to a career, the two were dear to one another's heart. Later, when she had lost her great beauty, she had retired out of the world to her chateau in the country and had not wanted any of her old friends to see her again. For many years she and he had not met. But they had kept up a correspondence which pleased them both, him because it was in itself inspiring to him, her because in his letters he addressed her as a woman who might still be desired. Herr Cazotte was a very discreet person and could keep a secret with anyone, but he made an exception with my great-grandmother and felt free to pass on to her any knowledge of his and even the secrets of his friends, aware that none of it would ever get any further. Most of my knowledge with regard to the story of Ehrengard I owe to his letters to her.

She expostulated with him on his fickleness, and he answered her:

Dear, adored Lady,
You call an artist a seducer and are not aware that you are paying him the highest of compliments. The whole attitude of the artist towards the Universe is that of a seducer.
For what does seduction mean but the ability to make, with infinite trouble, pa-

tience and perseverance, the object upon
which you concentrate your mind give forth,
voluntarily and enraptured, its very core and
essence? Aye, and to reach, in the process, a
higher beauty than it could ever, under any
other circumstances, have attained? I have
seduced an old earthenware pot and two
lemons into yielding their inmost being to
me, to become mine and, at that same moment, to become phenomena of overwhelm-
ing loveliness and delight.

But most of all to be seduced is the
privilege of woman, the which man may well
envy her. Where would you be, my proud
ladies, if you did not recognize the seducer
in every man within waft of your petticoats?
For however admirable she be, the woman
who does not awaken in man the instinct of
seducer is like the horse of the Chevalier de
Kerguelen, which had all the good qualities
in the world, but which was dead. And what
poor unworthy creatures would we men be,
did we not endeavor to draw forth, like the
violinist with the bow upon the strings, the

full abundance and virtue of the instrument within our hands?

But do not imagine, wise and sagacious Mama, that the seducer's art must in each individual engagement fetch him the same trophy. There are women who give out the fullness of their womanhood in a smile, a side glance or a waltz, and others who will be giving it in their tears. I may drink off a bottle of Rhine wine to its last drop, but I sip only one glass of a fine, and there be rare vintages from which I covet nothing but the bouquet. The honest and loyal seducer, when he has obtained the smile, the side glance, the waltz or the tears, will uncover his head to the lady, his heart filled with gratitude, and will be dreading only one thing: that he may ever meet her again.

It was a symptom of the Grand Duchess' altered politics that she did now view Herr Cazotte with a lenient eye, that during the sittings she lent a gracious ear to his converse, airily expressed her own opinions on life, and in the end hinted at her misgivings with regard to her son. The slightest of hints was sufficient, the painter read the Grand Ducal mind like a book, and like an aeolian harp responded to its inaudible sigh.

"Let me," he said, "endeavor to give words to my sentiments. It is true that, generally speaking, in a boy or a youth the qualities of inexperience and intactness, and of innocence itself, are looked upon as merely negative traits, that is, as the absence of knowledge or of zeal. But there are natures of such rare nobility that with them no quality nor condition will ever be negative. Incorporated in such a mind anything partakes in its soundness and purity. To the plastic unity of an exalted spirit no conflict exists, but nature and ideal are one. Idea and action, too, are one, inasmuch as the idea is an action and the action an idea. When Prince Lothar makes his choice he will do so in an instant and with the wholeness of his nature. Today he watches his young friends dissipating their hearts in petty cash, he does not judge them, but he knows that their ways are not his way."

The Grand Duchess was comforted by Herr Cazotte's speech, she listened to his advice, and together they thought out a project.

For some time the Grand Duke and Grand Duchess had been urging their son to pay a visit to such courts of Europe as had princesses of his own age, while on his side Prince Lothar had longed to make a tour to the great centers of art in the company of his learned friend. Obviously now the two purposes might be combined. Herr Cazotte, acting as both worldly and spiritual attaché to the youth, would imperceptibly lead his steps to the desired goal. Prince Lothar at once delightedly agreed to the arrangement and looked forward to his aesthetic pilgrimage. The Grand Duchess and Herr Cazotte also, with much zeal, looked round in every direction.

Herr Cazotte from the beginning had had his eyes on a particular court, that of Leuchtenstein. The principality of Leuchtenstein was about the size of the Grand Duchy of Babenhausen and its ruling house in age and purity of blood vied with the Grand Duke's own. The worthy Prince of Leuchtenstein had unfortunately lost his consort, but was fortunate in possessing five fair daughters. On a former visit to the court Herr Cazotte had painted the portraits of the young ladies and had all the time been feeling that for the task he needed the brush of Master Greuze. Since then the two eldest princesses had made pretty marriages, the third in age, Princess Ludmilla, by now was seventeen years old.

If the princely house of Leuchtenstein, Herr Cazotte reasoned, were running any risk of decline and annihilation, it was not from withering or from losing contact with this world. The noble family might, on the very contrary, perish from mere exuberance of life, like a tree through a long time blooming and blossoming to excess. Within the cluster of Leuchtenstein maidens the artist had scented a quality of unconscious seductiveness, that rose-like fullness and fragrance which guilelessly allured the passer-by to pick the flower. He led his steps, and those of Prince Lothar, to Leuchtenstein.

Many tales in the course of time have come to surround Prince Lothar's courtship.

It was said that the youth, inspired by Herr Cazotte's description of Princess Ludmilla, had insisted on making his first appearance at her father's court in disguise, in the role of a simple young pupil of the great painter. A serenade, composed by him, is still sung in Leuchtenstein and Babenhausen. Of these things I can tell you nothing with certainty, they shall be left to the imagination of romantic persons.

Be this as it may, the young princely worshipper of the Muses returned to his own court, craving nothing in the world but to marry Princess Ludmilla of Leuchtenstein.

The ceremonial demand in marriage was made and accepted. And on a bright October day, when the vintage was just finished, the city of Babenhausen welcomed its young Princess. Fresh and pure as a peony bud, tender and playful as a child, the bride made the loyal Babenhauseners scatter their very hearts with the rain of flowers upon the pavement before her coach.

A row of brilliant balls, banquets and gala performances ensued. The whole court was smiling, and old chamberlains with tears in their eyes witnessed the display of princely matrimonial happiness.

The young couple, like two instruments of different nature, melted together in melodious happiness. Princess Ludmilla, delighted to delight, led the dance, and Prince Lothar, still wooing what he had won, followed his young wife through all its figures. The Grand Duchess looked on and smiled. The glory of the house of Fugger-Babenhausen was to be maintained.

It was and it was not. On a day shortly before Christmas Prince Lothar came to see his mother and calmly and candidly, as he did everything, informed her that the Ducal heir, on whom her mind and heart had for so long been concentrating, was about to make his entry in the world a full two months before law and decency permitted.

The Grand Duchess was struck dumb, first with amazement, for she had never imagined the possibility of such a thing in *bonne compagnie*. Then with horror, for what would the nation think of a scandal in the ruling house—what, in particular, would the dubious branch of the house itself think, and make, of it? In the end with terrible wrath against her son. And with this last emotion came a crushing feeling of guilt. For had she not herself delivered her frail child into the hands of that demonic figure, Herr Cazotte, and had not Herr Cazotte, talking about Lothar, pronounced the sentence: "With him the idea is action." The Grand Duchess trembled.

The next moment she was folded in the arms of the miscreant himself. And in this embrace, the first that her son had ever offered her on his own accord, her whole being melted. The world was changed round her, slowly, like a landscape at sunrise, it filled with new surprising tinges of tenderness and rapture. And this, I may here state, was the first triumph of the cherubic child upon whose small figure so much of my tale does turn.

Before she had spoken a word the Grand Duchess had determined to side with her son and daughter-in-law. She would keep their secret even from her husband. She took no further decision at the moment, but when Prince Lothar had left her and she was again alone, she realized that a line of action would have to be found.

To her own surprise the Grand Duchess at once found herself longing for Herr Cazotte. The tail and cloven hoof of the gentleman faded out of the picture, she recalled his second remark about Lothar ("And with him the action is idea") and smiled.

But Herr Cazotte was away in Rome, painting the portrait of Cardinal Salviati. So the Grand Duchess spent the strangest Christmas of her life, with a dimly radiant Christmas tree somewhere in front of her and parcels of secrets in her drawers.

However, between Christmas and the New Year an event took place which gave her a kind of respite. On a sledge party in the mountains the two panached horses before the young princely couple's sledge shied at an old woman carrying wood, ran away and upset the sledge in a deep drift of snow. None of the passengers came to any harm, Princess Ludmilla's rosy face laughed up at her rescuers. But her mother-in-law was alarmed, she sent for the old physician-in-ordinary, Professor Putziger, and told him everything. Professor Putziger ordered his patient to stay in bed for three weeks; for that length of time the Grand Duchess felt a kind of safety.

A fortnight later Herr Cazotte returned from Rome, pleased with his portrait. The Grand Duchess at once sent for him. Although she felt it beneath her to lay any responsibility on him, the artist realized that he was here being taken to task as a person at home in the land of romance and as Prince Lothar's guide and mentor in it.

"Madame," said Herr Cazotte, "The Lord God, that great artist, at times paints his pictures in such a manner as to be best appreciated at a long distance. A hundred and fifty years hence your present predicament will have all the look of an idyll composed to delight its spectators. Your difficulty at this moment is that you are a little too close to it."

"I am very close to it, *mon ami*," said the Grand Duchess.

"Each of your loyal subjects," said Herr Cazotte, "did he know of the matter which now vexes you, would smile in his heart, for all the world loves a lover. At the same time he might feel it his duty to pull a grave face. You are feeling and behaving just like him, Madame. Do not let your own face deceive you."

"But what are we to *do?*" asked the Grand Duchess.

"Providence," said Herr Cazotte, "has stepped in to help us. We must not fall out of step with it."

He developed to the Grand Duchess a plan which, although it must have been conceived on the spot, seemed well thought through.

The Grand Duke and the nation of Babenhausen, he pronounced, would be informed, quite truthfully, that a hope for the dynasty was dawning. The date for the happy event, in the announcement to them, would be put down for the middle of July. They would further be informed that upon Professor Putziger's advice the Princess should keep to her bed for three months, and that even after that period she would have to live in utmost seclusion.

During these three months a country resort must be found, everything in it arranged as comfortably and harmoniously as possible, and a small trustworthy court formed. In April the precious patient would be escorted, with care, to the chosen residence and there, in the middle of May, the infant would actually be born.

It was upon the subsequent two months that the whole matter turned. That period alone would be really perilous, and the partisans of the rightful Grand Ducal house were here called upon to form as a stone wall of loyal hearts round an exalted secret. At the end of it, on the fifteenth of July, a cannonade—the cannonade, it was to be hoped, of a hundred and one guns announcing the birth of a male heir—from the old citadel of Babenhausen would proclaim to town and country the great and happy news.

Certainly one would have to be careful even after that date. The traditional pompous baptism must be held within a few weeks. Here it was a lucky thing that the old Archbishop was extremely short-sighted. After this great event the young princely couple might quite naturally take up their summer residence for the rest of the season. And about the end of September the proud Babenhauseners would be pluming themselves on their lusty and clever little Prince.

The Grand Duchess went through the plan carefully and approved of it. In further meetings between her and Herr Cazotte, at times joined by the young father-to-be, it was built up in detail.

The choice of the residence itself was entrusted to Herr Cazotte. After various expeditions this gentleman for Princess Ludmilla's place of confinement picked out the little chateau of Rosenbad, a rococo hermitage, charmingly situated on a mountain slope by a lake and among woods, and isolated from the rest of the world. For a month he devoted all his talents to fitting out and furnishing the place.

Next a list of the members of the small court was drawn up. Old Professor Putziger as a matter of course would be staying at the chateau in constant attention to the Princess. A distinguished *Oberhofmeisterin* was found in the Countess Poggendorff, who twenty-five years before had been maid-of-honor to the Grand Duchess herself. The Grand Duchess' old maid and valet were transferred from her service to that of her daughter-in-law. The roll was lengthening sweetly.

The Grand Duchess, participating in an intrigue, was rejuvenated by thirty years. She might to the one side partake of her consort's legitimate dynastic gratification, while to the other she kept herself pleasantly occupied by little tête-a-têtes with Herr Cazotte. She even undertook two trips to Schloss Rosenbad.

A problem presented itself with the nomination of a maid-of-honor to the Princess. The present one was not, to the mind of the Grand Duchess, all that could be desired, for she had three married sisters at court, all three notable gossips. The question when gone into proved more difficult than first assumed, for the young lady who was to hold the office would have to be of such birth, education and appearance as would to the eyes of the world justify her election. She would furthermore have to be young and sweet-tempered, since the Princess in her seclusion would want a companion of her own age and temperament. And where does one, these days, find a pleasant young girl of the highest society with the elevation of mind, the steadfastness of character and the unwavering loyalty of heart demanded by the situation? Tell me that, my dear Herr Cazotte!

Herr Cazotte sat for some time in silence with a thoughtful face. Possibly he had already made his choice, but was taking pleasure in letting the highborn maidens of Babenhausen pass muster before his inner eye.

In the end he said: "Ehrengard von Schreckenstein."

"Schreckenstein?" the Grand Duchess asked. "The daughter of that General von Schreckenstein who was my father-in-law's aide-de-camp?"

"The same," said Herr Cazotte.

"But my dear Herr Cazotte," the Grand

Duchess exclaimed after a moment. "The Schreckensteins are Lutherans!"

"They are?" said the painter, as if pleasantly surprised.

"One of the few old Lutheran families of the country," said the lady. "A very stern, indeed puritan breed. All military people."

"A most fortunate coincidence," said Herr Cazotte. "If the Roman Catholic mind has a greater picturesqueness, the Lutheran mind has a steelier armature—an armature, Madame, being that iron skeleton round which the sculptor builds up his clay."

"The General," said the Grand Duchess, "was first married to a von Kniphausen and by her had five sons, all in the army. Then later in life he married a Solenhofen-Puechau and by his second wife had this daughter. Where have you seen the girl? I seem to remember her now," she added. "Nothing much to look at."

"O Madame," said Herr Cazotte. "Speak not so. She has been presented at Court, and I have seen her. In a white frock. A young

Walkyrie. Brought up in the sternest military virtues, in the vast and grim castle of Schreckenstein, the only daughter of a warrior clan. An almost unbelievably fitting white-hot young angel with a flaming sword to stand sentinel before our young lovers' paradise!"

"*Gauche*," said the Grand Duchess thoughtfully.

"Young," Herr Cazotte agreed. "Long-legged. With big hands and a forehead like a Nike."

"I have been told, I think," the Grand Duchess remarked, "that the Schreckenstein girl is to marry her cousin, a von Blittersdorff, of my guards. Or that, although there be no official engagement, the marriage for a long time has been agreed upon by the families. Will not the girl blab in her letters to her fiancé?"

"Unless the young guardsman's birthday falls within our particular two months," Herr Cazotte answered, "I doubt whether the young lady will be writing him any letters at all. The Schreckensteins are not a literary family."

"I shall think the matter over," said the

Grand Duchess. "For mind you, this is a very important post on our list."

"The most important of all," said Herr Cazotte, "with the exception of one. Of that of a gentleman with sufficient knowledge of the world, and with sufficient deadly devotion to the house of Fugger-Babenhausen, to act as liaison officer and to be moving freely between the outside world and the enchanted castle. Him it may take us some time and trouble to find."

"That gentleman," said the Grand Duchess, "has already been found and already been appointed." With these words she gracefully gave Herr Cazotte her hand to kiss.

The great lady, after having thought the matter over, had an interview with General von Schreckenstein.

This gray-haired warrior, inflexible in his military doctrines, held vaguer views on sentimental matters, the which he took to be mainly women's domain. He listened to the flattering confidential princely communication and made no questions. The situation, he gathered, would involve no trifling with the sacred, fundamental principle of legitimacy. And no Schreckenstein had ever failed in loyalty to his Sovereign. He would, he said, inform and instruct his daughter.

Herr Cazotte himself later paid a visit to the castle of Schreckenstein. He was familiar with the plan and the history of the place and enchanted with its medieval ramparts and dungeons. He also enjoyed General von Schreckenstein's complete ignorance of his own name and work.

So the name of Ehrengard von Schreckenstein was entered into the Grand Duchess' list of the Schloss Rosenbad household.

❧

And with this settlement, my dears, the prelude to, or the first movement of my little story terminates. I shall name it "Prince Lothar." Now, entering upon the next chapter of the tale, we are moving from the town to the country, into the peaceful setting of big trees, clear lakes and grassy slopes. My second movement is a pastorale, and shall be named "Rosenbad."

Herr Cazotte in the last week of April wrote to my great-grandmother:

My Dearest Friend and Benefactress,

You ask me for a description of Schloss Rosenbad. Imagine to yourself that you be quietly stepping into a painting by Claude Lorrain, and that the landscape around you becomes alive, balsamic breezes wafting and violets turning the mountain sides into long gentle waves of blue! And imagine, in the midst of this delightful scenery, our small scene and temple of delight. You may mount the stairs at liberty and walk undisturbed from room to room: an artist and poet, you will then admit, has gone through the house before you and has made it speak.

You have seldom seen me satisfied with my own work, and often distressed by my own worthlessness. Do not, now, shake your head at my outburst of triumph. The triumph is not mine, and I take no credit for it. I am in service, "Ich dien."

The Goddess of Love, the Lady Venus herself, has entrusted me with the work, and I have only followed her instructions. In the landscape, the light, the season and the situation itself she has whispered to me and ordered me to re-erect, in the blue mountains, her ancient, sunken and slandered residence: the Venusberg.

How hard and happily I have worked in her employ. I have succeeded in preserving the charm of remoteness, reverie and decay of the place, and I have polished it, upholstered it in silk and colored it in tints of rose, making of it a nest of classic elegance and comfort. Look up and down, right and left, with your most critical eye—you will not find a single tone which be not harmoniously tuned into the harmony of the whole. Voluptuousness breathes through the rooms, stairs and corridors, voluptuousness lingers in the folds of the curtains and smilingly gazes at you from the tapestries on the walls. In these surroundings our young Princess cannot fail to give birth to an amorino.

I am holding a privileged post at the Venusberg Court as mediator between Rosenbad and Babenhausen. And what a happy côterie we form inside the magic ring! A particular charm is given to our daily life by the fact that our circle has had to be restricted to a minimum. We are gardeners and milkmaids, grooms and waiters in the service of the seaborn Goddess. I myself, as you know, am a fairly skilled chef and do often give a hand to old François.

The good Babenhauseners turn their eyes towards the Venusberg with loyal approval and hope, discussing the bulletins. We are silent, mentally each of us has a finger on the lips. But through our silence ripples of smiles are running. At times I hear the drops of the Venetian chandeliers jingling with subdued laughter and the jets of the garden fountains joining in.

Is not your boudoir as you open this letter filled with fragrance?

Your most deeply devoted
Cazotte

P.S. Walking in the garden this evening Prince Lothar said to Princess Ludmilla: "So here is Paradise." And with her head upon his shoulder his young wife echoed: "Paradise." I smiled benevolence on them, like an archangel assisting the Lord in laying out the garden of Eden, and smiling on the first human male and female. But the great landscape architect himself, when his work had been completed, on looking at it and listening to the Gloria and Hallelujah of his angelic chorus, will have felt the craving for a clear, unbiased eye to view it with him, the eye of a critic, a connoisseur and an arbiter. With what creature, in all Paradise, will he have found that eye, Madame? Madame— with the Serpent!

Your obedient servant, etc.
On the first of May he again wrote:

I saw, at a court ball, a girl in a white frock, the daughter of warriors, in whose universe art, or the artist, have never existed. And I cried with Michelangelo: "My greatest triumph hides within that block of marble."

Since then I have at times ventured to believe that it be this vision of mine which has caused our entire course of events and has, in the end, lifted my young eaglet off her native mountain peak to drop her in the flower garden of Rosenbad.

What will be now, to the true artist, the fine fleur of her being? In what act is a nature like hers, within the chosen moment, to give forth itself most exhaustively? I have pictured her in every possible situation and posture, in itself a sweet pursuit.

And I made my decision. In the blush.

You will not, I know, for a moment be thinking of the blush of offended modesty which might be called forth, from the outside, by a coarse and blunt assailant, if one coarse and blunt enough could be found. To the mind of the artist the very idea is blasphemy, he turns away his face from it. You will no more be thinking of the blush of anger, the which, from the outside, I myself —preserve me—might bring about. None of the two would, in any case, be what I want. Events from outside will, by law of nature, come to Ehrengard and will mean nothing at all to her. She will marry—and I do not envy the man who is to enter into relationship with the Schreckensteins, personally I should prefer to enter their dungeon—she will bear ten soldier sons, and it will mean nothing at all to her. What is really to happen to this admirable, this unique nature is to happen within herself.

So I shall in time be drawing my young Amazon's blood, not down onto the ground —for I dislike the sight of human blood outside the human body, it is the wrong color and mars a picture—but upwards from the deepest, most secret and sacred wells of her being, making it cover her all over like a transparent crimson veil and making it burn her up in one single exquisite gasp of flame.

If I have succeeded in placing her in surroundings and in a situation which might bring a blush to the cheek of another virgin, I do by no means wish her to blush in reluctance to, or from fear of, the perils round her. No, her blood is to rise, in pride and amour-propre, in unconditional surrender to those perils, in the enraptured flinging over of her entire being to the powers which, till this hour, with her entire being she has rejected and denied, in full, triumphant consent to her own perdition. In this blush her past, present, and future will be thrown before my feet. She is to be the rose which drops every one of her petals to one single breath of the wind and stands bared.

In high mountains, as you will know, there exists a phenomenon of nature called Alpen-Glühen.

Scientists will tell us that it is caused by a rare play of the spectral colors in the atmosphere, to the looker-on it is a miracle.

After the sun has set, and as the whole majestic mountain landscape is already withdrawing into itself, suddenly the row of summits, all on their own, radiate a divine fire, a celestial, deep rose flame, as if they were giving up a long kept secret. After that they disappear, nothing more dramatic can be imagined: they have betrayed their inmost substance and can now only annihilate themselves. Black night follows.

Tall white-clad mountains will naturally be a little slow in the uptake, but when at last they do realize and conceive, what glow, you heavens, and what glorification. And what void afterwards.

I have seen the Alpen-Glühen once, the moment is among the greatest of my existence, and when it was over I said to myself that I would give ten years of my life to see this once more. And yet after all it has been but a presage of my adventure with Ehrengard.

Your obedient servant, etc.

Cazotte

Princess Ludmilla was exceedingly happy at Schloss Rosenbad.

She was delighted to be out of bed, in the open air and country and in the company of people with whom she could speak openly. She felt affectionately towards each member of her small court.

Herr Cazotte, in the center of it, by now was an old friend. He played the piano to her French and Italian songs; entertained her with gossip and anecdotes; when she had no appetite he concocted with his own hands marvelous cosmopolitan dishes; and from his visits to town brought back fine old lace for the dainty princely cradle.

Countess Poggendorff, the *Oberhof-meisterin*, encompassed her young mistress with graceful attention. From the coquettish lace cap on her head to the tip of her dainty shoe, the tiniest lady's shoe in Babenhausen and a bit smaller than her foot, she was an emotionalist, and impressionable like a girl of fifteen. Once again within romantic surroundings and in an atmosphere of passion and danger she saw her own youth revived, charmed everybody and radiated a *languissant* benevolence on the household.

And as far as Princess Ludmilla's relations with her new young maid-of-honor were concerned, the Princess, heavy with the sweetness of life, like a bee on its way home to the hive, was unable to see in her companion anything less than a sister. When the two girls slowly made the round of the rose garden, Ludmilla, who was the younger and smaller, would lean on Ehrengard's shoulder, but how infinitely wiser and more experienced, how much the elder sister did she not feel the while. At times she was almost afraid to display her immense superiority, she would then become more tender in her manner and would only reveal her advantage in a kind of tender raillery.

She was intrigued by Ehrengard's lonely life at the Schreckenstein castle, asked her questions about her five tall brothers, whom she had seen at court, and shuddered at the description of the blizzards in the mountains and the ghosts in the old gray block of stones. She was keen to learn about her friend's handsome young fiancé and his courtship. Ehrengard, in order to supply the information expected from her, had to think a good deal more about Kurt von

Blittersdorff than till now she had ever done. Kurt, she informed the Princess, had fought several duels.

"But were you not terrified then, beside yourself with fear and grief?" Ludmilla asked.

"Kurt is a very good swordsman," Ehrengard replied. "He has taught me to fence too."

"Have you kissed him, Ehrengard?" Ludmilla enquired after one of her long pauses.

"Yes, I have kissed him many times when we were children," said Ehrengard. "He is my cousin. While he was at school he used to stay at Schreckenstein during his holidays."

After another pause Ludmilla asked: "Have you two ever had a secret together?"

"Yes," Ehrengard again answered. "When the boys had done something bad, and I helped them to keep it from Papa."

The Princess was silent, then suddenly exclaimed in a low voice: "Try to have a secret with him. Something that, in the whole world, only you and he know of. You will be feeling, then, that he is you and you are he."

Herr Cazotte wrote:

Ehrengard—like, I believe, most people of severely moral milieus—is not aware that she has learned any principles, and indeed does not know the meaning of the word principle. Her moral code she takes to be a codex of laws of nature, the which you need not explain or uphold since they will explain and uphold themselves.

She is a country-bred girl, and familiar with the facts of life. She knows at what date after the wedding a child should be born. With servant girls of Schreckenstein irregularities have occurred, she has watched the abhorrence and wrath in faces of old housekeepers and governesses, and to her, then, as by the very law of gravitation, the girl in question has been a fallen woman. But inasmuch as the one fundamental law of her own nature is the loyalty of the house of Schreckenstein to the house of Fugger-Babenhausen, in present circumstances the reversion of the rule is legal and logical. A moral volte-face of this kind might be difficult to an old trained casuist, but a young girl will accomplish it with a high hand.

The paradox of our relationship is therefore this: that while I am making her drink in by eye, ear, and nostril and by every pore of her clear skin the sweet poison of the Venusberg, it is I who am, in reality, teaching her and impressing upon her the nature and the necessity of moral principle. When she has fully appropriated the nature of principles and the necessity to herself of principles, then I am victorious, then the moment of my triumph has come.

In the meantime I am enjoying every mien and movement of my youthful victim. It has taken five hundred years of isolation, discipline, and consciousness of absolute power, and of total abstinence from and ignorance of the arts, to make these. A wild animal, when it believes itself unobserved, moves and gazes about in that same way. Diana once walked through the woods of

Arcady like that. At the same time she is, as the Grand Duchess pronounced, gauche.

Of an evening, while the Princess rested on her sofa, Prince Lothar would play chess with Ehrengard. To him the chessboard was a deeply fascinating symbol of life and worthy of his entire attention. Ehrengard had been taught the game by General von Schreckenstein who, by now cut off from actual military exertion, still liked to practice his strategic skill and to operate with cavalry, artillery and infantry.

Herr Cazotte wrote:

In many ways—although without possessing his talents or his sentiment—she is so much like the Prince that the two might well be brother and sister. When I spoke to the Grand Duchess of plastic unity of being, I might have been discussing the maid-of-honor. Both are strikingly straight and well-balanced. But while the balance of my young lord is heaven-aspiring, like that of a young tree striving towards zenith, the girl is bal-

anced to perfection in the manner of those
little toy figures with lead at the base of them,
which cannot be overturned.

Prince Lothar was an eager horseman as
well, and in the beginning of May, when to all
sides and in every way the landscape was getting lovelier, he invited his wife's maid-of-honor
to accompany him on his rides. At times Herr
Cazotte would join them.

Herr Cazotte wrote:

*Ehrengard has found the horses of our
Rosenbad stables too sedate for her taste, and
has asked to have her own mount brought
from Schreckenstein. It is a fine and fiery
black horse named Wotan, hard for anybody
to manage but its young mistress herself.
When those two lead the way, we are all
making light of hurdles or ditches. My Lord
Lothar admires Ehrengard as a fearless horse-
woman. I myself wonder whether the reckless
rides be not unconscious attempts at escape.
She is getting uneasy in the heavily-scented*

air of Rosenbad and begins to find it difficult
to draw her breath in it. Her whole vigorous
youthful constitution cries out for strong ex-
ercise. My gallant Ehrengard! You would
never consent to run away from a danger. Set
your mind at rest, from your present danger
you cannot run away.

On the eighth of May a little Prince was
born at Schloss Rosenbad.

As the first shrill, preternatural cry rang
from the Princess' room round which the household had been listening, the chateau trembled
and was changed from cellar to attics. A sigh
of happy relief ran through all rooms. But in
the very next instant the silence became infinitely deeper and more momentous. Who would
have the heart to betray the tiny defenseless
newcomer? Death to each inhabitant of the
house would be preferable.

A lovelier child had never seen the light of
day in Babenhausen. Professor Putziger himself
was surprised at the faultlessness of the infant
and put on an additional pair of glasses to ex-

mine it. The trusted midwife, who had once helped Prince Lothar into the world, was bound to admit that the son outshone the father. Countess Poggendorff cooed before the cradle: "*L'on se sent plus belle devant une telle beauté! L'on se sent plus innocente devant une telle innocence!*" From the silky topknot to the rosy toenails the baby was perfection.

A courier was at once dispatched to the Grand Duchess. The poor lady, for fear of publicity, had not dared to break off her stay with the Grand Duke at their usual watering place. She had passed the last weeks in a state of great nervous excitement by the side of her unsuspecting husband. Her sudden outburst of tears at the apparently insignificant tidings from Rosenbad, as a sign of unwonted weakness in his consort, made the Grand Duke resolve to prolong their sojourn at the bath.

A new figure, of great importance in the household as well as in this story, now made her appearance in the Rosenbad circle. Her name was Lispeth. Magnificently dressed in the costume of the province, with embroidered cambric and long silk ribbons, she was a pleasant sight, big and buxom, pink and white, with a round, gentle and genial face. She was the daughter and granddaughter of faithful gamekeepers to the Grand Ducal house, and already some time ago had been picked out by the Grand Duchess and Professor Putziger, with the utmost regard to physical and moral qualities, as nurse to its small hope.

The young mother, in the satin and lace of her four-poster, at the first sight of the young peasant woman had shed a few tears of jealousy. But she was soon won over to see her rival as a kind of second self, stronger and wiser and with more knowledge of life, for Lispeth had got two children beside the baby which she had left in order to give her warm bosom and heart to the little Prince, an arbiter and oracle in all vital matters. Her privileged position was acknowledged in the house, Countess Poggendorff and Herr Cazotte took trouble to ingratiate themselves with the country woman who spoke the strong dialect of the province.

The problem of the baby's christening had

now to be settled. The great ceremony within the cathedral of Babenhausen would be taking place towards the end of July. How then were things to be managed during the interval of ten weeks? To have a child christened twice is blasphemy. Yet could his devotees consent to expose their precious charge to any bodily or spiritual risks by leaving him unbaptized for that length of time? Lispeth took her place on the council as an expert on changelings and oafs. Steel, she declared, must always be kept in the cradle, rats or mice must not be mentioned, yarn must not be wound, and by no means must the name of the Devil be as much as whispered inside the walls of the chateau. Herr Cazotte, himself being a son of the people, enjoined all these precautionary measures.

Herr Cazotte wrote:

Ehrengard undoubtedly for the first time in her life and without knowing it herself, as altogether she knows very little about herself, has fallen in love. It will serve my purpose. To fall in love with the God of Love himself may well be, to a mind of her energy and collectedness, the first step towards a deeper, final fall. The guileless figure of Cupid, the embodiment of love, himself ignorant of and immune to the passion, is the most fatal of dolls. I have sometimes wondered at seeing mothers placidly encouraging their small daughters to play with dolls. A little girl is a deep creature and may by instinct know more about the facts of life than the elderly maiden governess who teaches her her ABC's. And while the Mama is looking to the future and reasoning that to her daughter the moment of supreme sacrifice will be lying a full fifteen years ahead, the daughter with her delicate roots in the dark mould of the past will be aware of that supreme moment of her existence, lying only five or six years back.

My young lady of Schreckenstein till now has taken no interest in infants. She has, she tells me, got nephews, but she has seen little of them and does, I understand, view them mainly as generals-to-be. The pathetic gracefulness of a baby to her is a new and surprising phenomenon. She does not smile and sigh over the little Prince as does our sweet Madame Poggendorff, she stands up straight by the cradle side, lost in contemplation. Once, as his nurse held him up, I saw her slowly raising his hand to her lips and passing the small fingers over them one by one, thoughtfully, as if a little alarmed by the softness and smoothness of the skin.

Am I jealous? By no means. I take it as a pretty compliment on the part of the God of Love that he should call, in the flesh, on his devoted priest.

Now that the maid-of-honor was partly relieved of her duty as companion to her mistress, she did not always know what to do with herself at Rosenbad and welcomed Herr Cazotte's conversation. It even became obvious to the small court that she preferred his company to that of others and would look round for him if she did not find him in the room or on the terrace.

The great artist was gentle and courteous, if a little impersonal, in his manner with the highborn maiden. From his rich treasury of knowledge he took out for her benefit strange tales of ancient times, theories of art and life and fancies of his own on the phenomena of existence. He entertained her, too, with narrations of his own eventful life, dwelling on the days when he was a poor boy in shabby clothes, or slightly touching on his triumphs at academies and courts, and sprinkling his talk with accounts of the life of outcasts in dark streets or with bits of scandal from sublime places.

He found that the girl had read little and lent her books from his exclusive library or read out to her in the shade of the big trees. Poetry, new to her, puzzled and fascinated her. Herr Cazotte had a voice made for reciting poetry and had often been asked to read by princesses and *beaux-esprits*. At times he would lower the book with a finger in it and go on reciting with his eyes in the tree crowns.

On a very lovely evening he had been reading to her in the garden and was slowly accompanying her back to the house, when he stopped and made her stop with him by a fountain representing Leda and the swan and repeated a stanza from the poem they had last read together. He was silent for a while, the girl was silent with him, and as he turned toward her he found her young face very still.

"A penny for your thoughts, my Lady Ehrengard," he said.

She looked at him, and for a moment a very slight blush slid over her face.

"I was not," after a pause she answered him slowly and gravely, "really thinking of anything at all."

He had no doubt that here, as ever, she was speaking the truth.

Herr Cazotte wrote:

You smile, dear friend, at my complaints that Ehrengard occupies my mind too much and is monopolizing it to such an extent that I am in sheer self-preservation longing for the moment when I shall have done with her and be free to take up other interests in life. And although you be the glass of matronly virtue to all Babenhausen, you will be asking in your heart: "Why does not the silly fool seduce the girl in the orthodox and old-fashioned manner and set his mind at rest?" My answer to your question is: "Madame, the silly fool is an artist."

He is at this moment an artist absorbed in and intoxicated by the creation of his chef d'oeuvre. Food and rest are nothing to him, he is fed by winged inspiration as the Prophet Elijah was fed by his ravens. Allow me to let you participate in the working of an artist's mind.

I insist on obtaining a full surrender without any physical touch whatever. I kiss the hands of our married ladies and have respectfully placed a kiss or two on Mistress Lispeth's broad brown hand, while I have hardly brushed with my own Ehrengard's slender, strong fingers. But how resolutely do not the hands of my mind caress every part of hers, how insistingly run over the inmost strings of her being, tuning them to wheel from them their deepest sounds and vibrations.

I might, upon your friendly advice, undertake to seduce the girl in the orthodox and old-fashioned manner, and the task might not be as difficult as it looks. All marble she is not; were she so, she would not interest me. She has within her fire enough for an artillery charge and warmth enough for a cow house, the Schreckensteins having been, for five hundred years, both condottieri and cattlemen. I might seduce her, for she is impulsive and unreflecting, in a particularly impetuous moment of hers. And, Madame, it would mean nothing.

For her ruin, in such a case, would be a fact and a reality. And she knows about facts and realities—as the daughter of a long line of men of action she very likely knows more about them than your humble servant. She might, in such a case, save herself by some real and actual measure. She might well, in one single, deadly collected movement, renounce the world and retire to desiccate, a dumb, tall mummy on horseback, upon her mountain. Or she might seize upon the idea of revenge and rouse her brothers and her young fiancé to kill me, a very brutal end to an artistic enterprise.

Set your mind at rest. She is safe within my hands and will be more thoroughly seduced than was ever any other maiden.

Pious people tell us that our moments of earthly delight be but echoes of a former, heavenly existence. I believe them. It will be so with Ehrengard von Schreckenstein when I have accomplished my task. From the moment when, in deep gratitude, I have bared my head to her and left her, any touch of physical delight within her life to her will be but the echo of my celestial embrace.

How will she, then, save herself? To the world I have never in the least compromised her, yet she will know herself to be ultimately and hopelessly compromised. The world did not grudge sweet Gretchen—the heroine of my gigantic namesake—her guilt, it admitted her crime of infanticide and her debt to the sword of justice. To that same world Ehrengard will still be on her pedestal, the snow-white virgin, and yet she will know herself just as clearly as Gretchen to be fallen, broken and lost. Will she not then, in her turn, in sheer self-preservation, be dependent on me as the one and only confirmer of her perdition, the unique guarantor of the loss, the blowing up of her virginity? Will she not for the rest of her life be dragging herself after me, wringing her hands, crying out my name incessantly, regularly, with the might of all the clocks of Babenhausen? Alas, Madame, she will not catch me up, for I shall be away painting other fair ladies, having handed her over, intact but annihilated, to the fond cares of a young husband who will never have the faintest notion that he is drinking up my remains.

And will not then, you ask me, her ruin be a fact and a reality? Verily, my friend, it will be so, inasmuch as the reality of Art be superior to that of the material world. Inasmuch as the artist be, everywhere and at all times, the arbiter on reality.

I have, on a trip to town, taken the trouble to look up our young guardsman. He is, by the way, shortly coming up to this neighborhood for the big maneuvers, but will naturally have no chance of recalling himself to his fiancée. I have found him to be all that I can desire for the role of a spiritual cuckold.

My heart kisses your hand.

Cazotte

P.S. Why should I not confide to you a fancy of mine which much occupied my thoughts at the time when I was a small lonely boy bewildered in existence, at the time before I met you? As you have been aware, I have never known the name of my father. Still, a father I will have had, and I thank him for contributing to giving me eyes, ears and a nose with which to enjoy the world. The little street Arab of Babenhausen took in, transported, the sights, sounds and smells round him. He was deeply in love with color and brilliancy and would follow the soldiers and the dashing officers in the streets, dwelling on the idea that one of these were his father. Now when in the early spring I visited the Schreckenstein castle this long-forgotten whim suddenly came back to me: why should not that imposing figure, General Schreckenstein, be my papa? We are alike in many ways. I, too, have got small ears set close to the head, and I, too, am fearless by nature. The General as a young guardsman will have had his amourettes in garrison towns, and to seduce and abandon a housemaid to him will have seemed a matter of no consequence. Yet the order of the Universe is sublime, graceful and inexorable. Inside it nothing is without a consequence, but your first move on the board may in the end pronounce you mate. A thoughtless move on the first night of July —for I was born, as all through our acquaintance you have been kind enough to remember, on the first of April, a true and guaranteed fool—may snow you under, finally, in your gala uniform and decorations and your towering castle. Unwillingly the father initiates the son into the law that things have got consequences, that even a case of seduction will have them, and the initiated brother passes on the knowledge to his young sister.

And what lofty spiritual heavenly court of justice will pass sentence on my case of lofty, spiritual, heavenly incest?

It was a kind of rite in the life of Herr Cazotte that he should pass the first night of July out-of-doors. Faithful to it, on that same night, shortly after the court and the household of Rosenbad had gone to bed, he walked out below pale stars in a pale sky, in a world dripping with dew and filled with fragrance. He first walked quickly to get away, then slowed down to gaze round him. As he did so his heart overflowed with gratitude. He took off his hat.

"What tremendous, unfathomable power of imagination," he said to himself, "has formed each of the smallest details here, and combined them into a mighty unity. I am no modest person, I think pretty highly of my own talents, and I venture to believe that I might have imagined one or the other of the things that surround me. I might have invented the long grass—but could I have invented the dew? I might have invented the dusk, but could I have invented the stars? I know," he said to himself as he stood quite still and listened, "that I could not have invented the nightingale.

"The blossoms of the chestnut tree," he went on, "hold themselves up straight like altar candles. The blossoms of the lilac seem to be rushing in all directions from the stem and the branches, making of the whole bush an exuberant bouquet, the flowers of the laburnum drop like golden summer icicles in the pale blue air. But the blossoms of the hawthorn lie along the branches like light layers of white and rosy snow. Such infinite variance cannot possibly be necessitated by the economy of Nature, it will needs be the manifestation of a universal spirit—inventive, buoyant and frolicsome to excess, incapable of holding back its playful torrents of bliss. Indeed, indeed: *Domine, non sum dignus*."

He strolled for a long time through the woods. "I am tonight," he thought, "paying my respects to the great god Pan."

The summer night lightened round him, the colors began to come out, tardily, as if reluctantly, in the grass and the trees. The wanderer's trouser legs were soaked high above his knees and set with burrs and thorns. In his pocket he had a round of bread and a slice of cheese, and he now sat down on the grassy slope of a small clear mountain brook to eat it, washing it down with ice-cold water from a small tin cup. Herr Cazotte, as far as food and drink went, was an ascetic. In his very young days he had been so from necessity, later, although he could value meat and wine to a nicety, by inclination, today he was keeping up the habit in order to preserve his figure. His simple meal finished, he leaned his back to a willow tree, and for a long time sat immovable, from the depth of his heart applauding the universe.

"And even little Johann Wolfgang Cazotte," he thought, "has been fitted in very prettily and is indeed at the moment indispensable to the mighty whole. As what?" After a pause he answered himself: "As a small, innocent and happy, wet and dirty satyr in the big dark woods."

He got up and started walking back. He had promised to assist Princess Ludmilla with the program for a little musical soiree, a surprise for Prince Lothar upon the anniversary of their first meeting. He was a punctual person, and as he walked he looked at his watch; he had plenty of time.

His path ran along the mountain lake. From time to time he stopped to let his eyes caress the landscape and his nose draw in the pure air. His walk would soon be over, and he would once more from the melodious solitude of the wood and the slope be back in the company of human beings who did not always understand him. He had sharp ears, and now he heard voices not far off, low, clear women's voices. He left the path and made his way through the shrubbery to get a view of the speakers.

Now, twenty feet away, somewhat below him where the lake narrowed and ended up, a couple of stone steps had been built into the green slope; here one could land a boat. Upon the steps were two female figures, in whom after a minute he recognized Ehrengard and her maid. Ehrengard was undressing, and the maid picking up and folding her garments. Just as he looked at her she let her shift drop to the ground and stood for a moment all naked, very quiet, gazing round.

Above the water sheet the haze was lifting like delicate layers of veils being withdrawn one by one. In the light of the coming sunrise it was roseate and opalescent, less white than the girl's body, the thin streamers clinging to her foot and knee like a lastly-shed, cobwebby garment. She stepped forth amid it, slender, strong, her head raised, her long tresses gathered together above it in a crescent. The maid collected her clothes and retired with them to the grass. The young girl seemed to be the only human being between the clear water and the clear sky. The trees and rushes were all her friends and playmates, unobserved like herself. She hesitated for a moment with one slim foot in the water, then went in, gently breaking its surface as she let it rise to her knee, bosom and shoulders. A little way out she stopped and lifted her arms to bind her hair tighter, as she got in deeper she filled her hands to bathe her face. She lingered in the water, moving slowly, a water nymph happily back in her element.

After a while she again ascended from the embrace of the lake. Her perfect solitude was broken as her maid came out from the bushes to wrap a big towel round her and, lowly chattering and chuckling, to rub her dry. Together they disappeared from view behind the shrub, their voices were still heard for a moment or two, then everything was silent once more, they had gone away.

Herr Cazotte became very grave. While watching the vision before him he had thought of nothing at all, his soul had been in his eyes. As now, slowly, he let notions and ideas come back to him, he realized that here he had been, as never before, elected and favored, over-whelmed with grace.

A unique motif had been granted to a

great artist, that was one thing. He had proved himself to be right, and more than right, in his valuation of the girl's beauty, that was another.

But the generosity of the Gods was more alarming and astounding still.

For their gift to him was of a direct and personal nature, the immortal powers had consented to cooperate with him in the purpose which had so long held him. Frolicsome they were, hilarious and magnanimous to excess. And dangerous, dangerous for a mortal, even for an artist, to associate with. He became still graver.

She would come back, of that he was certain. The Gods would not cheat him. Probably her early morning bathing in the lake was a recurrent event and a daily observance, which she was keeping secret to all the world with the exception of her maid.

The picture which he had here been ordered to paint—"Nymph bathing in a forest lake," or "The bath of Diana"—would be in itself a wonder and a glory, the crowning of his career as an artist. But more wonderful and glorious still would be the moment in which he was to set it before the eyes of its model.

In what possible way could he more fully and thoroughly make the girl his own than by capturing, fastening and fixing upon his canvas every line and hue of her young body, her complete, carefully hidden beauty, going over it, patting and dubbing every item of it with his brush, re-creating and immortalizing it, so that nobody in the world could ever again separate the two of them. It would be, unmistakably and for all eternity, Ehrengard, the maid from the mountains, and it would be, unmistakably and for all eternity, a Cazotte.

In the picture the face of the bather would be turned away. By no means would he betray or give away his maid-of-honor. He might show his masterpiece to Princes and Princesses, art critics and enraptured lay lookers-on, and to the girl herself at the same moment, and no one but he and she would know the truth. The connoisseurs round her would break out in delight at the beauty of the bathing figure; in little expert remarks they would, with their thumbs in the air, minutely go through this latest and loveliest nude of that great painter Cazotte. She would be, in the midst of the brilliant crowd, alone with him.

Her mind never worked quickly, it would take her two or three minutes to grasp her position. Three facts she would at the end of them have made her own. That she was beautiful. That she was naked—and already in the third chapter of Genesis such a recognition is reported to be fatal. And, lastly, that in being thus beautiful and naked she had given herself over to the Venusberg. And to him.

The figure on the canvas would remain chastely silvery before the ardent eyes of the spectators. But the maiden by his side would slowly become all aglow. Behind the shawl, silk gown, embroidered petticoats and dainty cambric, the straight, strong, pure body from heel to forehead would blush into a deep exquisite crimson, a mystical *rose persan*, which no clear water of a mountain lake would ever wash away.

Into that Alpen-Glühen upon which night follows!

No one in the world, and least of all she herself, would ever find words for the relation between her and him. But from that moment whenever he bid her farewell, he would be abandoning and forsaking her.

Herr Cazotte drew a deep sigh.

But indeed, indeed, he went on after a while, the Gods are dangerous playfellows, and he would have to be wary and watchful to the utmost degree. He must lie in wait, dead still, like the lion waiting for the antelope by the water hole. The faintest movement might ruin him forever. For had not, from the very beginning, he himself, the artist and arbiter, the true lover and servant of this young womanhood decreed that she were to blush not with indignation at an assault, but with ecstasy at a revelation, not in protest or self-defense, but in consent and surrender!

Herr Cazotte was of small assistance to Princess Ludmilla in the arrangement of her program. All through the evening he was so silent that in the end Prince Lothar laughingly cried to him: "Wolfgang, you are planning a new picture!" The painter looked up, grew a little pale, and after a moment very gravely answered: "Yes, forgive me. But I have got an order for a new picture."

The next day he travelled to Babenhausen in order to buy canvas, brushes and paint. And the following morning found him among the bush of the bank, setting up his easel and stretcher, and then waiting patiently for sunrise and for the vision of three days ago. The sunlight was on the higher slopes of the mountains and on the treetops when once more he caught the low, gentle women's voices approaching. The scene was the same as the first morning, and the whole of Herr Cazotte was in his firm hand as he put down his primary contours on the canvas.

Time was short, all too short, in a quarter of an hour she was gone. The sun shone on the lake and the landscape, but their soul had left them, leaving him himself in a vacuum as if he had suddenly gone blind. He took down his easel and collected his drawing things. He would have, every morning, this divine *quart d'heure*. For the rest of the day he kept the vision behind eyes closed to everything else. He locked the door to his study and kept the key in his pocket.

He worked on for a week, radiating a new mystic happiness, but silent, humble in mien and manner and particularly humble and submissive towards Ehrengard when the two were brought together by the daily life of the chateau. Only every morning he had a heart-rending moment when his nymph went away.

Then on the last day of the week her disappearance seemed to him more sudden than before, indeed inexplicably sudden. A sigh or a short subdued outcry, which could not have come from Ehrengard but might have been the maid's, went through the morning landscape— then it was like watching a doe in a wood: she was there, and then she was there no more, the space was empty.

He needed more tubes of paint and again went to Babenhausen. There in the colorshop he was struck by an instantaneous deadly apprehension. Ehrengard or her maid, he thought, might have spied him in the morning, and that might have been the reason for their supernatural disappearance. He dismissed the idea, he knew from experience that sooner or later in the course of a piece of work he would be the victim of some such terrible nervous misgiving. But he could not free himself of it, and on his return journey was both longing for and dreading his next meeting with Ehrengard. Would her face tell him without a word that there was to be no more bathing of Diana and that the glory of his life was never to be achieved?

He came back to Rosenbad late in the afternoon and found the ladies of the court assembled in the Princess' pale blue boudoir, which was filled like an aviary with twitter and trills of laughter.

During this last week the court had been curiously moved and agitated. For at the end of it the little Prince was to make his legal and ceremonial entry in the world. On Saturday the goal would be reached, the danger would be over, and therefore everybody was gay. But on Saturday, too, a strange, a dreamlike period would come to an end, the child would no longer be the secret of Rosenbad, and therefore everybody was a little sad.

The Princess today was *coiffée* for the first time and dressed in a pretty white negligée. She had watched the nurse bathing the baby, had snatched him from her aproned lap, and insisted on carrying him into her own room, still all shining like a figurine in the midst of a fountain. She was now, on the sofa, gently rolling him about on her knees and rubbing him in the lace of her peignoir. The Oberhofmeisterin, in an armchair by the sofa, repeatedly assured the mother that the child was really smiling. Ehrengard was standing up looking at the baby.

"O my dear friend," the Princess cried out at the sight of the painter, "you have come at the right moment. I feel, I am convinced, that never again, not even tomorrow, will he be as adorable as he is this afternoon. Do catch this perfect moment . . ."

"This momentary perfection," put in Countess Poggendorff.

". . . Pin it to your canvas and preserve it for the world to adore."

The child had grown lovelier with each of his sixty days, his small body was firm, smooth and dimpled, and as light as if he might at any moment lift himself and fly off. He was an easy and amiable baby and was seldom heard to cry. Herr Cazotte from time to time had been drawing up in charcoal and pastel small portraits of him, the which in due time, in September, would be shown in the Babenhausen gallery as illustrations of the infant's progress.

"Look at him, dear good Herr Cazotte," the Princess exclaimed. "Surely you will be needing a model for an amorino in a scene of love. I lend him to you for the purpose."

The gardener had just brought up a very large flat basket filled with fresh, abundant white stocks, and the lackey had placed it on the floor.

"Hand me the basket, sweetest Poggendorff," said Ludmilla. "I am sure that it is exactly like the basket in which the Princess of

Egypt found little Moses amongst the rushes. Poor, poor Princess, how she must have wept at the thought that he was not her own."

As the Oberhofmeisterin lifted up the basket, the Princess placed the baby upon the fragrant couch. "You have not looked at him nearly enough," she cried to Herr Cazotte. "Take the basket, Ehrengard, and hold it up for the Master to inspect."

At her request Ehrengard lifted the basket and the child from the Princess' knee, and on her strong arms presented them to Herr Cazotte. The painter, still reluctant to look her in the face, let his eyes rest on the baby. But the pose of her figure recalled to him a group by the great sculptor Thorvaldsen, "Psyche selling amorini." For a minute he stood quite still, his face like hers bowed over the fairy cradle. The scent of the stocks, an invisible cloud of Venusberg incense, encompassed their two heads. She was calm and happy, he felt; he might be calm and happy with her, with full confidence in the Gods.

"Princess," he said, "you have given me a

more than princely gift. For as the hart panteth after the water brook, so panteth the soul of the artist after his motif. And who knows whether the motif does not long for that work of art in which it is to be made its true self."

Lispeth appeared in the doorway, anxious about the unorthodox treatment of the baby. The little Prince was lifted from his bed of flowers, given back to the arms of his nurse, where he immediately began to squall, and carried away. Ludmilla drew Ehrengard down to her side on the sofa and put her arm round her waist.

"O Ehrengard," she said. "How I do wish that Prince Lothar and I had been even more thoughtless than we have, and that we had got a month more at Rosenbad."

The evening of that day was the most glorious of the summer. A golden light filled the air as golden wine fills a glass.

The Princess went to bed early. The Oberhofmeisterin, the maid-of-honor and the court painter made their usual tour of the garden. But Countess Poggendorff began to feel the air a little cool and was the first to return to the house, the two younger people following her slowly on the gravel path. Herr Cazotte wondered whether Ehrengard, as upon an earlier evening, was thinking of nothing at all.

As upon that earlier evening they passed the Leda fountain. Ehrengard slowed her steps, stopped and stood for a moment with the tips of her fingers in the clear water of the basin from which the breast and the proud neck of the swan rose towards Leda's knees. As she lifted her head, turned and faced Herr Cazotte, she was a little pale, but she spoke in a clear voice.

"My maid tells me," she said, "that you want to paint a picture. Out by the east of the house. I wish to tell you that I shall be there every morning, at six o'clock."

Herr Cazotte wrote:

> My dear good Friend,
> The damnable, the dynamic, the demonic loyalty of this girl!
> Yours in fear and trembling,
> Cazotte

Here, said the old lady who told the story, finishes that second part of my story which I have named "Rosenbad." It has gone a little slowly, I know—so, generally speaking, do pastorales. Now, to make up for the lost time, the last movement of my small sonata shall be a rondo, which perhaps you may even find to end up *con furore*.

❧

It has been told in the beginning of this tale that there existed in the Grand Duchy of Babenhausen a lateral branch to the dynasty. These fine people with their head, the Duke Marbod, a gentleman who had spent most of his life out of his own country and had married a lady-in-waiting to the Queen of Naples, we have been able to leave for a while to themselves, since they had been lying low from the time of Prince Lothar's wedding. Some of them had even shaken the dust of Babenhausen off their feet and taken up their residence elsewhere. Now unfortunately they come back into the tale as they came back into the country, sneaking upon a track and drawn by a scent.

For there is a strange quality about a secret: it smells of secrecy. You may be far from getting the true nature of the secret itself, you might even, had it been told you, be highly skeptical and incredulous of it—yet you will feel certain that a secret there be.

The early misgivings of the Grand Duchess in regard to the all too celestial nature of her son had been vague and undefined, she lacked knowledge of the world and of the nature of man to put them into words. Duke Marbod and his friends, who were of a grosser fabric, had had no scruples in setting up on their own a definite hypothesis of the case. Something about the Rosenbad establishment and the complete seclusion of the Princess and her court, set a cantankerous imagination running, and in the end a highly fantastic story circulating in the gang. Young Prince Lothar, it was declared, was incapable of being the father of a child, and Princess Ludmilla's pregnancy was all a farce. The ruling house, foreseeing its doom, was quietly preparing to hoodwink the nation, to carry through the pretence and in the end, in order to keep their rivals out of their rights, to present to a loyal people a child of obscure origin as heir to the throne. Absurd and unseemly rumors about pads provided for the transformation of the Young Princess' slim figure were made up—enough of that. The pack, as we ourselves will know, was running on a wrong scent; all the same, as we will also know, it was running on a scent.

Duke Marbod himself, who was never a man of many ideas, at the utmost reflected that it may always pay to fish in troubled water. But his partisans let their ideas multiply. In the end two of them, one a former officer of the hussars, the other a man about town, a wine merchant, took up their abode in "The Blue Boar," the inn of a village some five miles from Schloss Rosenbad, awaiting a chance to pry into the stronghold.

A very small and poor fish caught in their net was mistress Lispeth's husband, a young peasant named Matthias. This boy by his father-in-law, the gamekeeper, had been suspected of poaching and had long held a grudge against the whole of his wife's family. Now he felt himself ill-used beyond endurance by being robbed of his pretty wife. The mother of a suckling baby and of two children only a few years older had been tempted away from her home in order to act as chambermaid to a spoilt great young lady, who must needs have all her whims attended to, for, as his wife had definitely informed him, there was no baby to nurse at Rosenbad. The thing went against his peasant's sense of decency, it was as if you would have a fine milk cow cart flowers to market. On top of all he was from the very beginning jealous of Prince Lothar's valet.

Matthias had come up from his farm a couple of times and had been allowed into the lodge of the chateau to see his wife and give her news of the children. But his querulousness and jealousy on these visits had upset Lispeth, after each of them the little Prince had yelled his protest, and Professor Putziger had had to put an end to the meetings. Still the unhappy young husband would or could not go home, but came prowling round the forbidden area.

On the morning of the fourteenth of July he waylaid his wife as she was taking the air in the park and through the lattice of the gate told her that, convinced of her treacherousness, he would kill the valet or himself. Lispeth did not take his threats seriously, but she was terrified of a scandal at this moment and could see no other way out of the dilemma than to disclose part of the truth to her husband. Yes, there was a baby at Rosenbad. She could at the moment give him no further information, he must take it for what it was and might come to understand in time. If he would solemnly swear to her that he would go home immediately after, she would bring down the child to the gate in the afternoon, so that he could see it with his own eyes. Matthias took the oath, walked back to a small inn quite close to the chateau where he had left his mare and cart, and there to clear his confused mind emptied a bottle of wine. It was at this moment that he fell into the hands of Duke Marbod's intriguers.

The two gentlemen by this time had almost given up the hunt. They had not been able to get into touch with the Rosenbad household, only at a distance had they seen Prince Lothar, Herr Cazotte and Ehrengard riding by, and Herr Cazotte had been right inasmuch as that the presence of the young maid-of-honor averted suspicions of double dealing. They were about to return somewhat crestfallen to Duke Marbod, but had come up close to the gates for a last attempt. By chance they got into conversation with Matthias, who over his bottle babbled out the list of his misfortunes, his wife's shamelessness and the villainy of the whole court in barring out her lawful husband.

The gentlemen looked at one another.

In the eleventh hour they found themselves to have been right. Surprisingly, mysteriously, their own fancies and fabrications took shape before their eyes, and proof was at hand. After a short consultation, while pouring more wine into their informant, they gravely initiated him into the situation: a dangerous plot was in progress at the Schloss. They could at the moment give him no further information. But it was a matter of high treason, and very likely, as he had been suggesting, Prince Lothar's valet was at the head of it.

This much they could promise him, that in case he could manage to carry off the woman and the child and deliver them into their hands at "The Blue Boar," he would be rendering a great service to his country, and they would pay him out on the spot a reward of a hundred thaler. Matthias was not so much moved by these prospects as by the satisfaction of long-wanted sympathy, also in seeing his personal grievances exalted into an affair of state he got back some of his self-confidence.

Thus it happened that in the afternoon of the fourteenth of July the husband brought his cart to the gate of the park, was shown the child, and told his wife that he did now believe in her innocence and was ready to forget all. As the two were taking a final leave, he managed to lure the unsuspecting woman outside the gate and even to make her put her foot on the nave of the wheel and lift up the child in order that he might kiss it. At that moment he seized her round the waist with one arm and dragged her onto the seat of his cart, while with his other arm he slashed the mare wildly with the reins and made her start into a mad gallop. Lispeth gave one long, terrible scream. But a minute later they were at the foot of the hill in a thick cloud of dust, and once out of earshot from the chateau and the park the unhappy woman dared not cry for help. She clung to the child and the seat and burst into a storm of tears.

During the whole mad drive of almost an hour no word was exchanged between the abductor and the victim, and no argument put forth from either side. It would indeed have been difficult to catch any word spoken in the rumble and clatter which surrounded and followed the cart like a thick swarm of angry bees, or to think of any argument while the small vehicle was being flung up and down and from right to left on rough, stony roads. All the same husband and wife, pressed together, were in some way communicating and acting upon one another.

Lispeth had at once realized with deadly clearness that she was hopelessly in the power of the blunt, silent figure beside her. He had outwitted, lost and ruined her, and with her the Princess and the whole circle of people who had put their trust in her. She had thought him a fool, and he was a fool, but he was something else and worse, he had in him a dreadful cruelty which she had never suspected. She wept loudly and without restraint.

Matthias, who had vowed that no protest on his wife's part should move his heart, in the course of the drive was slowly being converted and brought into a state of contrition by that fine thing: the righteous fury of an honest person. Vaguely he felt the distance between the countrywoman in his cart, smelling from clean starched linen and bathed in artless tears, and the new urbane plotting friends smelling from pomade, waiting for him in the inn, and of the monstrousness of delivering the former into the hands of the latter. But tossed from side to side both bodily and spiritually he was incapable of forming any plan, and after a while left matters in charge of his mare.

This patient animal, possibly the most indignant of the group, could not go on forever at her first mad rate; as her master lost heart she slowed down. Lispeth then sat up a little, drew a deep breath and looked round.

Through the mist of her tears and the beginning dusk she saw a great many mounted soldiers galloping in the fields to all sides of her. She remembered the big maneuvers going on and somehow took courage, soldiers in uniform were decent people and would side with a woman against a madman and murderer. A short time later the road ran through a village and up to an inn which the mare knew, she stopped before its door. Matthias gave in to her, pushed his cap back on his head and silently, almost humbly, climbed down and helped his wife and the child to the ground. Dusk was coming on, there were lights in the windows of "The Blue Boar."

Behind them there was both high glee and merriment, and deep anxiousness.

The maneuvers were over. The officers were celebrating the occasion by a dinner in the big common room, from which loud talk and laughter rang. Here Kurt von Blittersdorff, who had distinguished himself in a cavalry attack, was being congratulated by his colonel. In a smaller room behind the hall there was silence. Duke Marbod's followers had not been prepared for the big gay gathering, they were afraid of being recognized and questioned, had chosen to lie low, and sat without words on two chairs, at times looking at one another.

Lispeth, Matthias and the child, like a second Holy Family of mystical inside relationship, were met at the door with the information that there was no room for them in the inn. Lispeth, sore-limbed and swaying on her feet with exhaustion, had only one thought: to find a place where she could feed the baby, and no words to express her need. But a kind of desperate determination in her mien and carriage, like that of a soldier dying on his post, moved the heart of a little maid of the inn, who herself had got young brothers and sisters at home, and who obtained for her a small room upstairs, where she could at last sink down on a chair and unbutton her bodice. The moment she had laid the child to the breast both became perfectly calm.

Matthias meanwhile slunk away to unharness the mare in the stable of the inn, highly nervous that his employers should somehow appear, or send for him, and happy when inexplicably they did not. He told the people of the inn that he had got nothing to do with anybody there and was going to leave as soon as his wife had had a rest. He then again slunk upstairs and sat down on a stool with his back to the wall in the exact manner of his friends down below. The little maid after a while brought up a candle and a tray with milk and bread and remnants from the officers' table.

During the time when these things were happening on the road and in the inn, emotions of a no less volcanic nature filled the rooms behind the silk curtains of Schloss Rosenbad.

When the child and his nurse were found missing, enquiries, at first only slightly uneasy, then inspired by growing fear and in the end by horror and dismay, were made in all directions. The baby and the nurse, it was said, had last been seen in the park. But a gardener's boy reported that he had observed Lispeth talking to a man outside the gate, and soon it was known that a cart with a man and a woman in it had been tearing down the road at incredible speed. There was no mistaking the fact that the little Prince had been kidnapped.

How, now, was Rosenbad to take in the truth and survive it? The cannons of the citadel of Babenhausen were held ready to proclaim, on the very next day, the birth of an heir to the throne, the flags of the palace were laid forth to be hoisted and fill the air over the towers with gay colors. Was the roar of triumph to be quelled in those iron throats and the sky to be left empty? Had the incessant watch of two months been in vain, and was the glory of Babenhausen to prove still-born? And oh, the child, the child—the trusting, laughing baby, the apple of the eye of Rosenbad—was he to be flung all alone into a hard world, possibly never to be seen again?

Two months ago when the very small voice had first been heard in its rooms, the house had been lifted off the ground to float, a temple of happiness, in the air above the lake and the green slopes. Now within one short hour it was overthrown as by an earthquake and was left roofless, open to all the winds of heaven, a ruin.

At first neither of the unhappy parents was informed of their misfortune. Prince Lothar had gone to town to bring his mother Herr Cazotte's latest miniature of the baby and would not be back till evening. Princess Ludmilla was studying the texts of her Italian songs for the concert and had given instructions that she was not to be disturbed.

But Countess Poggendorff in the garden room actually fell on her knees with the weight of all the falling stones of the chateau upon her delicate shoulders. When she got some of her strength back she rang the bell and sent for Herr Cazotte, and when he appeared she threw herself into his arms.

This heart-rending news, she declared in a faint and broken voice, must by all means be kept from the Princess, who might take her death from it, and meanwhile rescuers would have to be sent out to all four corners of the earth. But O my dear Herr Cazotte, who was wise and discreet enough to be trusted with a mission so momentous and so delicate!

Herr Cazotte at once ordered his small gig made ready and his cloak and hat brought down. While he waited he stood silent, with a thoughtful face.

As usual, he knew more than other people. He had seen Matthias on one of the man's vain expeditions to the chateau, he had even talked with him and had some of the offended husband's grudges confided to him. On one of his trips to town, upon a hot day, he had stopped at "The Blue Boar" to have a drink, and there had met the two conspirators, who were old acquaintances of his. He now put two and two together and blamed himself for having been so

absorbed in a single work of art as to overlook
the artifice of baser minds in the neighborhood.

But the terrible news was not unwelcome
to him. After his last walk by the Leda fountain
with Ehrengard he had passed a bad night and
had left his work untouched in the morning.
Now he saw that although they had been playing him a trick, those dangerous playfellows of
his, the Gods, were with him still. The course
of things was inspiring, and of all things in the
world Herr Cazotte really with his whole heart
wanted only one: inspiration. From the present
situation almost any other might arise, and Herr
Cazotte was a collector and connoisseur of situa-
tions.

The first of these presented itself when
Ehrengard came into the room, in her riding
habit and just back from her ride, and Madame
Poggendorff turned from Herr Cazotte to fall
on the neck of the girl, sobbing as unre-
strainedly as an hour before had Lispeth in the
cart and on the road. As soon as she was en-
lightened upon the catastrophe Ehrengard again
pulled on her riding gloves to go in pursuit of

the criminals. Countess Poggendorff begged her to go with Herr Cazotte in his gig, she did not like the thought of her facing these scoundrels all alone, and it was getting late. No, said Ehrengard, she was not afraid. Wotan was quite fresh, she had been out exercising Prince Lothar's mount for him, and she would be quicker on horseback than in a carriage. She knew all the roads and paths in the neighborhood, and if she were to stay out late she was used to riding at night.

Herr Cazotte did not try to hold her back. If she had the advantage of getting off before him, he on his side had a surer track to go upon. During the minutes in which he stood watching the tearful older and the flaming younger woman, a succession of charming pictures passed through his mind. He would be presenting the regained child to the girl to give back into its mother's arms, he might even be on his knees before her to do so. An amorino, the Princess had called her baby, an amorino indeed, joining, as with a garland of roses, a human couple. Would the girl not feel then for a vertiginous moment this particular amorino to be, spiritually and emotionally, her own child—and his! He himself got her into the saddle.

Wotan was in high spirits, when Ehrengard reined him in to question people on the road he reared, and she was so filled with indignation against the kidnappers on whose track she was trotting that she beat her mount with her riding whip. All the same she was happy, it was as if for a long time she had yearned to be angry. She was Ehrengard, no one could take that away from her, and, strangely, it was a privilege. The evening air was getting cooler, she rode through many spheres of fragrance: clover, flowering lime trees, and drying strawberry fields, through them all the ammoniac smell of the lathering horse was the strongest. She drew in her breath deeply, and ran on, with raised head and distended nostrils, a young female centaur playing along the grass fields.

She had the hunting instincts of her breed, it was not difficult to her to run the fugitives to earth in "The Blue Boar." The cart was still standing outside the stable, and she learned from an ostler of the inn that the man, the woman and the child were in the house, possibly, she thought, behind the lighted window above her head. She left Wotan in the man's care, ordering him to walk him up and down for half an hour and then to rub him well with a wisp of straw. There were, she noticed, a number of soldiers about the place, she felt happier still at this sight, they were people of her own kind, and it was as if she had got home.

Up in the small room behind the lighted window a temporary peace ruled. Lispeth had fallen into a short slumber with the child still at her breast. But Matthias was wide awake on his stool with his back to the wall. For a long hour he had been trying hard to sound the depth of his misfortune, from time to time also wondering what his fellow conspirators were doing, or thinking of him. The presence of his wife, however, the familiar sight of her suckling a baby and the familiar feeling that she would be able, somehow, to put things right, in the end had quieted his nerves. When she woke up, he reflected, he would drive her straight back to

Rosenbad. And possibly all might still be well.

He was startled out of this state of hope when the door was flung open and Ehrengard stood on the threshold. The girl in the ride had lost her hat, her long fair hair streamed down and framed her face and figure, to the guilty man those of a young destroying angel.

Lispeth, waking up too, saw the girl in the same light, but conscious of her innocence she at once welcomed the angel of revenge in a glance as expressive as an outcry. She remained perfectly still on her chair, only in a hardly perceptible movement of her arm she raised the baby's head so as to show that he was unhurt.

Ehrengard's gaze responded to Lispeth's in a declaration of perfect trust, then she turned to the kidnapper. The inviolable obligation of silence controlled the girl as well as the woman, she said not a word. But here, at the final goal of her ride, the old feudal consciousness of the right to punish seized and held the daughter of the Schreckensteins. She would have died rather than have foregone her office of chastiser.

She had left her riding whip with the horse

and was barehanded for the execution, she gripped Matthias by his long hair and three times knocked his head against the wall behind him till the room darkened and swam before his eyes. He gave out a row of low wails which, however, far from frightening his tormentor, infuriated her into striking him in the face with her fist, so that the blood spouted from his nose. In actual fear of his life, of being knocked to pieces by the strong young hands that held him, he made his cries for help ring through the house.

Down at the officers' dinner table the talk happened to have turned upon ghosts. One of the party had been recounting an old tale of "The Blue Boar" itself. A hundred years ago a jealous husband had followed his runaway wife and her lover to the inn, had found them together in a room upstairs and had dealt the seducer the treatment of Abelard. At certain times at night the gruesome scene was repeated in the room. At this moment Matthias let out his screams.

These were indeed pitiful enough to have moved the hearts of the dinner party, who probably feared the lot of the victim in the tale more than anything else in life. At the same time they were so far from being connected with any idea of romance that the short alarmed silence round the table was immediately swallowed up in laughter.

"You go up, Kurt," the colonel cried to that young officer, "and find out if it be ghosts or people. And come back whole yourself."

The tall young man pushed back his chair and left the room, followed by various loud and gay remarks. As he ran up the stairs, the screams from above were repeated.

He opened a door, and in a dimly lit small room caught sight of a deadly pale man pressed up against the wall by a slender young woman in a riding coat with long waves of golden hair flowing down her back. From a chair by the window a woman with a baby on her lap, with wide-open eyes but without a word, watched the scene.

When she heard the door open behind her, the Amazon let go her hold of the man and turned round.

"Ehrengard!" Kurt von Blittersdorff cried out in the highest amazement.

The girl's cheeks as she tossed back her hair were all aflame and her eyes shining. She opened her lips as if to cry his own name back, then stiffened, like a child caught red-handed.

The whole absurd situation was so much like one of their childhood romps that the young man almost burst out laughing. At the same time he felt uneasy about the girl's presence in the inn, with his fellow officers waiting for him downstairs.

"Ehrengard! What on earth are you doing here?" he asked.

The released sufferer profited by the respite to wriggle himself out of reach of his assaulter. He fumblingly ran his fingers through his hair, making it stand up straight like the quills of a hedgehog, and whimpered a couple of times. Although he was at the moment safe from molestation, he realized his position to be graver than before. Here was a gentleman, an officer, obviously a friend of his enemy and welcomed by her, unexpectedly on the stage. With three judges upon him what hope had he? Still, as a silence followed on the officer's exclamation he blindly groped for a way out and started on a harangue of defense.

"So God help me, Sir," he said, "I am a perfectly innocent man, and this is a very unfair attack on the part of the lady. That," he went on, pointing at the woman with the baby, "is my lawful wife. You ask her yourself, Sir, she will not deny it. Has the lady, has the lodge-keeper, has the Prince's valet, or has he himself, then, got any right to keep her away from me? They have not, Sir, and they know so themselves. For what God has joined together," he cried in a stroke of inspiration, "let man not put asunder."

He stopped for a moment, but his nerves could not bear the continued silence of the others in the room.

"So God help me, Sir," he started again, "it is I who am wronged. I want my lawful wife back, that is all I want. She tells me she cannot leave the child. Well, then let her take the child with her. I have not tried to stop her from taking the child with her. Only ask her if I have done so."

The lasting silence, Ehrengard's fury a little while ago, his wife's despair in the cart, and the persuasion and promise of the two gentlemen from town, if Matthias had been able to see these things as a whole, by now might have made the entire pattern dawn upon him. It was not so, his sore head reeled, anything might have thrown him in any direction. But hares, when the hounds are after them, in their wildest side leaps will show a kind of genius. Something in the atmosphere of the room suddenly told him where his chance of escape lay. It was with the child.

The child, who after the strenuous journey was now firmly asleep on Lispeth's bosom, was the mystery which his wife and the angry lady did by no means want solved. If he let out that he could do so if he wished, they might think more highly of him, they might even consent to buy his silence. As he spoke on he felt that he was on the right track.

"My wife, Sir," he said, "will tell you that

I have got no claim on the child, for it is not mine. If that is what the lady is going to tell you as well, let them tell you whose child it is."

Kurt gave Lispeth a short glance, then looked back at Ehrengard. Both women seemed to have been struck dumb by the man's speech. The situation, till now merely inexplicable, began to take on a different, a more momentous aspect. He must, he felt, put an end to a scene obviously beneath the dignity of his fiancée.

"Come," he said, "you cannot stay here. What have you got to do with these peasants? Why do you not leave them to settle their quarrels between themselves? I shall arrange at once for some convenience to take you back to Rosenbad."

He had not succeeded in getting one word out of her, neither did he do so now.

"There you see, Sir," cried Matthias triumphantly. "Neither of them will tell you."

There was a short pause.

"Well," Kurt asked in a steady voice. "Do tell me, Ehrengard. What child is it?"

At this moment they heard light steps coming up the stairs. It was Herr Cazotte who had arrived in his gig and who now entered the room.

He took in the situation in one glance. But he felt that at the moment and under the circumstances it did not fall to him to interfere. He placed his hat on the bed and after a minute sat down on the bed himself. There he remained, like some highly intelligent looker-on in a *fauteuil d'orchestre*, keenly interested in the drama on the stage and in full understanding with the fact that none of the *dramatis personae* took any interest whatever in him himself.

"You see, Sir," Matthias repeated in the same way. "They will not even answer you, neither of them."

Kurt, moved by a new strange, deep concern, again followed Matthias' lead.

"What child is it?" he asked.

Ehrengard still met his eyes and still did not answer.

"But if you will not answer me," Kurt said lowly, "I cannot help this woman or interfere with her husband."

She stood up straight, as if pondering his words.

"If you will not answer me," he said, "How am I to understand that you be here at all?"

Ehrengard said: "It is my child."

The young man had drunk a good deal during dinner, but up in this room he had believed the effect of the wine to have left him. Now at her declaration his head failed him, he must, he realized, have drunk more than he had been aware of. He laughed.

"Say that again," he cried. But as he would by no means have her say it again he went on: "Are you all mad up here? Come away with me."

"I shall say it again," said Ehrengard, and after a moment: "It is my child.

"You may ask Lispeth," she went on, "she will bear me up. This man, who is really, as he tells you, her husband, has kidnapped both the child and his nurse. I have gone after them and have found them here."

There was a long pause.

"It will," said Ehrengard, "as you say, be the best thing to get a carriage and go back. It is good of you to offer to help me. But I cannot accept your help unless you will give me your word that when you have brought me back to Rosenbad you will leave me forever."

Slowly and solemnly she once more announced, "For it is my child."

Kurt had grown very pale, his mind ran wildly through the time in which he had not seen her. His instinct of self-preservation cried out to him that she had gone mad. Again he laughed, a short pathetic laugh. But he could not go on laughing in front of her deadly earnest face, in a little while he became as grave as she.

"You will have to believe me," Ehrengard said. "I have never in my life lied to you."

He stood on looking at her. There had been, he now saw, a change in her since their last meeting six months ago. With the candle behind her and her mass of hair hanging down, she seemed to float in a mist of gold, much lovelier than he had ever seen her, much lovelier than any woman he had ever seen, a goddess or a demon. How was it that he had known her so long, had played with her, ridden with her, wrestled with her, had known that some day he was to marry her, and that until this hour he had not known that she was the most lovely thing on earth, and the one thing necessary to his happiness? This state of mind of his lasted for about a minute, then he knew for certain that he had always known.

It took him some time to form an answer. His faith in her, of so many years, together with his new need of her, contracted his throat and made it impossible for him to get out his voice.

"You will help me, then," said she, "and take me home. Then we must part. You must never speak of me. You must never think of me."

To Ehrengard, too, something was happening as here she stood up straight, face to face with Kurt's straight figure. She too felt, in a new way, the depth of life. There was a sweetness in it which till now she had never known of, there was a terrible sadness as well. She would never have believed, had anybody told her, that to meet and to part with Kurt von Blittersdorff could mean so much. The recognition at this moment was, she felt, the outcome of her stay at Rosenbad.

"Yes," Kurt said at last. "I shall do as you ask me. I shall go now and get the carriage to drive you back. I shall then leave you forever. I shall not speak of you more than I absolutely need. I shall try, as you say, not to think of you."

There was another pause.

"But," he went on slowly and lowly, "there is one question to which I must have an answer from you. I have no right to ask you. But neither have you any right to ask me never to think of you again. And that cannot be done, I cannot possibly leave off thinking of you, unless you answer it. Who is the father of the child?"

A silence. Neither the young man nor the girl could have told whether it lasted for a minute or an hour. The other people in the room sank through the floor, he and she were alone as on a mountain peak.

"It will be, Ehrengard," he said, "a secret between you and me, a thing which, in the whole world, only you and I know of."

Ehrengard had grown as pale as he. So colorless did her face become that her light eyes seemed dark in it, like two cavities. Then she turned and looked straight at Herr Cazotte. Under her glance the gentleman rose from the bed.

The girl's glance was strong and direct, like an arrow's course from the bowstring to the target. In it she flung her past, present and future at his feet.

She lifted her arm, like a young officer at his baptism of fire indicating to his men the entrenchment to be taken, and pointed at him.

"It is he," she said. "Herr Cazotte is the father of my child."

At these words Herr Cazotte's blood was drawn upwards, as from the profoundest wells of his being, till it colored him all over like a transparent crimson veil. His brow and cheeks, all on their own, radiated a divine fire, a celestial, deep rose flame, as if they were giving away a long kept secret.

And it was a strange thing that he should blush. For normally an onlooker in a *fauteuil d'orchestre* would grow pale at seeing the irate hero of the stage suddenly turn upon him. The actual situation held very grave possibilities to Herr Cazotte. A duel might be the immediate consequence of it, and Herr Cazotte, as it is known, disliked the sight of human blood outside the human body. Any gallant warrior of Babenhausen, knowing Kurt von Blittersdorff's reputation with a sword or a pistol, might have gone white, even white as death.

But Herr Cazotte, who was an artist, blushed.

Here ends the story of Ehrengard.

❧

But as I gave you a prelude to my story, said the old lady who told it, I shall give you an epilogue.

No duel took place. By the mediation of Prince Lothar and Princess Ludmilla a full understanding was obtained. A week later the betrothed couple Kurt and Ehrengard were present at the baptism of the new-born Prince in the Dom of Babenhausen.

Upon this occasion the girl wore, across the bodice of her white satin frock, the light blue ribbon of the Order of St. Stephan, the which is a distinction given to noble ladies for merits in the service of the house of Fugger-Babenhausen.

Herr Cazotte to the surprise of the court was not present at the ceremony. He had been called back to Rome to paint a portrait of the Pope.

It was here, now, that he had that famous liaison with a *cantatrice* of the Opera which caused much talk and made his acquaintances smilingly alter his name to that of Casanova.

When the Grand Duchess heard of it she was upset.

"I had really," she said, "during that time at Rosenbad, come to have such faith in Geheim-rat Cazotte."

ABOUT THE AUTHOR

ISAK DINESEN (1885-1962) was the nom de plume of Baroness Karen Blixen of Rungstedlund. Born of an old Danish family, she carried forward its tradition of making contributions to Danish literature while establishing a distinguished niche for herself in English as well as Danish letters. Her father gained distinction as a writer after he had served as an army officer and come to America, where he lived for several years as a trapper with the Pawnee Indians in Minnesota. Two of his books were published in Denmark under the pseudonym of Boganis, a title conferred upon him by the Pawnees. Her brother, Thomas Dinesen, a soldier in the First World War and an author of repute, was awarded the Victoria Cross for extraordinary valor.

The author of *Anecdotes of Destiny* was married to a cousin, Baron Blixen, in 1914 and went with him to British East Africa, where they established and successfully operated a coffee plantation. In 1921 she was divorced from her husband, but she continued to manage the plantation for another ten years, until the collapse of the coffee market forced her to sell her property and go back to Denmark. Her book, *Out of Africa*, records many of her experiences in the Colony with a painter's feeling for its sweeping landscapes and a sure-handed wizardry in communicating the character of its people. It was selected by the Book-of-the-Month Club and was received with acclaim by critics and readers alike.

Prior to the publication of *Out of Africa*, Isak Dinesen had established a firm place for herself in America with her first book, *Seven Gothic Tales*. That volume and *Winter's Tales*, her second collection of stories, were also Book-of-the-Month Club selections. Her third collection, *Last Tales*, was published in 1957. Four more stories with African settings were published in *Shadows on the Grass* (1961).

In 1957 Isak Dinesen was elected to honorary membership in the American Academy and National Institute of Arts and Letters. Reserved for foreigners who have made unusual contributions to the arts, honorary memberships in the academy-institute are limited to fifty.

VINTAGE BELLES—LETTRES

V-418   AUDEN, W. H.   *The Dyer's Hand*
V-398   AUDEN, W. H.   *The Enchâfed Flood*
V-342   BECKSON, KARL (ed.)   *Aesthetes and Decadents of the 1890's*
V-271   BEDIER, JOSEPH   *Tristan and Iseult*
V-512   BLOCH, MARC   *The Historian's Craft*
V-544   BROWN, NORMAN O.   *Hermes the Thief*
V-75   CAMUS, ALBERT   *The Myth of Sisyphus and Other Essays*
V-30   CAMUS, ALBERT   *The Rebel*
V-314   CLARK, ELEANOR   *The Oysters of Locmariaquer*
V-349   CURTISS, MINA (tr.)   *Letters of Marcel Proust*
V-535   EISEN, JONATHAN   *Age of Rock: The Sounds of the American Cultural Revolution*
V-655   EISEN, JONATHAN   *The Age of Rock 2*
V-112   GIDE, ANDRE   *Journals, Vol. I: 1889-1924*
V-113   GIDE, ANDRE   *Journals, Vol. II: 1924-1949*
V-363   GOLDWATER, ROBERT   *Primitivism in Modern Art*, Revised with 58 illustrations
V-402   GOODMAN, PAUL   *Hawkweed: Poems*
V-449   GRAY, FRANCINE DU PLESSIX   *Divine Disobedience*
V-438   HELLER, ERICH   *The Artist's Journey into the Interior and Other Essays*
V-663   HERRIGEL, EUGEN   *Zen in the Art of Archery*
V-456   JONES, ITA   *The Grubbag*
V-235   KAPLAN, ABRAHAM   *New World of Philosophy*
V-337   KAUFMANN, WALTER (tr.)   *Beyond Good and Evil*
V-369   KAUFMANN, WALTER (tr.)   *The Birth of Tragedy and the Case of Wagner*
V-436   KAUFMANN, WALTER   *Nietzsche: Philosopher, Psychologist, Antichrist*
V-401   KAUFMANN, WALTER (tr.)   *On the Genealogy of Morals and Ecce Homo*
V-437   KAUFMANN, WALTER (tr.)   *The Will to Power*
V-452   KESSLE, GUN, photographed by, with JAN MYRDAL   *Angkor*
V-230   LEEDOM, WILLIAM S.   *The Vintage Wine Book*
V-329   LINDBERGH, ANNE MORROW   *Gift from the Sea*
V-296   MACDONALD, DWIGHT   *Against the American Grain*
V-193   MALRAUX, ANDRE   *The Temptation of the West*
V-55   MANN, THOMAS   *Essays*
V-593   MERWIN, W. S. (trans.)   *The Song of Roland*
V-452   MYRDAL, JAN, photographed by GUN KESSLE   *Angkor*
V-337   NIETZSCHE, FRIEDRICH   *Beyond Good and Evil*
V-369   NIETZSCHE, FRIEDRICH   *The Birth of Tragedy and The Case of Wagner*
V-401   NIETZSCHE, FRIEDRICH   *On the Genealogy of Morals and Ecce Homo*
V-437   NIETZSCHE, FRIEDRICH   *The Will to Power*
V-639   OUSPENSKY, P. D.   *Tertium Organum*
V-672   OUSPENSKY, P. D.   *The Fourth Way*
V-373   PAUSTOVSKY, KONSTANTIN   *The Story of a Life*

V-598	PROUST, MARCEL	*The Captive*
V-597	PROUST, MARCEL	*Cities of the Plain*
V-596	PROUST, MARCEL	*The Guermantes Way*
V-594	PROUST, MARCEL	*Swann's Way*
V-599	PROUST, MARCEL	*The Sweet Cheat Gone*
V-595	PROUST, MARCEL	*Within a Budding Grove*
V-24	RANSOM, JOHN CROWE	*Poems and Essays*
V-691	RUKEYSER, MURIEL	*The Speed of Darkness*
V-109	SATURDAY EVENING POST	*Adventures of the Mind*
V-415	SHATTUCK, ROGER	*The Banquet Years*, Revised
V-278	STEVENS, WALLACE	*The Necessary Angel*
V-85	STEVENS, WALLACE	*Poems*
V-194	VALERY, PAUL	*The Art of Poetry*
V-347	WARREN, ROBERT PENN	*Selected Essays*
V-468	WATTS, ALAN	*The Wisdom of Insecurity*
V-592	WATTS, ALAN	*Nature, Man and Woman*
V-665	WATTS, ALAN	*Does it Matter?*
V-298	WATTS, ALAN	*The Way of Zen*
V-256	WILDE, OSCAR	*De Profundis*
V-580	WILLIAMS, MARGARET (tr.)	*The Pearl Poet*
V-360	WIMSATT, W. R. and BROOKS, C.	*Literary Criticism*
V-546	YATES, FRANCES A.	*Giordano Bruno and the Hermetic Tradition*

VINTAGE CRITICISM,
LITERATURE, MUSIC, AND ART

V-418   AUDEN, W. H.   *The Dyer's Hand*
V-398   AUDEN, W. H.   *The Enchàfed Flood*
V-269   BLOTNER, JOSEPH and FREDERICK GWYNN (eds.)   *Faulkner at the University*
V-259   BUCKLEY, JEROME H.   *The Victorian Temper*
V-51   BURKE, KENNETH   *The Philosophy of Literary Form*
V-643   CARLISLE, OLGA   *Poets on Streetcorners: Portraits of Fifteen Russian Poets*
V-569   CARTEY, WILFRED   *Whispers from a Continent: The Literature of Contemporary Black Africa*
V-75   CAMUS, ALBERT   *The Myth of Sisyphus and other Essays*
V-626   CAMUS, ALBERT   *Lyrical and Critical Essays*
V-535   EISEN, JONATHAN   *The Age of Rock: Sounds of the American Cultural Revolution*
V-655   EISEN, JONATHAN   *The Age of Rock 2*
V-4   EINSTEIN, ALFRED   *A Short History of Music*
V-632   ELLMAN, RICHARD (ed.)   *The Artist as Critic: Critical Writings of Oscar Wilde*
V-13   GILBERT, STUART   *James Joyce's Ulysses*
V-646   GILMAN, RICHARD   *The Confusion of Realms*
V-363   GOLDWATER, ROBERT   *Primitivism in Modern Art*, Revised Edition
V-114   HAUSER, ARNOLD   *Social History of Art*, Vol. I
V-115   HAUSER, ARNOLD   *Social History of Art*, Vol. II
V-116   HAUSER, ARNOLD   *Social History of Art*, Vol. III
V-117   HAUSER, ARNOLD   *Social History of Art*, Vol. IV
V-438   HELLER, ERICH   *The Artist's Journey into the Interior and Other Essays*
V-213   HOWE, IRVING   *William Faulkner: A Critical Study*
V-20   HYMAN, S. E.   *The Armed Vision*
V-12   JARRELL, RANDALL   *Poetry and the Age*
V-88   KERMAN, JOSEPH   *Opera as Drama*
V-260   KERMODE, FRANK   *The Romantic Image*
V-581   KRAMER, JANE   *Allen Ginsberg in America*
V-452   KESSLE, GUN, photographs by, and JAN MYRDAL   *Angkor*
V-83   KRONENBERGER, LOUIS   *Kings and Desperate Men*
V-677   LESTER, JULIUS   *The Seventh Son*, Vol. I
V-678   LESTER, JULIUS   *The Seventh Son*, Vol. II
V-90   LEVIN, HARRY   *The Power of Blackness: Hawthorne, Poe, Melville*
V-296   MacDONALD, DWIGHT   *Against the American Grain*
V-55   MANN, THOMAS   *Essays*
V-720   MIRSKY, D. S.   *A History of Russian Literature*
V-344   MUCHNIC, HELEN   *From Gorky to Pasternak*
V-452   MYRDAL, JAN and photographs by GUN KESSLE   *Angkor*
V-118   NEWMAN, ERNEST   *Great Operas*, Vol. I
V-119   NEWMAN, ERNEST   *Great Operas*, Vol. II
V-24   RANSOM, JOHN CROWE   *Poems and Essays*
V-108   SHAHN, BEN   *The Shape of Content*
V-415   SHATTUCK, ROGER   *The Banquet Years*, Revised
V-186   STEINER, GEORGE   *Tolstoy or Dostoevsky*
V-278   STEVENS, WALLACE   *The Necessary Angel*
V-39   STRAVINSKY, IGOR   *The Poetics of Music*

V-100   SULLIVAN, J. W. N.   *Beethoven: His Spiritual Development*

V-243   SYPHER, WYLIE (ed.)   *Art History: An Anthology of Modern Criticism*

V-266   SYPHER, WYLIE   *Loss of the Self*

V-229   SYPHER, WYLIE   *Rococo to Cubism*

V-458   SYPHER, WYLIE   *Literature and Technology*

V-166   SZE, MAI-MAI   *The Way of Chinese Painting*

V-162   TILLYARD, E. M. W.   *The Elizabethan World Picture*

V-35   TINDALL, WILLIAM YORK   *Forces in Modern British Literature*

V-194   VALERY, PAUL   *The Art of Poetry*

V-347   WARREN, ROBERT PENN   *Selected Essays*

V-218   WILSON, EDMUND   *Classics & Commercials*

V-360   WIMSATT, W. and C. BROOKS   *Literary Criticism*

V-500   WIND, EDGAR   *Art and Anarchy*

V-546   YATES, FRANCES A.   *Giordano Bruno and the Hermetic Tradition*

VINTAGE FICTION, POETRY, AND PLAYS

V-158 AUDEN, W. H. and C. ISHERWOOD *Two Great Plays: The Dog Beneath the Skin and The Ascent of F6*

V-601 AUDEN, W. H. and PAUL TAYLOR (trans.) *The Elder Edda*

V-673 BECK, JULIAN and JUDITH MALINA *Paradise Now*

V-342 BECKSON, KARL (ed.) *Aesthetes and Decadents of the 1890's*

V-271 BEDIER, JOSEPH *Tristan and Iseult*

V-321 BOLT, ROBERT *A Man for All Seasons*

V-21 BOWEN, ELIZABETH *The Death of the Heart*

V-48 BOWEN, ELIZABETH *The House in Paris*

V-294 BRADBURY, RAY *The Vintage Bradbury*

V-670 BRECHT, BERTOLT *Collected Works*, Vol. I

V-207 CAMUS, ALBERT *Caligula & 3 Other Plays*

V-2 CAMUS, ALBERT *The Stranger*

V-223 CAMUS, ALBERT *The Fall*

V-245 CAMUS, ALBERT *The Possessed*, a play

V-281 CAMUS, ALBERT *Exile and the Kingdom*

V-626 CAMUS, ALBERT *Lyrical and Critical Essays*

V-135 CAPOTE, TRUMAN *Other Voices, Other Rooms*

V-148 CAPOTE, TRUMAN *The Muses Are Heard*

V-643 CARLISLE, OLGA *Poets on Streetcorners: Portraits of Fifteen Russian Poets*

V-28 CATHER, WILLA *Five Stories*

V-200 CATHER, WILLA *My Mortal Enemy*

V-679 CATHER, WILLA *Death Comes for the Archbishop*

V-680 CATHER, WILLA *Shadows on the Rock*

V-140 CERF, BENNETT (ed.) *Famous Ghost Stories*

V-203 CERF, BENNETT (ed.) *Four Contemporary American Plays*

V-127 CERF, BENNETT (ed.) *Great Modern Short Stories*

V-326 CERF, CHRISTOPHER (ed) *The Vintage Anthology of Science Fantasy*

V-293 CHAUCER, GEOFFREY *The Canterbury Tales*, a prose version in Modern English

V-142 CHAUCER, GEOFFREY *Troilus and Cressida*

V-723 CHERNYSHEVSKY, N. G. *What Is to Be Done?*

V-146 CLARK, WALTER VAN T. *The Ox-Bow Incident*

V-589 CLIFTON, LUCILLE *Good Times*

V-173 CONFUCIUS (trans. by A. Waley) *Analects*

V-155 CONRAD, JOSEPH *Three Great Tales: The Nigger of the Narcissus, Heart of Darkness, Youth*

V-10 CRANE, STEPHEN *Stories and Tales*

V-531 CRUZ, VICTOR HERNANDEZ *Snaps: Poems*

V-205 DINESEN, ISAK *Winter's Tales*

V-721 DOSTOYEVSKY, FYODOR *Crime and Punishment*

V-722 DOSTOYEVSKY, FYODOR *The Brothers Karamazov*

V-188 ESCHENBACH, WOLFRAM VON *Parzival*

V-254 FAULKNER, WILLIAM *As I Lay Dying*

V-139 FAULKNER, WILLIAM *The Hamlet*

V-282 FAULKNER, WILLIAM *The Mansion*

V-339 FAULKNER, WILLIAM *The Reivers*

V-381 FAULKNER, WILLIAM *Sanctuary*

V-5 FAULKNER, WILLIAM *The Sound and the Fury*

V-184 FAULKNER, WILLIAM *The Town*

V-351 FAULKNER, WILLIAM *The Unvanquished*

V-262 FAULKNER, WILLIAM *The Wild Palms*

V-149	FAULKNER, WILLIAM	*Three Famous Short Novels: Spotted Horses, Old Man, The Bear*
V-130	FIELDING, HENRY	*Tom Jones*
V-45	FORD, FORD MADOX	*The Good Soldier*
V-187	FORSTER, E. M.	*A Room With a View*
V-7	FORSTER, E. M.	*Howards End*
V-40	FORSTER, E. M.	*The Longest Journey*
V-61	FORSTER, E. M.	*Where Angels Fear to Tread*
V-219	FRISCH, MAX	*I'm Not Stiller*
V-8	GIDE, ANDRE	*The Immoralist*
V-96	GIDE, ANDRE	*Lafcadio's Adventures*
V-27	GIDE, ANDRE	*Strait Is the Gate*
V-66	GIDE, ANDRE	*Two Legends: Oedipus and Theseus*
V-656	GILBERT, CREIGHTON	*Complete Poems and Selected Letters of Michelangelo*
V-473	GOODMAN, PAUL	*Adam and His Works: Collected Stories of Paul Goodman*
V-402	GOODMAN, PAUL	*Hawkweed*
V-654	GOODMAN, PAUL	*Homespun of Oatmeal Gray*
V-300	GRASS, GUNTER	*The Tin Drum*
V-425	GRAVES, ROBERT	*Claudius the God*
V-182	GRAVES, ROBERT	*I, Claudius*
V-717	GUERNEY, B. G. (ed.)	*An Anthology of Russian Literature in the Soviet Period*
V-255	HAMMETT, DASHIELL	*The Maltese Falcon* and *The Thin Man*
V-15	HAWTHORNE, NATHANIEL	*Short Stories*
V-476	HOROWITZ, ISRAEL	*First Season*
V-489	HOROVITZ, I. AND T. McNALLY AND L. MELFI	*Morning, Noon and Night*
V-305	HUMPHREY, WILLIAM	*Home from the Hill*
V-727	ILF AND PETROV	*The Twelves Chairs*
V-295	JEFFERS, ROBINSON	*Selected Poems*
V-380	JOYCE, JAMES	*Ulysses*
V-484	KAFKA, FRANZ	*The Trial*
V-683	KAUFMANN, WALTER	*Cain and Other Poems*
V-536	KESSLER, LYLE	*The Watering Place*
V-134	LAGERKVIST, PAR	*Barabbas*
V-240	LAGERKVIST, PAR	*The Sibyl*
V-23	LAWRENCE, D. H.	*The Plumed Serpent*
V-71	LAWRENCE, D. H.	*St. Mawr and The Man Who Died*
V-315	LEWIS, ANTHONY	*Gideon's Trumpet*
V-553	LOWENFELS, WALTER (ed.)	*In a Time of Revolution: Poems from Our Third World*
V-537	LUKE, PETER	*Hadrian VII*
V-673	MALINA, JUDITH AND JULIAN BECK	*Paradise Now*
V-136	MALRAUX, ANDRE	*The Royal Way*
V-479	MALRAUX, ANDRE	*Man's Fate*
V-180	MANN, THOMAS	*Buddenbrooks*
V-3	MANN, THOMAS	*Death in Venice and Seven Other Stories*
V-86	MANN, THOMAS	*The Transposed Heads*
V-496	MANN, THOMAS	*Confessions of Felix Krull, Confidence Man*
V-497	MANN, THOMAS	*The Magic Mountain*
V-36	MANSFIELD, KATHERINE	*Stories*
V-137	MAUGHAM, SOMERSET	*Of Human Bondage*
V-78	MAXWELL, WILLIAM	*The Folded Leaf*
V-91	MAXWELL, WILLIAM	*They Came Like Swallows*
V-221	MAXWELL, WILLIAM	*Time Will Darken It*

V-489	McNally, T. and I. Horovitz and L. Melfi *Morning, Noon and Night*
V-562	McNally, Terence *Sweet Eros, Next and Other Plays*
V-489	Melfi, L., I. Horovitz, T. McNally *Morning, Noon and Night*
V-593	Merwin W. S. (trans.) *The Song of Roland*
V-306	Michener, James A. *Hawaii*
V-718	Nabokov, V. (trans.) *The Song of Igor's Campaign*
V-29	O'Connor, Frank *Stories*
V-49	O'Hara, John *Butterfield 8*
V-276	O'Neill, Eugene *Six Short Plays*
V-18	O'Neill, Eugene *The Iceman Cometh*
V-165	O'Neill, Eugene *Three Plays: Desire Under the Elms, Strange Interlude and Mourning Become Electra*
V-125	O'Neill, Eugene Jr. and Whitney Oates (eds.) *Seven Famous Greek Plays*
V-586	Padgett, Ron and David Shapiro (eds.) *An Anthology of New York Poets*
V-478	Parone, Edward (ed.) *Collision Course*
V-466	Plath, Sylvia *The Colossus and Other Poems*
V-594	Proust, Marcel *Swann's Way*
V-595	Proust, Marcel *Within A Budding Grove*
V-596	Proust, Marcel *The Guermantes Way*
V-597	Proust, Marcel *Cities of the Plain*
V-598	Proust, Marcel *The Captive*
V-599	Proust, Marcel *The Sweet Cheat Gone*
V-600	Proust, Marcel *The Past Recaptured*
V-714	Pushkin, Alexander *The Captain's Daughter*
V-24	Ransom, John Crowe *Poems and Essays*
V-732	Reeve, F. (ed.) *Russian Plays*, Vol. II
V-297	Renault, Mary *The King Must Die*
V-564	Rudnik, Raphael *A Lesson From the Cyclops and Other Poems*
V-16	Sartre, Jean-Paul *No Exit* and Three Other Plays
V-65	Sartre, Jean-Paul *The Devil and the Good Lord* and Two Other Plays
V-238	Sartre, Jean-Paul *The Condemned of Altona*
V-586	Shapiro, David and Ron Padgett (ed.) *An Anthology of New York Poets*
V-330	Sholokhov, Mikhail *And Quiet Flows the Don*
V-331	Sholokhov, Mikhail *The Don Flows Home to the Sea*
V-153	Stein, Gertrude *Three Lives*
V-85	Stevens, Wallace *Poems*
V-141	Styron, William *The Long March*
V-63	Svevo, Italio *Confessions of Zeno*
V-178	Synge, J. M. *Complete Plays*
V-601	Taylor, Paul and W. H. Auden (trans.) *The Elder Edda*
V-750	Tertz, Abram *The Trial Begins* and *On Socialist Realism*
V-713	Tolstoy, Leo *The Kreutzer Sonata*
V-202	Turgenev, Ivan *Torrents of Spring*
V-711	Turgenev, Ivan *The Vintage Turgenev* Vol. I: *Smoke, Fathers and Sons, First Love*
V-712	Turgenev, Ivan Vol. II: *On The Eve, Rudin, A Quiet Spot, Diary of a Superfluous Man*
V-257	Updike, John *Olinger Stories: A Selection*
V-605	Williams, John A. and Charles F. Harris, (eds.) *Amistad 1*
V-660	Williams, John A. and Charles F. Harris, (eds.) *Amistad 2*
V-580	Williams, Margaret (trans.) *The Pearl Poet*